By C.S. POE

The Mystery of Nevermore

Published by DSP PUBLICATIONS
www.dsppublications.com

# THE
# MYSTERY
## OF
# NEVERMORE

SNOW & WINTER: BOOK ONE

## C.S. POE

# DSP PUBLICATIONS

Published by
DSP Publications

5032 Capital Circle SW, Suite 2, PMB# 279, Tallahassee, FL 32305-7886 USA
www.dsppublications.com

The Mystery of Nevermore
© 2016 C.S. Poe.

Cover Art
© 2016 Reese Dante.
http://www.reesedante.com
Cover content is for illustrative purposes only and any person depicted on the cover is a model.

ISBN: 978-1-63477-069-9
Digital ISBN: 978-1-63477-070-5
Library of Congress Control Number: 2016902730
Published August 2016
v 1.0

For Josh, the Master of Mystery.
You gave me the courage to find my voice again.

# THE
# MYSTERY
## OF
# NEVERMORE

SNOW & WINTER: BOOK ONE

## C.S. POE

# CHAPTER ONE

SOMETHING WAS rotten.

I didn't mean in a figurative sense. I meant something smelled like it was decaying.

"Shit," I muttered. I stood at the door of my antique shop, hand to my nose.

Tupperware. It had to be an old lunch.

It was a wintry, miserable Tuesday in New York City, two weeks' shy of Christmas. The snow was coming down heavily at seven in the morning, blanketing the city and producing an eerie, muted effect. I had shown up early to my business, Snow's Antique Emporium, in downtown Manhattan, with the intention of going through some newly acquired inventory. Instead, I was dripping melted snow onto the welcome mat and trying to pinpoint that god-awful stench.

I quickly hung up my jacket and hat and changed out of my boots into an old pair of worn loafers beside the door. I ran my fingers through my unruly hair and smoothed the front of my sweater while walking down the tiny, crowded aisles. I stopped to turn on old lamps as I followed the smell. The glow of the lights was subdued, creating a cavernous look for the shop.

At the counter that had an old brass register on it, I took the step up onto the elevated floor, scanning the shop. It smelled even worse here. I reached into my sweater pocket and replaced my sunglasses with black-framed reading glasses. Turning on the bank lamp, I winced and looked away from the light.

I stared at the door standing ajar to my right. It was a tiny little closet that served as an office, with a computer and chair and mini fridge all tucked away for my use.

Does forgotten Thai food smell like death after two days?

I walked in, opened the fridge, and hesitantly sniffed a few cartons. Okay, I needed to do some serious cleaning, but what seemed like a half-eaten burrito was not the source of the odor.

I walked back to the register, groaning loudly as I looked around. Something had to have died—a rat, perhaps? I cringed at the thought of finding a New York City rodent in my shop, but I crouched down and started shoving aside bags and boxes used at checkout while I looked.

The front door opened, the bell chiming overhead. "Good morn—what's that smell?" my assistant, Max, called. "Sebastian?"

"Over here," I grumbled.

Max Ridley was a sweet guy, a recent college grad with an art degree he realized rather too quickly wasn't going to pay his rent. He was smart and knew his history. I'd hired him the same day he'd come in to fill out an application. Max was tall and broad-shouldered—a handsome young man who was maybe bisexual or maybe just out to experience it all. I'd heard enough stories over morning coffee, reading mail, and pricing antiques to know Max's preference seemed to be mostly anyone.

Call me old-fashioned, but I'm a one-man sort of guy.

"God, the weather sucks today. Do you think it'll be busy?" Max asked as he strolled through the shop.

"Usually is," I said, looking up over the counter.

"What did you leave sitting out?"

"Nothing. I think a rat died or something."

"Can I turn on more lights? It'll be easier to find."

"I already have a headache," I said absently. I crouched back down to finish moving out the supplies from under the counter.

I was born with achromatopsia, which means I can't see color. We have two types of light receptor cells in our eyes, cones and rods. Cones see color in bright light, rods see black and white in low light. My cones don't work. At all. The world to me exists only in varying shades of gray, and I have a difficult time seeing in places with bright lights because the rods aren't meant for daylight purposes. Usually I wear sunglasses or my special red-tinted contacts as an extra layer of protection....

"I forgot my contacts. And the snow was too bright."

"Even for shades?"

"Yes. *Damn*, where is that smell coming from?" I asked while standing.

Max motioned to the register. "Smells the worst right here."

"Yeah." I walked back to the steps and promptly fell forward when the creaky floorboard underfoot skidded sideways.

Max lunged out and grabbed me before I could plant my face on the floor. He held me tight, my face smooshed against his armpit. "Did you have another fight with Neil last night?"

"Why?" I asked as I pulled myself free from his hold.

"You've got some bad mojo following you around this morning."

"It wasn't a *fight*. It was—you know, I'm not talking about it while the smell of rot continues to permeate my shop." I turned back to the step and bent to examine the floorboard that had become free.

Bad idea. The stench of decay filled my nostrils, and I fought back the urge to gag.

"I think you found it," Max muttered, looking down over my shoulder. "I'll get a bag."

I nodded silently, holding my nose while I looked into the opening under the floor. It—*the thing*—wasn't dark, like a dead rat. It didn't appear to have fur, but I'd be lying if I said I had great vision when it came to close-up details.

"Max? Come here."

"What?" His voice came from the office before he joined me with a garbage bag. "What's up?"

"Look in there."

"Oh come on. You don't pay me enough for that."

"No, I mean, I don't think that's a rat."

Max got down on one knee and glanced inside before quickly pulling back. "What the hell!"

I stared at the floor. "Tear up the planks! Here, here!—It is the beating of his hideous heart!"

"What is that?"

"Poe," I replied.

"God, you're so weird, Seb," Max muttered.

"What else am I supposed to say?" I asked, pointing at the rotting flesh. "It's a *heart*."

"Who did you kill?"

"I'll call the cops."


HAVING TO explain to the dispatcher that I needed police not because of a dead body, but there was a body out there missing an essential part, was certainly the strangest thing I'd done in some time. I'll admit the situation piqued my interest, but there are 101 things in life I simply don't have the patience for, and finding someone else's rotting heart in the floorboards of my shop just about topped the list.

Max sprayed nearly an entire can of air freshener while we waited after the phone call. "Smells like fresh laundry," he stated while reading the can.

"Oh good," I said.

"Laundry and *death*," Max corrected after a pause. "Sometimes *I* want to die instead of dragging my dirty clothes to the Laundromat."

"Max." I sighed.

"Sorry."

I crossed my arms, looking toward the back of the shop at the piles of boxes that had been left there. When new inventory arrived, it needed to be carefully inspected, priced, and arranged in the shop. If it was too priceless for the shop, it needed to be listed for auction, not sitting in a damn box on the floor. Those and several more were collecting dust in my apartment. So much for finally getting around to it all this morning.

There was a rap at the door, and I walked over to unlock it. "Good morning."

"Sir," one of the uniformed officers said. "We got a call—"

"There's a body part in my floor," I quickly answered, leading them through the aisles toward the register.

It was pretty clear they'd been sent to dispel whatever fear or confusion the dispatcher thought I was experiencing, yet they followed without complaint or comment. The first officer removed his cap as he bent down to the opening I pointed at. He only glanced inside before shaking his head and rising.

"Brigg," he spoke to his partner, and the woman approached.

I watched them confer briefly before she got on her radio. "So," I said, "do we need some hazmat team or something?"

"Can I get your name, sir?" the officer replied as he removed a notepad from his belt.

"Sebastian Snow."

"And do you run this business?"

"Yes."

"Own the building?"

"No. I wish."

He looked up. "Approximately when did you suspect something was in the store?"

"You mean—*that*?" I asked while looking down at the floor. "When I opened the door this morning, I could smell it. It was about seven."

"Does anyone else have access to the store?" The officer looked over my shoulder at Max.

"Max has keys, but only I and—only I have access to the security code," I explained.

The truth was, my partner of four years, Neil Millett, also had keys and the code, but mentioning his name around cops was a bit tricky. He was a detective with the NYPD's forensic investigations unit, and very much in the closet. So much so that the only people who knew we were living together were Max and my father. Neil didn't want other officers knowing he was gay, and when I was twenty-nine with a heart all aflutter for a sexy detective, I didn't mind. Now I was thirty-three, and it was wearing me out.

The officer wrote down a few notes. "Do you have cameras? You have a lot of expensive-looking items in here."

"I have one, but it's been on the fritz for the past month." I had been suffering from a lack of mental stamina lately and just hadn't found the energy to give a shit about a number of things, camera included.

It wasn't like me. I knew that.

Neil made a point of bringing up my recent attitude. A lot. It only pissed me off more.

The officer continued taking down my contact information, then asked for Max's as well. A few more basic questions followed, and then Brigg led two plain-clothed cops from the front door toward us. Glancing around the now congested aisle, I saw yet another woman entering, carrying some sort of medical kit.

The overhead lights, which I never used, were switched on without warning, and the entire room was washed out of sight. I hastily covered my eyes and turned away, stumbling and reaching around the countertop. Max went to the other corner to avoid the police and the heart, grabbed my sunglasses, and handed them over just as someone spoke my name.

"Mr.... Snow, is it?" a woman asked.

Turning as I put on my shades, I was confronted with the two new cops. The woman who spoke was maybe my age and couldn't have been an inch over five feet, with a strong build and closely cropped hair. The other, a man, was tall and big and filled out his suit with nothing but muscle. He looked older than Neil, who was thirty-seven. His hair was light, so I guessed it was what I have been told is blond.

I squinted to better study him. He had freckles. A lot, actually. I kind of had a thing for guys with freckles. Cheeks, nose, forehead—he had freckles all over, and it gave him a sort of sweet look initially. Maybe his hair was red instead.

"Sebastian Snow," I agreed.

The woman took the lead, extending her hand to shake. "I'm Detective Quinn Lancaster, and this is my partner, Detective Calvin Winter."

"Uh, hi."

Lancaster smiled. "How's business been, Mr. Snow?"

"Fine," I said, confused. It was strange to be looking down at such a short figure of authority, but she had an air of confidence I wasn't willing to question.

"What can you tell me about your clientele?" Lancaster continued.

I shrugged while crossing my arms. "Regular folks, some with big money, some looking for curiosities. Corporate types, hipsters—I get a little of everyone in here."

She nodded. "Would it be all right if you removed your sunglasses, sir?"

"I can't."

Lancaster looked up at Winter briefly before asking, "Why's that?"

"I have a light sensitivity. If you turn the overheads off, I will," I said while pointing up.

Winter turned away and gave an order to one of the uniformed officers. The lights died and the shop was once again illuminated by the strategically placed lamps.

"Better?" Lancaster asked, her tone not mocking or unkind.

I pulled the sunglasses back to rest on my head as I put my regular glasses back on. "Thank you," I said briskly.

"That's called photophobia, isn't it?" she asked.

"I have achromatopsia."

"I see." She didn't bother for more details. "Has anything out of the ordinary happened in the past few weeks?"

"Nope."

Lancaster frowned. "Who found the body part?"

"I did, when I came in. I smelled something awful and started looking for it."

"Have there been any break-ins or stolen items?" she asked.

"No," I said. "What's this about? I'm assuming something bigger is at play here, otherwise you two wouldn't be grilling me."

"Why do you say that?" Lancaster asked.

"I live with a cop" was what I wanted to say. Four years of stories from Neil had, admittedly, given me an unhealthy interest in *whodunit* mysteries.

Instead, I just shrugged.

Winter spoke for the first time. "Do you know Bond Antiques?"

"Yeah, on Bond Street and Lafayette," I confirmed.

"How is your relationship with the owner?"

"I fail to see what that has to do with anything," I responded. "Mike Rodriguez and I have known each other for a while."

"How do you get along?" Winter asked.

"He's competition," I stated. "What's going on?"

"Sebastian!" called a familiar voice.

Ignoring the towering mountain that was Detective Winter, I looked around him to see Neil walking through the shop, shaking snow from his coat. I was immediately both happy and frustrated to see him, which didn't seem like the right response. I hadn't called to tell him what happened, so there should have been no reason for his appearance.

I turned to the counter. Max raised his hands up defensively and shook his head.

"What's going on?" Neil asked upon reaching us. He looked at the two other detectives and removed a badge from inside his coat. "Detective Millett, CSU."

Lancaster didn't seem interested. "Detective Lancaster, homicide," she replied with a nod. "My partner, Winter. We haven't requested forensics yet."

"Homicide?" I echoed. I mean, sure, I guess technically a heart without a body could mean something more sinister was at work besides a medical cadaver showing up to class and some poor student flunking when he had no heart to dissect.

I looked at Neil. He seemed concerned and maybe nervous, and for a minute, I was happy because he was worried about me. The annoyance I had been harboring toward him all morning suddenly washed away, and I had the urge to reach out for a hug.

"Sebastian is—a friend," Neil said.

"*Friend*," Winter repeated in a tone I didn't like.

"He called me."

*Goddamn it, Neil.* He was so convinced he'd lose his shield for having a life outside his job, that after four years I was still just his *friend* in public.

"We're in the middle of asking Mr. Snow some questions," Winter said before looking back at me. I swear his gaze was intense enough to strip me down to bare bones. "Mr. Rodriguez's business was broken into Sunday night."

"I'm sorry to hear that," I answered, turning away from Neil. "Was anything stolen?"

"The investigation is still underway. He pointed a finger at you, though."

"M-Me?" I asked in surprise. "What—Mike thinks *I* broke in?"

"Why would he say that?" Winter asked.

"I have no idea," I quickly answered.

"Where were you Sunday night?" Lancaster asked. "After eight."

I could feel Neil's desperation rippling off his body. I had been at home with him. I believe around eight we had been fucking, which had ended prematurely and dissolved into an argument until about nine. *That's* where I had been.

"Home," I said simply. "Look, I'm not answering any more questions without a lawyer, if that's what I need. I called because I found a human heart in my shop, and now you're accusing me of robbing someone."

Neil's hand was on my elbow next, and he was excusing us while dragging me away. Stopping near the back of the shop, he let go and turned to tower over me. "What the hell is going on?" he whispered.

"What's going on?" I repeated. "What are you doing here?"

"I'm a cop, Sebby—"

"Don't call me that."

"What human heart? Why didn't you call me?"

I honestly hadn't thought to ring Neil. Maybe a year or two earlier, the first reaction I'd have had would be to call my cop boyfriend to come solve this peculiar little problem. Now, he hadn't even crossed my mind. It was disconcerting.

"Nice lie you told, by the way," I said instead. "I *called* you? Why the hell did you come if it wasn't to be here for me?"

"Stop it," he ordered in a harsh whisper. "We're not having this argument again."

"Go back to work, Neil. Everything is fine," I said stubbornly.

"You didn't…." He hesitated.

"Tell them about you? No. I know the drill."

Neil gritted his jaw. He looked angry. He turned back to the other detectives before saying, "Is that Calvin Winter?"

"What? Yeah, why?"

"Be careful what you say to him."

"*Why*, Neil?" I repeated.

"Because I hear he's a homophobe," Neil said.

Without thinking I replied, "*You're* a homophobe."

Neil looked back at me with a strange expression I couldn't place. "Real nice, Sebby," he said after a moment.

I couldn't take it back, but when I stared up at Neil, when all of our recent arguments over the past month came rushing back, I didn't care and didn't want to take it back.

"Go back to work," I said again. "We'll talk at home, behind locked doors."

I was making him angry, and I couldn't stop myself. I don't know what had gotten into me lately. Neil and I had been at each other's throats for weeks. I provoked him, or something he said got under my skin in ways it never did before.

Neil didn't say another word. He turned while zipping up his coat and brushed by the other detectives in silence on his way out.

I took a breath. It was shaky. I was being cruel to the most important man in my life.

I pushed my glasses up the bridge of my nose as Lancaster left the woman with the medical supplies and walked toward me with a smile.

"Good news, Mr. Snow."

"Oh boy."

"It's not human."

*Who, Neil?* "The heart?"

"It's a pig's heart," she replied.

"A minor relief." I took another breath, working harder than necessary to calm myself. "So can I open for business?"

She spread her hands. "There's been no foul play, although it seems like someone wanted to pull a prank on you. I highly suggest you invest in some tighter security."

*No foul play.* My gut said otherwise. Two detectives—from homicide, no less—had shown up right away, and I played twenty questions regarding the unfortunate pig and Mike Rodriguez, the latter of which I found extremely strange. Why would time be wasted to send out detectives for something that proved to be nothing? And it still didn't explain how the pig heart ended up in my shop to begin with.

Lancaster thanked me for my time, to which I muttered some pleasantry. She turned to leave with the medical examiner.

Winter, however, approached me. "Your friend seemed upset."

I frowned while looking up. I was on the shorter side, only five foot nine, and both Neil and Winter stood a good half a foot taller. Neil was a leaner build, like myself, which was a stark contrast to the brick body that was Detective Winter. He was close enough again that I could study his freckles—which to me actually looked like gray blemishes. They'd be clearer if I invaded his personal space or looked at his skin with a magnifying glass.

Neither of those do I recommend doing to someone you've just met.

In comparison, his light-colored eyes were so brilliant and sharp, it was almost unnerving. They reminded me of minerals on display at the Museum of Natural History. They were gorgeous, but also maybe just a little weary. They looked like they'd seen something that had hardened and tired him considerably.

Winter swallowed up the air around me. He was both intimidating and somewhat comforting to be in the presence of. He smelled nice too. Some kind of spice—really different from Neil's cologne.

"I didn't break into Mike's shop," I said again. For the record.

His gaze shifted slightly to the boxes behind me. "What's all this?" I looked over my shoulder, then back at him. "New inventory."

"From where?"

"Bond Antiques," I retorted. "Jesus. It's from an estate sale."

He reached into his suit coat next, and I wouldn't have been surprised if he pulled his gun with the way I was shooting my mouth off. Instead, he handed me a business card. "Should you conveniently remember something."

"Like slaughtering some pigs?" I shoved the card in my pocket.

"Have a good day, Mr. Snow." He turned and walked out of the shop.

THE STORM seemed to have scared off the day's foot traffic, which on any other afternoon would have worried me, being so close to the holidays when the sales are needed. But I couldn't concentrate on anything business-related. My salad sat beside me at the register, half eaten and getting soggy as it settled into the pool of vinaigrette dressing. I held a magnifying glass to the mail as I read.

"Why not get bifocals?"

I looked up to see Max staring at me, pulling up the spare stool to sit. "What?"

"The magnifying glass is sort of silly. You pull them out of pockets like you're an old-timey detective."

"I tripped down the stairs wearing bifocals when I was younger," I answered while setting the glass aside and stacking the junk and bills together. "Broke my arm."

"Yikes." Max reached out to push my salad around with the fork. If he planned on scalping my meal, the sogginess must have changed his mind. "So why was Neil here?"

"I don't know." I stood, brought the mail into the office, and dropped it on the desk.

The morning had been resting heavily on my mind. Usually I was closed on Mondays, but holiday demands often changed my schedule, so I had been open yesterday. When I closed the shop last night just after six, it gave someone a thirteen-hour window to break inside. Max and I had spent the remaining hours of the morning going through the Emporium, and from what we could tell, not a single item had been misplaced.

It was *that* concept that puzzled me the most. Why break into an antique shop, get past the security alarm, only to steal nothing?

So someone came in, put a decaying pig heart under the floorboards, and hightailed it without taking so much as an old button?

More upsetting was the matter with Mike Rodriguez. I had worked for Mike for a few years before going into business for myself. I respected his knowledge and the success of his shop—he'd been in this line of work for over twenty years now—but he was a cranky old fuck. He hadn't liked me all that much when I worked for him, and I'm certain he felt slighted, to say the least, when I took everything I had learned to open the Emporium.

Mike specialized in higher-end antiques. Georgian and Victorian furniture, clothing, paintings, and other works of art. It wasn't where my interests were, and the Emporium was cluttered and stuffed instead with books and old documents, maps, photos, and every little gizmo and gadget from another century. People enjoy the odd and bizarre, like Victorian glove stretchers or tear bottles. The Emporium was doing very well after only a few years of business, and I suspected Mike was insulted.

I walked back out of the office, leaned against the doorframe, and crossed my arms. Mike and I weren't exactly on friendly terms these days—we certainly weren't mailing each other Christmas cards—but how the hell had he come to the conclusion that I should be looked at as a possible suspect? Had he waited three years to seek revenge against me? And it wasn't even revenge so much as insulting my integrity and character.

"Man, look at it coming down," Max murmured as he stared out toward the front door, watching the storm continue.

"Jingle Bells" started to play on the shop's speakers. Dashing through the snow, all right. The city was getting buried.

"Why don't you get out of here early, Max."

"Really?"

"Yeah. The subways are going to be a wreck, I bet," I said while walking to the counter.

"Are you leaving?"

Honestly, I wanted to swing by Mike's place and ask him what was going on, but it didn't seem like the smartest idea. Maybe I'd give him a call. That was less threatening. As much of an asshole as he was for accusing me of doing something like breaking into his place of business, we had a long history and I *did* want to make sure he was okay.

"Probably."

"I'll walk out with you, then," Max replied as he stood and started cashing out the register for me.

The shop phone rang, and I reached to take it off the receiver. "Snow's Antique Emporium."

"It's me."

*Neil.* I collected myself. "Hey."

"Busy?"

"We're closing up early. The weather's getting bad, and Max has to take the subway to Brooklyn."

"I'm ducking out," he replied. "I'll swing by for you."

"I can walk home."

Neil took an aggravated breath. "Sebby, please don't argue with me just once this month, okay? Let me pick you up."

Why was I getting angry at him for wanting to drive me home instead of making me walk in this nasty weather? "All right. Thanks."

"Want me to grab anything for dinner?"

"I thought I'd cook," I said offhandedly. I was getting sick of takeout. Neil couldn't cook to save his life, so it was up to me if we wanted a homemade meal.

"That sounds great," he replied happily. "I'll be there in twenty, tops." He hung up, and I put the phone down.

"Neil's coming to pick me up," I said to Max. "I'll finish closing. Why don't you get out while you can."

Max laughed and finished his counting. "Thanks, Seb."

"I'll call you tomorrow if the weather looks like we may have trouble opening."

"I'll plan to come in unless I hear otherwise." He was out the door within moments, disappearing into the storm.

I locked the front door and collected my belongings. I packed my laptop into my messenger bag. On the off-chance we stayed closed, I could at least start cataloging the inventory I had at home. Of course, I'd been telling myself that for two weeks and never seemed to have the energy for it.

By the time I'd shut off the lights, secured the shop, and changed into my winter attire, Neil's black BMW was parked out front.

The car had been another source of aggravation between us. I don't have a license because of the amount of work those with achromatopsia have to go through in order to be permitted to drive. It isn't worth the headache when I live in a city with such incredible public transportation. That being said, I had agreed to buy a car with Neil and pay for it together so we could vacation out of New York every once in a while.

Neil has expensive taste. He wouldn't settle on anything less than a new luxury coupe. I didn't understand the point—we'd save so much money with a decent used car. That argument had ended with me saying that I'd refuse to help with the payments, to which he had stubbornly agreed and told me to fuck myself. Out of childish spite, I had tried to refuse every ride offered thus far.

The car was warm when I opened the door and sat in the passenger's seat. The windshield wipers worked hard to keep the heavy, sticky snow off the glass. Neil was listening to some Christmas tunes and looking like his cool, sexy self. I had to admit he looked good behind the wheel of this car.

He smiled. "Ready?"

"Yup."

Neil pulled back onto the road, taking it slow down the streets already buried in snow and brown slush. "You may get snowed in tomorrow if this keeps up like the weather predictions claim."

"Will you have to go in?" I asked.

"Public servants don't get snow days. Warm enough?"

I muttered a response and fell silent. We lived in a cramped, too-small-for-two Manhattan apartment not far from my store. It wouldn't usually take so long to reach, but the road was completely buried, and cars ahead were already slipping and sliding. Neil wasn't taking chances by driving fast.

I looked at his profile, seeing the same handsome face I'd known for years. He told me he had brown eyes and sandy brown hair, comparing it to coffee with too much cream in it. Whatever the color, he had always been attractive to me, and he aged wonderfully. I saw the man I had fallen in love with, staring at him.

Why had we been fighting so much?

My good old dad said it was because I was losing my mind being shoved back into the closet for the sake of Neil's paranoia. I had denied it for years, that it would eventually make me nuts, but lately it seemed like Pop had been on to something. I had been out since college, and I was proud of who I was. Neil had been my first *serious* relationship, and it had thrown me for a spin to learn he wasn't out.

It still threw me.

"I'm sorry," I said quietly.

"For what?"

"For giving you attitude this morning." I stared at my hands. "Why did you come to the Emporium?"

He sighed. "I was in the right place to overhear detectives being dispatched to the address. I thought something was wrong—something happened to you."

"Thanks for being worried." I snorted and shook my head. "That sounds weird."

"I get what you mean." He removed one hand briefly from the steering wheel to pat my thigh.


NEIL DROPPED me off on our street and went to find a place to park. I let myself into the building, hiking the three floors of old, rickety stairs to our one-bedroom apartment. The pipes were clanking loudly as the water heaters were turning on. I hung up my coat and hat and put my boots in the closet. I dropped my bag on the foot of our bed before turning on a few lamps around the apartment.

I know Neil didn't like living in such a dark home, but he was polite and dealt with it without a word of complaint so I didn't need to wear sunglasses inside. I had tried to keep my condition a secret from him for a long time. It got really hard when he'd ask something like "Could you grab my navy blue button-down for me?" or "Pass the green salsa?" while eating Mexican. It ended up coming out when he found my collapsed walking stick in my bag one evening while searching for a condom.

I laughed quietly to myself, opening the fridge in the kitchen. That had killed the mood. I thought then and there he'd break up with me. Both boyfriends I had had before left me because of my condition. It wasn't life-threatening, but it was a burden, I guess. Neil had stayed with me, though, and that mattered.

I heard Neil at the door, removing his coat and shoes while I was chopping onions and peppers in the kitchen. I tossed the diced veggies into a pot to let them cook while I opened two cans of tomato sauce.

"Spaghetti?" Neil called, the smell familiar.

"We need to go shopping," I answered. "Not many other options."

He stepped around me and opened the fridge. "Want a beer?"

"Sure."

He popped the tops off two bottles, set one on the counter beside me, and leaned back against the opposite side. "So tell me what happened this morning."

I recited the story again for what felt like the hundredth time while I doctored up the sauce with salt, pepper, Tabasco, and whatever spices I could find deep in the cupboard. "But it wasn't human. It was a pig heart."

"What did the detectives say?"

I shrugged. "Lancaster told me to open for business and get better security."

"And that Winter fellow?"

I looked over my shoulder. "Why don't you like him?"

"I told you why."

"He let the questioning about Mike drop and left." I had turned back to stir the sauce, but paused and looked at Neil. "You haven't heard anything about that, have you? Mike's break-in?"

Neil shook his head before taking a swig of beer. "Someone else's case, not mine."

"Why do you think Mike would accuse me of breaking into his store?"

"Because he's a prick."

"Yeah, but—"

"But nothing," Neil interrupted. "He's always had it out for you, Seb."

Taking a drink of beer, I considered my next comment. "I was thinking about giving him a call tonight."

Neil stared at me as if I'd grown a second head. "You're not stupid, are you?"

"Excuse me?"

"Sebby, stay the hell out of it. Let the police investigate what happened to Mike, and don't be an idiot and harass him."

"Who said anything about harassment? I was just going to see if he's all right."

"Doesn't matter," Neil replied. "The police don't need to see you've been contacting him after he pointed his finger at you in the first place, okay?"

Neil had a valid point, of course, and who would know better what a cop would think than another cop?

Taking a drink and giving dinner my full attention, I zoned back in when I heard him saying my name.

"Seb, promise you won't stick your nose where it's not supposed to be."

"Why do you think I will?"

That question made Neil laugh. "Because you like the thrill. The two hundred mystery novels on the bookcase in the living room say so."

"I don't have *two hundred*," I said defensively. But so what? I liked a good brainteaser.

"Seb," he said again, more sternly.

"I *won't*," I insisted, getting annoyed. "I get it." Before Neil could say another word, I said, "How the heart ended up in the shop has yet to be explained."

"Hmm?"

"How'd a pig's heart get under the floorboards, Neil?" I asked while turning. "I didn't put it there, and I was the one to close up last night. I didn't forget to lock the gate or set the alarm."

"It was probably a prank," he said simply, shrugging.

"A prank?" I echoed. "By who?"

"I don't know. Kids—*teenagers*. Someone sick in the head. Come on. You've been busy as hell at the Emporium. You and Max can't keep an eye on everything all the time."

Again, what Neil said could have very easily been true. Minus today, we had been slammed since before Thanksgiving. There was always a handful of customers roaming about at one time, inventory coming in, items going out for auction—I *couldn't* always watch everything.

"But what's the point?"

"What's the point of a hotdog-eating contest?" Neil countered with a laugh. "People do stupid things sometimes, Seb."

"I guess. It's a little dramatic, though. 'The Tell-Tale Heart.'"

"The what?"

"Poe," I said. "It is the beating of his hideous heart!"

"Oh, yeah, I think I remember reading that in school," Neil replied thoughtfully.

"An old man with a blind eye is murdered and cut up. The murderer thinks he hears the heart under the floorboards where he put the body,"

I explained. "He goes mad with guilt while the police are there looking into a possible disturbance."

"Well, damn."

"Good thing I'm only legally blind," I said sarcastically.


NEIL AND I watched some police procedural drama while we ate, which really was just Neil complaining for forty-five minutes that the forensics team was handling the scene incorrectly, and *no one* got DNA results back that quickly. Disgruntled, he ended up channel-surfing before finding *Home Alone* and settling on that.

"I always wanted to do this," he said as we sat in the dark, sipping wine later in the evening.

"Be Macaulay Culkin?"

"Catch bad guys," Neil replied.

"You do," I pointed out. "Just with big-boy toys. You're a little too old for tar on the stairs and BB guns."

Neil wrapped an arm around my shoulders, and I got comfortable in his embrace. It was nice to be enjoying the evening together and not fighting about stupid shit. Neil must have been thinking the same thing, because he leaned close and kissed the top of my head.

"Hey," he murmured.

"Hey, what?" I responded, looking up. Believe it or not, my vision was considerably better in the dark. Neil's finer details were easier for me to see here.

"Why don't we hightail it out of here?"

"To where?" I laughed.

"The next room over." Neil leaned forward, setting our glasses on the coffee table before getting to his feet.

I stood, taking Neil's offered hand, and let him lead me into our cramped bedroom.

He stopped to put my bag against the wall and shut the door.

"Afraid someone will see?"

He paused before turning to look at me. "To keep the cold air out, Seb," he corrected in that voice I'd come to learn as the *Sebastian, you're being irrational* tone. I did not like it, because he used that tone on me whenever a discussion of his sexuality reared its ugly head.

Neil reached out, grabbed my waist and the back of my head, and kissed me hard. He tasted a little sweet and a little bitter, which about summed up our relationship. He had lost his suit coat and tie since arriving home, but I quickly helped with the remaining shirt and trousers. Neil was busy tossing aside my slacks and sweater when he laughed against my mouth.

"What?"

"You dress like a grandpa," he whispered.

"I like that sweater."

"It's older than you."

"I'm not trying to win a fashion contest."

Clothes shopping was stressful for me. Department stores were so bright, and there was apparently a concept of *clashing colors*. My idea of adding new options to my wardrobe was heading out to secondhand shops with Pop, letting him grab a dozen items in dark colors he says won't hurt anyone's eyes if I mix and match, then we're out in ten minutes.

"We'll get you a nicer sweater," Neil said, kissing my neck.

"I like that one," I replied.

"It's from Goodwill."

"So? I don't need some three hundred dollar Ralph Lauren sweater when that one does a fine job of keeping me warm," I said defensively.

"Are you done, Sebby?" Neil asked, pulling back to stare at me. "Do you really want to argue right now?"

I didn't, of course not. I was sick of fighting, tired of every conversation ending in one of us getting frustrated with the other. Staring at Neil in the near dark, a familiar and awful thought came to mind again.

I wasn't what he really wanted.

It was stupid shit like the sweater. What did it matter if I wore something a little frumpy? He wanted to have me wear something chic and fashionable, like the damn car.

"Seb?"

I shook my head, wrapped my arms around his neck, and kissed Neil, trying to get back into the mood.

*When was the moment our relationship turned?*

He pushed me down onto the bed, kissing and sucking down my chest and stomach.

*When we moved in together, maybe.*

I was turned onto my belly, and the snap of a bottle preceded a warm, oily finger pressing into me.

*When had I grown so defensive? So bitter and resentful toward my partner?*

Neil's hands were on my hips, raising me up before he pushed in roughly.

I gritted my teeth as he started thrusting.

*I didn't like who I had become.*

# CHAPTER TWO

"WE'RE EXPERIENCING record snowfalls for New York City in December," the meteorologist on television said the next morning.

I sat at the little table just outside the kitchen, watching the TV screen from across the room while eating a bowl of Lucky Charms and drinking coffee from my Cheshire Cat mug. When hot liquid was put inside, the cat on the outside vanished, leaving only his grin. *It's the most curious thing!*

"—thirteen inches overnight, with an expected ten to sixteen more throughout the day. We urge residents to stay inside. Winds will reach speeds of forty miles per hour across Manhattan and the outer boroughs, with speeds up to sixty on Long Island."

I grunted at the woman and took another bite of soggy marshmallows. I had already texted Max and told him to forget coming into the city. The MTA had halted service of the buses and subways after the mayor cited safety concerns. The City That Never Sleeps was at a standstill.

I picked up a book I'd left on the table the other day, opened it to the bookmarked page, and read with one of my many magnifying glasses.

Neil came out of the bedroom while pulling his suit coat on. "Mysteries and cereal?" he asked with a frown.

"Sure," I muttered before looking up from the page. "Murders don't wait till after breakfast, Watson."

Neil made a face. "You're not Sherlock." He motioned to the bowl. "That's pure sugar."

"I'll remember to make an appointment with my dentist," I replied before taking another bite.

He didn't rise to the bait of another argument. "You're staying home today, right?"

"Yeah. Max can't get into the city anyway."

I was going to use the day to go through the boxes of inventory that were stacked up here, like I had told myself I would do the night before. But I just hadn't been feeling that old thrill, the excitement I got from going through the untold treasures and mysteries inside each new shipment of antiques. It was like someone put a cup over a flame and snuffed out the oxygen. I missed the rush.

I didn't feel like the same Sebastian I had been even earlier in the year. Not since Neil moved in.

"Something similar must have happened to Mike," I said offhandedly. I set the magnifying glass down and opened the cereal box to refill my bowl.

"What?" Neil was adjusting his hair in the mirror on the wall near the door.

"If the detectives who are investigating his break-in are the same that were called to the Emporium yesterday."

"Drop it, Sebby. You're just wasting energy thinking about it."

"How can you *not* find it strange?"

"I do, but Detective Lancaster is right. There wasn't a crime."

"Someone broke in."

"We talked about this yesterday."

I stirred the cereal into the milk. "Just a quick conversation with Mike would put it all into perspective."

"Seb, I'm serious," Neil said as he turned to stare at me. "If you go over there, I'm not bailing you out of jail when you get arrested."

"Well, it's good to know where you draw the line in this relationship."

Neil shook his head and grabbed his shoes and coat. "I'm leaving." He looked back as he zipped up. "Don't go over there."

"Yes, warden," I said while raising my hand to mock salute him. "Will you call to make sure I don't break curfew too?"

"Cute, Sebby." He opened the door. "Be good."

"I'm not twelve, Neil," I called, but he shut the door as I spoke.

My phone rang from the tabletop not more than a moment later, the caller ID flashing "Dad."

"Good morning, kiddo," said William Snow cheerfully. "Some storm we're having, huh?"

"Hey, Pop."

"I'm not interrupting anything, am I?"

"No. How are you?"

"A little restless. Maggie and I couldn't go for our walk. Staying home today?" he asked.

I hummed in response around a mouthful of cereal. "Not much point in opening the Emporium, I figured."

"Neil home too?"

"No, he had to work." I looked back at the television. "Any plans for the day?"

"Nah," Dad replied lazily.

"Mind if I come over?"

"Of course not, but there aren't any taxis out."

"That's all right," I said while standing and bringing my bowl to the kitchen sink. "I'll slip and slide my way over there."

"Everything okay, Sebastian?"

"Sure," I said, as if saying it out loud would convince me it was true. "I'll see you soon." I said good-bye and hung up.

I went back into the bedroom and pawed through the pile of laundry on the floor of the closet. I tugged on a pair of faded Levi's and pulled on a probably white, maybe gray, T-shirt. In the bathroom I stared at my face in the mirror and rubbed my cheeks while I considered shaving.

Not worth the effort.

I ran my fingers through my hair a few times, washed my face and brushed my teeth, put on deodorant, and then popped in my red-tinted contacts. They made my—according to Pop—*hazel* eyes a very dark brown, but they were a great protection that made wearing my regular, prescription sunglasses possible.

I regretted the decision to go out the minute my boots sank into the unplowed sidewalks. The snow was still coming down hard, and the city was frighteningly quiet. I passed a few other brave souls who were trudging through the storm as I made my way downtown toward my father's apartment.

The streets were empty, the rumbling of snowplows echoing nearby. Nearly everything was closed, save for a lone dry-cleaning shop and the café next door to it. I stopped in long enough to make a purchase of fresh donuts to use as a peace offering for when Pop inevitably started griping about my lackluster appearance. Twenty-five minutes later, which on any day that wasn't Snowpocalypse should have taken about fifteen, I finally reached my dad's building.

I stood on the doorstep, waiting to be buzzed in while shaking snow from my coat and scarf. I grew up in this building. It was one of those architecturally gorgeous, prewar complexes. Dad had been a tenant since he was a teenager and was one of the lucky folks to have a rent-controlled home. Otherwise he probably would have been forced into the outer boroughs after his recent retirement. The buzzer rang and the door unlocked. I hurried inside, took the stairs up to the fourth floor, and knocked.

"It's open!"

I pushed the front door open in time to be assaulted by a huge pit bull. She jumped on her back legs and licked my face and sunglasses. "Oh, Maggie, *come on*, every time!"

"Down, girl," my father said sternly. "You only ever do this to Sebastian," he chastised quietly when his princess hurried to his side, tail wagging happily.

"Hey, Pop," I said with a huff while shutting the door. I took off my coat and scarf, hanging them up before removing my sunglasses to wipe them clean on my shirt.

"I was worried you got lost in the wild, arctic tundra," Pop said with a chuckle.

"Yeah, nearly," I answered. I retrieved my glasses from my coat before setting the box of donuts on the counter.

Pop looked sideways from filling the coffee machine with grounds. "What's that?"

"From Little Earth."

"My favorite."

"I know." I pulled out a tiny bag inside the box to reveal two dog biscuits. Besides being locally famous for their killer donuts, Little Earth was every pup's favorite stop on walks because of their homemade treats. "Promise to stop jumping on me?" I asked Maggie.

She obediently sat, looking up with anxious excitement.

I held the biscuits out, and she snatched them both in one bite. "Sure," I told her. "You'll jump again."

"Did you just roll out of bed?" Pop asked as he finished starting the coffee, only to turn and stare at me with an unhappy expression.

"I brushed my teeth," I replied while leaning back against the counter and looking around.

The apartment hadn't changed much in thirty-some odd years. It was one big, open space, with the long, well-equipped kitchen on the right just as you walk in. There was a small dining table near the large bay windows, and a couch in the middle, surrounded by bookshelves stacked to capacity and a decent entertainment system I had helped Pop set up a few years prior. The bathroom was down the hall, as was my old bedroom, now an office Dad hardly used since his retirement. The master bedroom stood just behind him, at the end of the kitchen. The curtains all around the room had been closed in preparation of my visit, and the lamps were all switched to the lowest settings.

"Well, you forgot your hair," my dad said. He got my attention when he reached out to pat down stray strands. "And didn't I teach you to shave?"

I laughed quietly, rubbing my cheeks. "It's my unexpected day off."

He grumbled something and retrieved two mugs from a cupboard and a plate for the donuts. "Maggie was supposed to have training today, but all of the shelters are closed."

"That's probably for the best."

Dad was sixty-three and just recently retired after thirty years of teaching American Literature at New York University. He couldn't handle the free time, and before he had cracked, I suggested adopting a dog. Enter his little princess, Maggie. Pop and she now spent their spare time volunteering, helping to rehabilitate other rescued pit bulls in the city.

Maggie ran across the kitchen carrying a squeaky toy, stopped at my side, and held it up.

"New toy?" I asked while taking it and tossing it gently across the room.

"It's good to get new toys," Pop said. "Dogs can get bored."

Maggie brought the toy back, squeaking away. I tossed it again before watching my dad. I looked like him. He had aged with a grace I hoped was hereditary. We had the same dark brown hair, he said, though his was actually more gray at this point, and I don't just mean according to my eyes. We both had strong eyebrows and what my ex-boyfriends called cute and dorky facial expressions. Sexy was not an adjective my dad and I heard, put it that way.

"Coffee?" Pop asked.

"Sure."

He put some cream into both mugs. "You sounded upset on the phone." He started pouring fresh coffee.

"Did I?" I asked, taking the cups and walking to the table with them.

"How's everything with Neil?" Dad asked next.

I slowly sat, then turned back to watch him come over with the plate of donuts. "Fine."

Pop eyed me critically while taking a seat. "Really." It wasn't a question.

"Things are okay," I amended. "It's been a bit up and down, that's all."

"Mostly down," Pop said. He broke a donut in half and took a bite.

I didn't argue as I took a donut for myself.

"It's not healthy, Sebastian."

"The donuts?"

Dad didn't think it was funny. "You went through enough crap in school. You shouldn't have to deal with this drama in your thirties."

"Dad, I got shit in school for my wardrobe, not for being gay. Remember that time I accidently wore purple pants with a yellow shirt?" I still didn't understand why that was such a fashion no-no, though.

"Doesn't matter," he said while waving a hand. "But you're an adult. I'm not going to sit here and chastise you on your choice in partners."

"I appreciate that," I muttered. I wiped my hands together before leaning back and resting them behind my head. "Something strange happened at the Emporium yesterday," I said, steering the conversation far, far away from Neil.

After I regaled my story to Dad, he asked, "'The Tell-Tale Heart'?"

I laughed quietly. "That's exactly what I thought."

Pop knew his literature inside and out, especially such a gifted, tortured soul as Edgar Allan Poe. We had him to thank for the modern detective story, Dad would always tell me growing up. He helped to shape science fiction as we know it today and made coded messages popular. Pop could go on and on about American writers and their contributions to literature.

"It's weird, right?" I asked.

"Definitely not in the holiday spirit. How'd it get in your floor?"

"I don't know. Neil figured someone pulled a prank the other day, and Max and I were too busy to take notice."

Pop considered that thoughtfully as he started on his third donut. "I didn't hear anything about Mike's shop in the news. That's a shame, though."

"I guess it's still an open investigation." I sipped my coffee, watching my dad get distracted by Maggie. "Hey, Pop," I said quietly while setting the mug down. "Can I ask you something?"

"Sure, kiddo," he answered while rubbing Maggie's big head.

"Why'd you never get married again, after Mom left?"

Pop paused and looked back up. "Well, that came out of left field."

"Just curious," I said with a shrug.

"I was too busy raising you."

"You're not raising me anymore."

"A father's work is never done."

"I don't want to see you lonely. That's all."

He snickered. "Do you think I'm lonely, Sebastian?"

I wisely kept my mouth shut and just shrugged.

"I'm not. But do you want to know something?"

*Do I?* "What?"

"It's not smart to project your own feelings onto others."


NEW YORK City has over eight million residents.

*Eight million.*

And I was lonely.

I had been with Neil for four years. I had fallen head over heels for that smart, sexy cop, and six months ago I had finally asked him to move in with me. I remembered thinking what a milestone it was. Neil wouldn't want to hide anymore if he wanted to live with me. He'd be out, and when we were seen together, people would know I was his partner.

I snorted to myself while walking down the sidewalk after finishing my visit with dad.

We lived together in that little apartment, and I had never felt farther away from him in all our four years together. Everything had gone to hell six months ago, and I was only just coming to terms with it.

Merry *fucking* Christmas, Sebastian.

It was cold and the wind was fierce enough to push me around, but I decided to go talk with Mike. I didn't need Neil's permission or approval. I was a goddamn adult, and if I wanted to ask Mike where he got off accusing me of stealing, I would.

Even though it wasn't a far walk from Pop's, by the time I got to Bond Street, I was sufficiently frozen through. The cars parked along the sides of the street were buried in over a foot of snow, but I could still pick out the back fins of Mike's famous 1957 Chrysler New Yorker. It was supposedly painted an official color of *shell pink*, but the neighbors just called it the Peptomobile.

I guess it'd be funny if I knew what color Pepto-Bismol was.

At least Mike was sure to be home. He lived in one of the apartments directly above his storefront. I walked toward the doorstep on the right that allowed access to the upstairs, but stopped suddenly. Bond Antiques was dark inside, but the heavy front door was ajar just enough to swing lightly in the wind. Snow was piled up in the partially open doorway.

The hair on the back of my neck stood as I watched the door creak back and forth. Turning to look up and down the street, I couldn't see anyone coming or going. My hands began to sweat in my jacket pockets as I stepped back from the door. I hurried to the apartment buzzer and hit Mike's number.

No one answered.

"Come on, you grouch," I muttered, hitting it again and again.

I jogged to the road to look up at the apartment windows, but between the snow and my vision, I couldn't tell if there were lights on or not. Mike could have simply run down to his shop to grab something. He was probably inside while I stupidly stood on the curb.

But why wouldn't he turn the lights on?

Why leave the door open in this storm?

*Creak.*

*Creak.*

Mike really needed to oil the hinges of the front door. And I nearly laughed out loud that *that* was suddenly the foremost thought in my mind.

My next immediate thought was to call the cops, but tell them what? I was standing outside the building of the business whose owner had, in so many apparent words, accused me of breaking into his shop? I grabbed my phone from my pocket and pulled up the telephone keypad.

That suddenly seemed like a good idea, because what if the shop had been broken into again?

I had hit nine and one before stopping. What was I doing? I could go to the door and check myself. This was ridiculous.

"Mike?" I called into the dimness, knocking on the door as I slowly pushed it open.

*Creeeeeak.*

Jesus Christ.

"Mike? It's Sebastian Snow," I called again, taking a step inside. "You left your damn door open. The floor is all wet." I was talking to a silent room. "I'm coming in, okay?"

I took another step before shutting the door behind me and cautiously looking around. The relative darkness of the shop, in part because there was no sun to shine through the big glass windows, made it easier for me to make out the shapes of chairs and tables. I hadn't been by his shop in a while, and the layout was new.

I felt guilty about tracking snow and slush across the antique wood floors as I made my way around displays. It should have been obvious by now that Mike wasn't here and that the door being left open meant something was wrong and that I should leave, but I did what any idiot would do—kept searching. The silence wasn't exactly right. It was like when you enter a room you know someone else is in and you can just hear that person's very existence—but not *quite*.

A shiver went up my spine, and I nervously wiped my hands on my jeans. I paused at the entrance of the T-shaped floor plan near the rear, with high shelving all around. The displays immediately ahead looked to be ladies' accessories—brooches and gloves, that sort. I couldn't see what was down the left or right aisles without entering.

*Mike isn't here. Mike isn't here. Get out, you idiot!*

But there was no obvious danger present, and I just needed to be certain a thorough search had been made before I considered calling the police for real to report… whatever I thought it was I needed to report. I took a quiet breath and moved forward. Turning left first, I walked straight into something furry. I yelped and jumped back, looking up and then ahead.

*What the fuck!*

It looked to be a cat. But—dead. Certainly dead. It had to be dead. The poor creature was hanging by a rope tied around its neck.

My heart raced, my breath coming out in short, panicked gasps as I looked up to see where the rope had been thrown around the blade of a ceiling fan. Nope. I was not having any of this. I turned, slipped on the wet floor, and grabbed a shelf to stay upright. A figure stood unmoving and staring at me from the right section of the T. Absolutely freaked, I hauled ass back to the entrance of the layout and made a hard right, running along the outer side of the T for the door. I didn't get far before I tripped over something big and firm on the floor, crashing straight down on top of it.

I fell in something sticky.

"Oh my God," I heard myself whisper as I braced my hands on the floor and shakily raised myself.

Mike stared up at me through lifeless, half-lidded eyes, a chunk of his head missing. Blood pooled and congealed all around him like a halo.

# CHAPTER THREE

TODAY SUCKED.

And the Understatement of the Year Award goes to: Sebastian Snow. I had called the cops after that. Of course.

Those few seconds after finding Mike were almost surreal. I had fallen back on my ass, stumbling away from the body. My hands and jacket were covered in blood. For a moment I sat on the floor in a daze, my heart slugging against my chest as I tried to catch my breath.

*What do I do?*

*Holy shit.*

Then a lightbulb flickered in the recesses of my mind. Detective Winter. He had given me his card yesterday. I had considered throwing it out but ultimately stashed it into a pocket. Suddenly no other plan of action seemed better or safer than calling him. He was already dealing with Mike's case—he'd help. He'd know what to do.

I wiped my shaking hands on my Levi's and fumbled through my pockets, eventually retrieving his card. I dialed and put the phone to my ear.

One ring. Two. Three.

*Jesus. Please, please, pick up.*

I was getting to my feet, feeling lightheaded and ready to vomit, when there was a gruff greeting on the other end.

"Detective Winter."

"I-I need help," I instantly said. Nothing like getting straight to the point.

"Who is this?" Winter's tone was strong and concerned.

"Sebastian Snow."

"Snow?"

"I—yesterday, you came—"

"I remember who you are. What's wrong?"

How to explain this? I took a deep breath and, in a voice that may have come across as too calm, said, "There's been an accident at Mike's shop, Bond Antiques."

I turned to the displays. Someone had been standing in there. Why hadn't they come after me? They were the one who did that to Mike—*right*?

"What sort of accident?" Winter asked.

I didn't respond, zoning out of the call as I warily approached the entrance of the T again. If I ran outside now, the killer would get away and no one would know what happened to poor goddamn Mike. I was shit scared but kept moving forward.

"Sebastian? Are you there? Sebastian!" he said more firmly.

"*Shh*," I hissed.

"Are you okay?"

I was nearly at the turn. Something wasn't right. This guy, or girl, should have come out by now. They should have heard my call, even heard Winter through the phone. I steeled myself and turned the corner.

The person was still standing there, wearing a heavy Victorian gown with a matching hat on their head.

Because it was a mannequin.

"Oh, fuck me," I whispered, letting out a breath.

"Talk to me, now," Winter ordered. "Are you hurt?"

"No," I said quietly, feeling like a moron. "But, Mike is."

"I'll have an ambulance sent—"

"It's too late for that."

There was a brief pause on his end before he said, "I'm on my way. Don't move."

The following ten minutes, I stood at the counter in the store, staring at Mike. Every time I looked away, my gaze wandered back, like if I didn't keep an eye on him, he'd get up and start coming after me for a replacement brain. I swallowed the bile threatening its way up my throat.

I wasn't even able to wait outside. I think my current state—soaked in blood—would worry the neighbors.

When I felt like I couldn't stand one more second alone in that shop without losing my mind, an ambulance showed up with its lights on but no siren. Three cop cars pulled up, followed by an unmarked car, which Winter and Lancaster climbed out of. They rushed across the sidewalk and to the door, uniformed officers following.

Winter immediately paused when I turned to face him.

"I can explain," I stated, holding up my bloody hands as an act of submission, but I think it gave off the wrong signal.

"Where is he?" Winter demanded, then looked in the direction I pointed. He turned and gave orders for the store to be checked, and the officers split off to lock down the location. Both Winter and Lancaster pulled SIG P226s from their holsters. Winter moved forward first, with Lancaster following close behind as backup.

Interesting partner dynamic. I *knew* she wasn't in charge, despite having taken the lead in questioning me the day before.

They were gone for several moments before the scene was declared secure. Officers came back to the front door, a few stepping out to cordon off the front of the shop.

Winter was on his phone, giving stern orders to some unlucky soul on the other end. When he hung up, he was standing near Mike's body, looking down. He crouched to examine without touching. After a pause, he stood back up, asking for lights to be turned on as he studied the floor.

One of the officers found the shop lights, and I winced slightly as the room blew up white and pushed my sunglasses back onto my nose with a bloody knuckle.

Winter took careful steps around my melted-snow-and-blood trail, eventually making his way back to me. "Mr. Snow."

"Detective Winter."

"Do you give all of the men in your life a murder case for Christmas, or just the really special ones?" he asked, hands in his pockets as he stopped to tower over me.

*Shit.* Why had calling him seemed like a good idea?

"Can I explain?"

"Please," he said. I swear he nearly growled.

I started to give him an abridged story—Dad's house to Mike's shop, to no Mike, to dead Mike. "Want me to tell it to you backward?" I asked after finishing.

"Why?"

"Because you look like you're sizing me up for a jumpsuit, and if I were lying, it'd be harder for me to get the facts straight backward," I answered.

That made him snort. "Is that so? Why'd you enter the shop when it was clearly closed?"

"I told you, the door was open."

"And you didn't think that was strange?"

"Well—no, I did, but Mike lives right upstairs. I thought maybe he had just run down for something."

"Why continue when no one answered your entrance?"

"I don't know," I admitted. "Something didn't seem right."

"Why didn't you just call the cops?"

"I did." I pointed at him.

Winter frowned and was silent for a moment, like a man desperately collecting his patience. "What happened when you called me?" he finally continued.

I glanced down at my sticky hands. "In the T display, over in the back. I—there's a cat back there."

"A cat?"

"Yes, but it was dead. I mean, it was hanging by a noose. I ran, and a stupid mannequin behind me looked like a person, and I was spooked. I didn't see Mike, and I tripped over him. Face-first."

"Ah."

"And so, I thought the mannequin was the person who killed Mike. You knew who I was and who Mike was. I didn't think I should call anyone else. Look, can we do this later? I really want to change."

Winter shook his head and pointed a blunt finger at me. "Don't move."

"Come on, Detective! I'm covered in blood!"

The prick was already walking away.

I moved to look around the corner, watching him go into the T display with Detective Lancaster. I huffed and crossed my arms before quickly uncrossing them. So much for this jacket. And jeans. I'd have to scrub my skin raw in the shower too.

I was left to stand there under the eye of a uniformed cop who kept a hand on his belt, ready to put a bullet in my knee if I tried to duck out. That's when the gravity of the situation began pushing down on my shoulders. I told myself everything would be fine. They'd confirm everything I'd said with evidence analysis done by someone like Neil.

Oh God.

"Neil...." Was going to kill me.

I was doing my best to come up with a bearable story besides *I resented being treated like a child and wanted to defy you* when Winter was approaching me with a short, middle-aged woman. "So, about changing," I said again.

"We need your clothing."

"You what?"

"Evidence." He nodded at the woman who had just come in a moment before.

"I'll need you to hand over the jacket and jeans, and whatever is underneath," she confirmed while putting on latex gloves.

"I didn't kill Mike!" I protested while looking back at Winter.

"You're covered in his blood," he pointed out. "You were found alone on his property with the body."

"I called *you* after finding him!" I said, voice rising.

"I'm only taking your clothes," Winter said sternly, moving a step closer and already filling up the space around us. "But if you keep it up, I'll be more than happy to book you and then strip you."

Wow.

I swallowed audibly, clearing my throat. "Can I make a phone call?"

"Why?"

"I don't have anything to wear. Just—let me make a call, please?"

A moment of internal deliberation was followed by a curt nod, and Winter backed off.

I pulled out my bloodstained phone and picked Neil from the contacts.

"Seb?" was the first thing he said. "Is everything okay?"

"No," I admitted. "Can you go home—"

"I'm at work."

"I know, but listen. I need you to go home," I said quietly, glancing up to make sure Winter wasn't listening in too much, but he was speaking with the woman waiting to see my nether regions. "I need you to grab a change of clothes for me, and a coat. Come over to Bond Antiques."

"What's going on?"

"I'll explain when you get here, but please hurry."

Hurry he did. Neil was there in just under twenty minutes, which couldn't have been safe in this storm, but I was thankful since the blood was fairly dry and crusty and making me extremely uncomfortable at this point. I watched Neil flash his badge and gain immediate entrance into the shop. He was carrying a backpack and looking around warily.

"Detective Millet?" Winter asked, intercepting Neil before I had a chance to shock him with my appearance.

Neil turned at the call of his name. "Oh, Winter. Hello."

"You part of my evidence team? You're late."

Neil shook his head. "No… I'm not…." He paused, sort of at a loss with the situation.

"Neil," I called.

He looked over his shoulder, and I was able to discern his startled expression from the distance between us and with the lights on, which meant he was probably going to freak the fuck out in three, two, one….

"Seb? What the hell?" he asked, approaching me. "Jesus! This isn't yours, right?"

"No. Neil, I'm sorry I had to call. But they need to take my clothes into evidence, and I didn't want to sport a onesie, courtesy of the NYPD."

"Evidence for what?" Neil demanded.

"Mike's dead." I motioned to myself. "I mean, no, no! I found him. I tripped over him. His head was—can I just have the clothes?" I asked tiredly and grabbed for the backpack.

"No, tell me what happened."

"So you and Mr. Snow are close?" Winter asked, having come up behind Neil silently.

"Friends," Neil replied sternly.

I was too stressed to give a shit about this lie and let it slide without remark.

"Friends with keys to each other's apartments?" Winter continued.

"I'm just here to drop off clothes," Neil warned in a tone with the underlying threat of *back off, man*. He looked at me and thrust the pack forward. "I'll talk to you later." He was walking out the door before I could think of something to say.

Winter turned his gaze on me, and I stared back up at him. Of all the serious issues I could have been focusing on, I was instead obsessing over his curious-looking eyes again. And those freckles. God, he even had them down his neck, disappearing under the collar of his shirt. I started to consider just how extensive that freckle trail was—

"Get those clothes off." He pointed expectantly at the woman who appeared at my side again to collect the damning evidence.

"Winter," Lancaster called as she stepped into the store again with a man who had to be the city medical examiner.

Winter gave me one last glare before leaving.

I learned the evidence woman's name was Martha Stewart—no relation, she added—and she had no sense of privacy.

"Honey, if you think I'm trying to sneak a peek, you've got nothing to worry about," she said, carefully putting my jacket into a collection bag and labeling the front.

"No? Why's that?" I asked, trying my best to ignore the fact I was now naked from the waist up in a cold room, with half a dozen cops nearby and a coroner shoving a liver thermometer into the body of my former boss.

"You aren't my type," she indicated while putting away my T-shirt next.

"I bet you say that to keep all the boys from blushing."

"I got a wife, sweetie," Martha said casually. "Pants. Come on. I've got a lot to do here."

I had never unbuttoned so quickly for anyone, but she was about to start tapping her foot. "You're not my type either, Martha."

"Oh, I can tell," she said, chuckling to herself.

"What does that mean?"

"It means you sure aren't checking out my goods when you've got a ginger to ogle."

Instead of vehemently denying the fact that I found Detective Winter even remotely attractive, I asked, "So his hair's red?"

She stared curiously.

"I can't see color," I clarified.

"Oh. Yeah, it's red. Well, more orange, like that fiery color. You know."

"I don't know, but I'll take your word for it," I replied. I glanced back toward Mike. The coroner was crouched beside him, talking to Winter, who did a real good job at looking like a sexy, imposing badass you'd see in a TV drama. And I had to pause while undressing because I was now painfully aware that I had an erection.

Of all places, times, and people to be aroused by.

"Hey," Martha said, snapping her gloved fingers.

"Can I put my new shirt on?" I asked, stalling.

She sighed heavily and picked up her camera. "Hold on. I need to photograph."

"Whoa, what, all of me?"

"I've never met such a prude," she mumbled. "Hold your hands out, palms down." Martha took several photos of my hands at different angles, as well as my chest, where a small smudge of blood had ended up. Upon finishing, I was allowed to put on my new shirt, which had given my body enough time to stand down from saluting.

I quickly finished stripping, having to pause for another photo before Martha deemed me finished, and she waited expectantly as I made myself proper. "Pleasure to meet you, Martha," I said, unsure what else I was supposed to tell a woman after I stripped and posed for her. Would "thank you" have been better?

She hummed absently in response while putting her camera aside and gathering up the bags. "Want a word of advice?"

I paused, one arm through the sleeve of a jacket that was more suited to cool autumn weather than the shitstorm outside. "Sure?"

"Don't go giving Winter a hard time, or he'll book your ass faster than you can say *heartless*."

What did that mean? "Uh...."

"He's seen it all," she said in a tone of warning. "And has patience for none of it." Martha left me alone after that.

I pushed my sunglasses back up and crossed my arms over my chest. I was suddenly freezing, but it wasn't a chill that shook me to the bone. Fear, that's what it was.

*Let's take a step back, look at this objectively.* Neil had taught me a lot about crimes and evidence, and I needed to use that to my advantage. I had zero interest in becoming a suspect—or worse, being arrested by Detective Winter.

Rigor mortis starts to set in around two hours after death, and the human body can decrease in temperature at an average rate of one point five degrees per hour. I needed to factor in, however, that the shop door had been open for who knows how long, which could affect the temperature reading on the body. If rigor was setting in, I could suspect poor Mike had been dead since....

I turned to squint at the wall clock behind me.

The officer who had been watching me the entire time asked, "Got somewhere to be?"

THE MYSTERY OF NEVERMORE                    39

"I can't read the time."

He glanced at the wall. "Just after twelve."

All right. I had been there close to an hour, which means it had been around eleven when I found Mike. So at a minimum, he was killed around eight that morning. I had alibis. Pop, the one employee at Little Earth—hell, I'd even drag Neil into this if it meant my head.

When I looked up from counting points off my fingers, Winter was standing in front of me, a strange expression on his face. Amused? Indulgent? Curious? It was hard to tell.

"Hi," I said.

"I've got some more questions."

Lancaster was giving orders in the background to have space made as a gurney was brought in and Mike's body was placed on it. So long, Mike....

"Where were you at seven this morning?" Winter asked.

*Ah-ha!* "Mike has only been dead a few hours?"

"Answer the question."

I knew it. Rigor mortis started with the face—the eyes, jaw, down the neck. His entire body wasn't affected yet, which meant he had to have been attacked when I was around other people. Given, also, how much snow had piled up in the doorway, it roughly corresponded with what the news had been saying about the city's expected precipitation per hour.

"Seven? I was home."

"Doing what?"

"Thinking about getting out of bed."

"Do you live alone, Mr. Snow?"

I felt the muscle in my throat jump. If I said yes, I would be lying to a cop, which was never good. If I said no, Winter would want the contact information of the second individual.

Would Neil mind?

*Of course*, but given the circumstances, would he be willing to out himself to a fellow detective, who he believed was a homophobe, if it meant the safety of his boyfriend?

It concerned me greatly that I didn't have an answer to that question.

"No, not exactly," I heard myself answer.

Winter looked expectant.

"I live with my boyfriend. He was home. He'd vouch for me."

"I'm sure he would," Winter said in a tone I couldn't quite place. "I'll need his contact information." He took out a pad and pen from inside his coat.

I quietly repeated Neil's cell number, watching as Winter wrote it down. There was no going back now. "Neil Millett."

He paused and looked up. "CSU?"

"Yeah."

Winter made a sound that was sort of a snort and a laugh. He wrote down Neil's name.

"What's that?" I asked.

"Nothing, other than I'm not surprised."

"What, that I'm gay?"

"That was easy to see," he replied, not looking up.

I had no idea. I never thought I came off particularly *gay*. "I didn't realize I left my neon sign on."

"I'll be in touch with Mr. Millett," Winter said.

"Oh joy."

"Walk me through your morning."

"Since seven?" When he nodded, I took a breath and said calmly, "Laid in bed for a while. Neil got up to shower. I went into the kitchen and made coffee and had breakfast. I watched the news. Neil went to work a little before eight. My father called as he left, and then I got dressed to go see him. I stopped at Little Earth—bought donuts and dog biscuits. I left Pop's around quarter to eleven." I proceeded to give him Pop's contact information and address, and the same for the café. "I couldn't have hurt Mike, and you know it," I said. "Right? He was killed around seven. That's what the examiner thinks."

Winter didn't respond as he put his notepad back into his pocket and adjusted his suit coat.

"I can't drive, and Neil had the car anyway. You know I walked to all of these places and that there's no way I'd have had enough time. It went down like I said," I insisted.

"Pick all this up from Millett?"

"No, I base this all off the infallible facts of *CSI* and *Law & Order*," I retorted.

To my surprise, Detective Winter did not throttle me then and there.

"I don't have any reason to want to hurt Mike," I tried next. "Ever. What's the point? Where's the motive?"

"Motive isn't the most important factor."

"Of course it is," I said defensively.

"You're not a suspect," Winter said quietly, changing the subject.

The relief that went through me nearly knocked me to the floor. "Really?" *Don't act so surprised.*

"Really," he said gruffly. "But I don't want you leaving the city, understand?"

"What am I going to do, walk to Jersey?"

"I ought to arrest you on grounds of being a smartass."

"Probably," I agreed. I raised my hands. "Can I please wash this off?"

"Go out to the ambulance." Winter nodded at the uniformed officer. "See that Mr. Snow, here, is cleaned up and then drive him home."

The officer nodded and asked for me to follow him.

It was around lunchtime when I got home.

# CHAPTER FOUR

I WAS undressed and turning on the shower within minutes of walking through the door. I threw the clothes Neil had brought me into a pile on the bathroom floor before stepping into the tub. I lathered my body with soap, grabbed the washcloth, and scrubbed every inch of myself. It didn't matter that the paramedics had helped clean my hands. Touching a dead body—no, *falling* into the congealed blood of a dead body—will make anyone want to shower.

I put my hands against the tiles afterward, leaning forward to let the spray hit the back of my head. I was exhausted. Murder was tiring. How did people like Detective Winter deal with it day in and day out?

*Fiery orange, you know?*

Color, I have learned, was a very complicated concept. There wasn't just orange; there were different shades, all subtle and unique, each capable of producing a different emotion or reaction. So what was fiery orange like?

Calvin Winter, with hair like an orange fruit? A pumpkin? I thought some construction signs were orange.... Even fiery as a description was difficult for me. Some people told me fire was yellowish, while others said more red. Or it could be like burning gas in a stove, which I've learned is actually blue.

But these color names meant nothing to me.

To me, Calvin was gray. His eyes were gray, and his freckles were gray. I'd never experience that exact shade of red hair he had. So why did a man—who was the same color to me as a sunset or dog shit—seem to stand out from the muted world around him in a way no one ever had? I couldn't explain.

Not entirely.

Calvin—and when had he gone from Winter to Calvin?—was hot and I won't deny that. He was so different from Neil, and not just in build and hairstyle. He was a little rough and a little hard, but he had an intriguing energy and a sort of guarded personality. And when he'd been on the phone with me, he sounded genuinely concerned, nothing like the *heartless* comment Ms. Martha Stewart had made.

Neil hadn't been concerned. At least not about me personally. I had been stuck in the middle of a murder scene, and Neil didn't even stay to make sure I was okay.

I raised my head and wiped my eyes. The hot water was cleansing, and both my body and mind were feeling better. Then I remembered I had gotten hard looking at Calvin earlier. *Unbelievable.* It's not like he had touched me or told me he wanted to do wicked things with me. *Hell,* he hadn't even been looking at me.

He'd actually been paying more attention to a dead man than me.

I leaned back against the wall, pressing the heels of my hands to my eyes. Was it okay to find someone else attractive when you were in a committed relationship? It'd been a while since anyone but Neil had made my cock ache as bad as it had at Bond Antiques, and it usually required a bit of effort on Neil's part to get me there.

Just thinking of sex in the same breath as Calvin made me reach down to touch myself. That was not good. It was not healthy, right? Fantasizing about another guy, and definitely not one I could have, because I was dating Neil. More or less. And because Calvin was not into guys. I didn't get the homophobe vibe Neil did, but I certainly wasn't getting fellow gay man either.

But by then I was hard again, and it didn't fucking matter if Calvin was gay or straight. I closed my eyes and imagined his hand instead of mine. Big and muscular, with callused palms able to give just the exact amount of pressure and speed I needed. I thought about what it must be like to be naked with him. His strong form surrounding me. His entire body nothing but solid muscle, chest dusted with light hair, and freckles all over.

*All over.*

Jesus, I'd never been so turned on by freckles in my life.

A little harder, a little faster. I was vaguely aware of my own heavy breathing. In my fantasy Calvin was pressed roughly against me, my cock between us as he stroked. He dipped his mouth close to my ear, then bit and sucked the lobe. He wanted to fuck me, and I wanted it bad.

I opened my eyes when I came suddenly.

*Well, then.* So there was that little truth. Maybe Calvin had no interest in fucking me for real, but that didn't change the fact that I would have bent over for him in a heartbeat. I cleared my throat in an *I'm embarrassed by myself* manner, washed once more, and turned off the water.

Dried and changed into a third set of clothes for the day, I walked into the front room and sat on the couch before turning on the television.

It was still snowing, I was being told. Stellar news reporting.

"There is another storm front on the tail of this, which is expected to hit New York City within forty-eight hours. There will be a small window when citizens can go out and unbury cars and get shopping done before they can expect to be blanketed by another ten to fifteen inches," the weatherman said.

"Awesome."

I stood back up, went into the kitchen, and searched the cupboards for food while convincing myself I hadn't just jacked off to fantasies about a cop who had been almost ready to handcuff me this morning. Okay, that wasn't entirely true. Calvin said I wasn't a suspect, but that threat to stay in the city told me I was definitely at the top of their person of interests list. I shuddered. Not a place I wanted to be.

I popped the top off a soup can and poured the New England clam chowder into a pot. I watched the contents bubble. Something about that crime scene had been weird. What had Mike been attacked with? A butcher knife? It was such a massive slice in his head....

I swallowed the sour taste coming up my throat.

No, weirder than that. It had been—

"The cat," I said suddenly. The poor animal that had been hanging from a rope around its neck. What had that been, a warning perhaps? Had Mike gotten mixed up with the wrong sort of people and walked in on someone leaving it?

What struck me as more bizarre than the cat itself was that that story was familiar.

I ran out of the kitchen and shoved aside a few boxes of the estate winnings I was hoarding to get to the bookshelf in the front room. The news anchors were discussing alternate side of the street parking rules being suspended for the next day while I knocked several stacked books off the cramped shelves. One too many mystery novels starring an English spinster and her cat; I had long ago run out of places to put them all. Near the bottom was a well-worn and battered copy of *The Complete Tales and Poems of Edgar Allan Poe*.

Growing up with a parent like my father, literature was important in our home. To my Pop's horror, I had never been one for the likes of Faulkner or Hemingway as a kid, but I had at least loved Poe. A depressed man with a twisted, tortured soul and mind. He made more money after his death than he had his entire life as a writer.

I snatched the book, holding it close to my face while reading the table of contents. There it was, page 387, "The Black Cat." I hurried to the table, sat, and grabbed the magnifying glass to help with the fine print. I now remembered reading this in junior high and how profoundly disturbed I had been by it. The details of the story had faded with the years that I refused to reread it. Everything but the death of the cat.

Pluto. That was his name.

"One morning," I read, "in cold blood, I slipped a noose about its neck and hung it to the limb of a tree."

And there it was. A cat hanged to death.

What were the chances the cat left in Mike's shop was black?

I looked back down at the pages, shaking my head. This was weird.

No. This was fucked up. Maybe I was reading too much into it, but why did short stories of Poe come to mind in both this situation and at my shop yesterday? I kept reading, refreshing myself with the disturbing story that involved a man lost to madness after becoming an alcoholic. He had killed his wife with an axe—

"To the head."

Something was burning.

I looked away from the book before jumping up and running into the kitchen. So much for lunch. I wasn't that hungry anyway. I turned off the burner and yanked open the blinds of the small kitchen window. I winced and squinted slightly, fumbling with the latch before thrusting the window up and using a potholder to guide the smoke out.

I took a long, deep breath. What were the facts? Mike's shop had been broken into on Sunday night, and the old curmudgeon had pointed an accusing finger at me. Tuesday morning, I found a pig's heart rotting under the floorboards, and by Wednesday morning, Mike was found dead in his shop. Then there was the curious addition of the cat.

I wondered what the circumstances of the break-in had been. The detectives hadn't offered any details yesterday. Something undoubtedly strange had to have occurred, or someone as stiff-lipped as Mike Rodriguez wouldn't have called for help. And not that I had exactly been paying close attention earlier at his store, but it didn't appear to have been ransacked. Everything was in order, from what I could tell.

I stuck the pot of burned soup in the sink and turned the water on.

I was missing something.

What did Poe have to do with this? Anything? I couldn't have been imagining the connection to his writing—could I?

What Mike and I had in common was pretty basic. We both owned antique shops and lived in Manhattan. That was it. I had worked for him, but that had been years ago. We weren't friends, but hardly enemies. I was thirty-three. Mike had to be in his midfifties. I was a gay man in a committed, shitty relationship. Mike was straight and had been a long-time bachelor.

I started scrubbing the pot and thought about calling Calvin. Maybe this was an important revelation in—whatever exactly this case was. The same person could be behind the pig heart in my shop and the untimely demise of Mike. I briefly considered that the heart could have been a warning for me.

But about what?

Was I going to get smashed over the head next?

"You are not a cop," I told myself sternly. "What happened to Mike is awful, but it's not your job to find the guy. Stay out of it, or you're going to get arrested."

That would have been enough to stop a regular person from getting caught up in a murder case. Hell, maybe under different circumstances, I would have heeded my own warning too.

But I was angry.

Angry at Mike, angry at Neil, angry at a lot of people.

And my business had been tampered with.

I felt justified.

I wiped my hands dry on my jeans while searching for my cell. I held it close enough to read and went through previous contacts, picked out Calvin Winter's cell, and pressed Call.

He didn't answer, and instead his recorded voice told me to leave a message.

"Uh—hey. It's Sebastian. Snow. Sebastian Snow...."

*He knows your name. Shut up and get to the point.*

"Look, I had an idea about who may have hurt Mike. It's a bit farfetched, but if you don't mind, give me a call back?" Halfway through the message, I began to feel like an idiot.

I was a civilian, not a detective. My ideas weren't going to help. The people who cracked these cases were Neil and Calvin.

Maybe I should bounce the idea off Neil. *If* he planned on talking to me again.

I realized I had been silent for an exceptionally long period. "Sorry to waste your time." I hung up quickly.


I CRASHED hard afterward and slept through the rest of the afternoon. I think what initially woke me was the pair of cardinals that nested in the tree outside our bedroom window. Cardinals mated for life. I had learned that one afternoon many years back, when I first moved into this apartment.

Lucky them. I bet they got along great.

I rolled over onto my back in bed. My eyes hurt. I'd fallen asleep with my contacts in.

Great.

The room was pretty dark, and the fuzzy numbers on the alarm said something like 6:DS, so I assumed Neil would be home anytime. I sat up, grabbed my glasses off the nightstand, and put them on before standing.

I heard a kitchen cupboard open and cans being moved around. Speak of the devil.

Opening the bedroom door, I rubbed the back of my head absently. I wondered if Calvin had grilled Neil on his morning whereabouts to confirm my alibi. When I stopped in the doorframe between the kitchen and front room, Neil turned to glare at me.

Roger that, sir. And target appears hostile. Proceed with caution.

"Hi, Neil," I said, leaning against the frame and crossing my arms.

He didn't reply. He did slam the cupboard door shut hard enough to rattle plates inside another.

"So—"

"Your friend paid me a visit at work," Neil interrupted.

"My friend?"

"Detective Winter," he retorted, turning to look at me.

"Ah-ha."

"Don't *ah-ha*, Sebby. You told him. You fucking *told* him!"

"That I had an alibi that would keep me out of jail?" I argued back. "You're damn right I told him, Neil! And where do you get off like this? I was at a murder scene today, and you didn't even stay to make sure I was okay!"

"What did I say to you this morning?" Neil asked as he approached me. "I told you not to go to Mike's. You promised, and what did you do? You got yourself involved!"

"Technically I never promised…. Besides, I could have been hurt—!"

"That would have been your own damn fault!"

I was stunned speechless for a beat. No matter how angry I could have been at Neil, if he had been in trouble, I know I'd have not given one single shit about arguments in the past. What would have mattered was his health and safety.

"You're unbelievable," I said.

"Fuck you, Sebastian," he said through clenched teeth. "You told a cop that I was gay. That's official now! That's in the books! Do you know how quickly it will get around? You've endangered my entire livelihood!"

I threw my hands up. "Right, I forgot. This is all about you, Neil. This entire relationship from the start has been what's best for you!"

"Sebby—"

"Stop calling me that! God! I hate it!"

Neil shook his head and made to move around me in the doorway.

I stopped him by taking a step forward. "No," I demanded. "You're not going to just leave the room without talking to me." I reached out to put a hand on Neil's chest, but he shoved me.

Hard.

I hit the doorframe as he barged past me. "How do you think I feel?" I called as he went toward the bedroom. "Being someone you're ashamed of for *four* years. I can't even walk too close to you in public without you getting weird."

"Shut up, Sebastian."

"I needed you today, Neil!" I followed him into the bedroom. "I was scared and could have been thrown in jail. I needed my partner, and you just *left* me!" I watched him shove clothes into a bag. "Where the fuck are you going?"

"I'd rather sleep in my car than look at you right now, Seb."

"That's nice. Really nice," I snapped back. "We're at a critical juncture in our relationship and you're walking out."

"That's right," Neil said while looking up. "I am. I don't want to talk to you. I don't want to listen to you. You've made me so angry, Sebastian, that—I can't even yell because I'm beyond it."

"What does this say about us, Neil?"

What was happening? Did he honestly expect to have our relationship stay a secret forever? I couldn't live like that. The reality—having to give Neil up if he didn't get comfortable dating me—hurt a lot.

He wasn't answering me, just finished filling his bag with a few more items.

"Neil," I said again, my voice desperate.

He shouldered the bag and pushed me aside with it as he left the room.

I turned and followed, feeling like a pathetic puppy. "You're really just going to walk out?"

Silent treatment.

"Neil, I can't live like this," I said, squaring my shoulders.

He put on his jacket and boots at the door.

"Neil! Goddamn it!" I couldn't fight—couldn't get my point across—if he wouldn't even meet me halfway. "If you walk out, I'm changing the fucking locks."

"Piss off, Seb." He opened the door and left.

# CHAPTER FIVE

"YOU LOOK like shit."

"Thank you."

The Emporium was able to open the next morning, the storm having ended sometime during the night. The mayor had lifted the ban on driving, and the MTA, however briefly before the next storm, was running. With delays.

*Of course.*

Max was over an hour late getting to the shop, but frankly I didn't mind.

I had been sitting in my office, staring at the black computer screen when he came in.

"It's not meant to be interpreted as a compliment," Max continued as he tried to fix his hair after taking his winter cap off.

"I know, but seeing as I feel worse than shit—"

"A tapeworm in cat crap," Max offered helpfully.

"Yeah, sure. Anyway. The *just shit* is a compliment."

Max turned and pointed at the counter. "I brought you a coffee."

I looked up with what was certain to be a pathetic smile, because Max suddenly looked so concerned. "Thanks." I stood.

"Neil?" he guessed. Not that it was hard.

I wished I had some minor aggravation to complain about, like the water heater in my apartment building broke, or the college kids who lived above me had a party until four in the morning. Something.

*Anything.* But the reality was, my super was extremely good at his job, and the kids above me were the bookish sort.

"It's fine," I said while waving my hand. I eyed the four cups. "Why so many?"

"They released new flavors," Max explained. "Two for each of us!"

I grabbed one of the coffees that looked like it had my name scrawled on the side and took a sip. Another sugary concoction from Starbucks, but Max loved them. He was trying to sway me in their favor, but I liked my coffee dark and bitter.

Maybe that said something about me. I set the cup aside and reached for a piece of saltwater taffy I left in a bowl on the counter. Bitter coffee and old-man candy.

"—Japan has the cherry blossom flavor," Max was saying.

"The what?"

"*Sakura*, isn't it? In spring, they have pink fraps. I want to go so I can try one."

"I'm sure there's a better reason to take a trip around the world."

"Why would you go to Japan, then?" he asked while sipping his drink.

"Me? In the Land of the Rising Sun? Come on. I'd be stricken blind," I teased lightly.

Max laughed. "What do you need done today?"

I took a deep breath and another sip of my nutmeg-caramel-mocha-soy-whateverthehellthiswas, which did *not* go well with taffy, and then nodded toward the back. "We ought to go through the boxes."

"Finally?" he asked with a grin.

"Spring cleaning," I replied.

"Little early for that," Max remarked.

"I need a fresh start," I said.

Hearing myself say that was—strange. Had I meant what I said to Neil the night before, about changing the locks? Did he understand what I had implied by that? Did *I* understand it in the heat of the moment?

I guess I had.

"Get a pair of gloves and the clipboard. Start with box one."

"Yup, I got it," Max said, leaving with his coffee to do as asked.

I fished my cell out of my pocket and raised it close to pick my dad from the contacts. I knew what he'd say about this. I didn't even need to hear it.

Not really.

Maybe.

"Dad?"

"Hey, kiddo. Everything okay? I tried calling you yesterday."

"Did you?" *Uh-oh.*

"Around eight."

I had turned my phone off after Neil left. I wanted to make a point, on the off-chance he tried to call during the evening. "Sorry, Pop. I had my phone off."

"What's going on with Mike Rodriguez? A detective called me yesterday about your visit."

"Mike's dead, Dad," I said quietly, glancing up, but Max was far in the back of the shop.

"Good lord!"

"It's complicated—not really why I called," I admitted selfishly.

"You have something that'll top this?"

"Well, no, but…. Neil walked out last night."

There was a long pause on my father's side. So much so that I thought the call had been dropped. "Dad?"

"Is he coming back?" he finally asked.

I wasn't sure and told him as much as I sat on the stool behind the counter. "I don't know what to do, Pop."

"It's your life, Seb. I can't tell you how to live it."

"You could give me a few pointers," I joked. "Shit hit the fan because I told that detective I lived with Neil. I had to. He was questioning me."

I heard my dad sigh. "I know why you're torn about this, Sebastian."

"Do you?"

"You've been together for a while. It's… not easy having your heart broken."

I felt an unexpected lump form and cleared my throat. Like father, like son. My mother had walked out on my dad and me when I was about six years old. My memories of her aren't great, but my father's devastation? *That* I remembered with painful clarity.

The shop door opened, and I heard Max go to greet the customer. I turned my back to continue the call with my dad. "Maybe we just need some time apart," I said lamely.

"Seb," my dad started.

"Sebastian?" Max called.

"Hold on, Pop." I turned. "What is it?"

Max pointed. "It's your detective."

"My—?" *Neil?*

No.

Calvin stepped into view from around a pillar. "Good morning."

My heart did a sudden jump of excitement, which was definitely not what I thought I should be feeling. "I, uh, sorry, I've got to go, Pop. Can I call you later?" I hastily said good-bye before hanging up and walking down the steps to meet Calvin.

"How's everything here?" he asked.

I looked at Max, who got the hint and excused himself. "Fine," I said, looking up. "Free of any ritualistic dismemberments."

"Good," he said simply, as if he were expecting that as my response.

"Am I under arrest?"

"No, but if you want to see the inside of a cell so badly, just ask," Calvin replied.

I was caught off guard by the smartass response.

Then he did something I hadn't seen yet. He smiled.

"So you can be rendered speechless," he stated. "I'll be."

I didn't really know how to answer. I squinted a bit to get a better read on Calvin's expression. Despite the smile, he looked tired. Haggard, but holding it together. "Have you slept? Since yesterday?"

He consulted his watch, like he really didn't know what time it was. "No."

To my surprise I asked, "Do you want some coffee?"

"That'd be nice."

I led Calvin over toward the register and picked up the second coffee Max had purchased for me. "I don't know what crazy flavor it is," I warned.

"I'm not picky," he said while taking it. "Thank you."

I watched him take a drink. "Not that I don't enjoy your company," I said casually, "but why are you here?"

"You called me."

"I did?" *Butt dial?*

"Yesterday."

"Oh. Right. I didn't mean to waste your time. It was a mistake."

"You said you may have an idea about Mr. Rodriguez's murder. That's not a waste of my time."

"Why didn't you just call me back?"

"I prefer these conversations happen in person." Calvin took another sip. "So?"

"So *what*?"

He looked more tired. "What did you want to tell me?"

I shook my head. "Sorry. I'm sorry, I... had a bad night." It could be argued that Calvin was the reason. If he hadn't talked to Neil—but no. It was childish to pass the blame. The fact was, Neil was a thirty-seven-year-old man that was ashamed of himself.

And me, by proxy.

"I'm sure," Calvin muttered.

"What?"

"Detective Millett." He looked up from studying the secret language of the barista on the coffee cup. "I assume you don't need me to say more."

I deflated a little. "No," I admitted. For a beat there was no sound but that of Max using a box cutter. "Anyway. It's kind of an out-there proposal." I looked back up, Calvin watching and waiting in polite silence. "Do you know much about Edgar Allan Poe?"

A flicker of something betrayed his stoic features. I wasn't certain what it had been, but I could tell I now had his undivided interest. "He was a writer," Calvin supplied. "Poems and short stories, essays, and criticisms. Known for his mystery and macabre. Expelled out of West Point. Married his first cousin, Virginia Clemm. He died under mysterious circumstances in Baltimore, 1849."

I was surprised but not really sure why. It had been sort of a rhetorical question, but Calvin knew more than I expected, which was rude because who was I to say that he wasn't the literary sort? Or even someone intrigued by the mysterious death of a mysterious man? I was judging Calvin based off my knowledge of Neil, who wasn't much of a reader of fiction.

"Ah... that's right," I stupidly answered. "Have you read much of his work?"

Calvin took a sip of coffee.

"Specifically 'The Black Cat.'"

"I have not," he answered.

"A madman kills his pet black cat by tying a noose around its neck and hanging it from a tree," I explained. "The guilt from the killing of the first cat causes the man to try to kill a second, but he ends up murdering his wife instead."

"I'm sure you're reaching a point."

I frowned at the interruption. "He kills her with an axe to the head. It's considered one of his most gruesome tales."

"With good reason."

"What color was the cat? Yesterday, at the shop?"

"Right, because you have achromatopsia."

"You remember that?"

He pulled out his cell phone and scrolled briefly before reading out loud. "Complete achromatopsia is a nonprogressive visual disorder, which is characterized by decreased vision, light sensitivity, and the absence of color vision. Affects 1 in 33,000 Americans. Individuals with complete achromatopsia have greatly decreased visual acuity in daylight, hemeralopia, nystagmus, and severe photophobia."

"I wouldn't say *severe*," I muttered.

"I don't notice nystagmus with you," he stated, pocketing his phone and staring at me.

Nystagmus was the involuntary movement of the eyes, sometimes called *dancing eyes*.

"My, I'm flattered," I replied while mockingly holding a hand to my chest. "I had it as a child. It got better as I got older. Only happens once in a while."

"No color, huh?"

"Nope."

He nodded thoughtfully and drank his coffee again. "Interesting."

"Is it?" *Not really.* "I'd say it's more of a pain."

"Has this been officially diagnosed?" Calvin asked.

"Of course it has. You think I play blind for attention?"

"People do a lot of crazy things for attention."

I snorted and crossed my arms. "I'll give you the number of my ophthalmologist. Can we talk about the cat, please?"

"The cat was black," Calvin answered. "Is this your theory? Some crazed madman is reenacting stories of Edgar Allan Poe?"

"I, uh, not exactly," I said. *Was* that my theory? All I knew was the resemblance to Poe's writing was uncanny and disturbing. "'The Black Cat' is often compared to 'The Tell-Tale Heart' because of the similar guilt the narrator experiences over his murder."

"Is that so?" Calvin didn't sound interested.

"'The Tell-Tale Heart' is about—"

"I know what it's about," he said over me. "I had English 101 too."

"Then you'll find it hard to deny that what happened in my shop on Tuesday morning is exactly like that story."

"Not *exactly*, unless you found the rest of a body today," Calvin said.

"Er, no, but the focus of the story is the heart."

"It was a pig's heart."

I threw my hands up. "Look, all I'm saying is, it's weird. *Really* weird. Have there been any other deaths lately that—"

"You're not privy to that information," Calvin quickly answered.

"I'm not asking for case details."

"You're a civilian. I appreciate your theory, but let this go. Don't start thinking you can play amateur sleuth just because you know a thing or two about crime scenes."

"I'm not!" I protested.

Max dropped a box in the back, and the crash echoed through the shop. Calvin startled abruptly, almost comically, and dropped his coffee. The lid popped off, and the hot liquid shot all over my counter. He was frozen in place for just a second, long enough for me to see the noise had actually, *truly*, frightened him.

He blinked and looked down. "Shit. I'm sorry."

"No, it's okay." I left to fetch a roll of paper towels from the office and brought them back to soak up the sugary, sticky mess. "Max?"

"Sorry, sorry! It was only books!" he said back.

"*Only* books? Are they okay?" I left the mess and hurried off the steps and down the tight aisles. "Let me see."

Max opened the box on the floor, motioning to the antiques. "All present and accounted for."

"What happened?"

"Spider." He grinned sheepishly.

I crouched down, eyeing the contents. "Go through these next. Make sure the spines and corners are okay. Some of these look like original bindings by the publisher."

"All right. Sorry, Sebastian."

I left Max's side and returned to the register to see Calvin tossing the soiled paper towels in the wastebasket. "Don't worry about that. I'll clean it."

He looked at me. "I'd better go, if there was nothing else you needed to tell me?"

I shook my head. "No, that was it."

Calvin stepped down and nodded. "I'll be in touch."

I was surprised. "Will you?"

He looked to be contemplating his own choice of words. "I'm sure you'll worm your way into my case again."

"Gee, thanks."

That made him laugh, and without another word, Calvin turned to walk out of the shop.

THE REST of the day at the Emporium was comfortably busy. I didn't have time to dwell on Neil, which was a relief. What spare time I did have was dedicated to eating my sushi lunch, brought to me by a very well-tipped delivery boy, and fixating on Calvin's cases.

Or I should say, case.

Because my little fiasco was a closed book. Nothing more than a prank. Right?

And yet, two antique shops in the same week had experienced an event very reminiscent of Poe, and one had ended with a fatality. What if I had caught the individual in my shop planting the heart? Would I have been cut up and put under the floor, just like in "Tell-Tale"?

Yeah. I wasn't obsessing over this.

I popped a tuna roll into my mouth while endorsing a few checks that had been delivered by mail. I needed to stop at the bank on the way home. I should buy some food too.

I could ask Neil—

No. I wasn't going to think about him, about our relationship that he had essentially crumpled into a ball and thrown in the trash last night. He hadn't called, texted, hadn't done anything to indicate he was sorry. And *I* certainly wasn't apologizing. I had nothing to apologize for.

*"The Black Cat" isn't one of Poe's terribly common stories*, I thought instead, while refusing to acknowledge I was directing my thoughts of Neil to an equally unhealthy topic.

"Max?" I called from my office. I looked out the open door at the register, where he was wrapping a small trinket in tissue paper for a customer. "What do you think of when I say Edgar Allan Poe?"

"'The Raven,'" Max offered. He handed over the sale to the older woman, flashing one of his killer smiles and thanking her for her business before warning her to be safe on the slippery sidewalk.

Kind of obvious, but I guess Max had a point. If there was one work that Poe was known for above all else, it was probably "The Raven." It gave me an idea, and I turned to power the desktop computer on.

The welcome screen's brightness levels had been readjusted. I swore, typing the password in and immediately lowering the settings. "Set the levels on the computer back to normal when you're done," I called to Max.

"Sorry! You know, they technically *are* set at normal," he teased. Max poked his head in. "Sorry," he added again.

I waved him away and resumed eating sushi while scanning recent newspaper headlines. Nothing jumped out as unordinary, but then again, it took quite a bit to rattle the nerves of a native New Yorker. I took a different approach and checked out the NYPD's crime statistics for the end of the year.

Overall crime was down 20 percent from the same time the year before. Well, that was good news, I supposed. Ah, but there's always an asterisk to these comments. Murder was up. An interactive map told me just where in particular too.

The outer boroughs mostly, but my neighborhood, the East Village, had a surprising number of red flags. I enlarged the map and clicked for crime details. One murder and over a dozen burglaries. I considered the murder in particular for a moment. It wasn't Mike's death, as the web counter appeared to be a week behind.

Despite the number of people who lived in New York, the neighborhoods were pretty tight. News travels. A murder would have been talked about, however briefly. A few minutes of surfing the Internet brought up nothing of substantial interest, though.

Open case, still?

A lost life the media claimed to be unimportant?

I could ask Neil—*no*.

I could ask Calvin—he told me to stay out of it. *That* sounded familiar.

I took off my glasses and rubbed my face in aggravation. I don't know what I had been expecting to find, maybe www.reallifepoemurders.com? I put my glasses back on and tried that.

It wasn't a real domain. I was almost relieved.

I went back to the crime map and realized, with a sort of grim curiosity, that I could enlarge the map and see the exact cross streets of each recorded crime in my neighborhood. The murder was just a little north of my apartment and shop. I opened another page and scoured the neighborhood, but the East Village was a rich and trendy area, and I had no way to know for certain if the crime had occurred in one of the first-floor storefronts or in one of the many apartments above.

I couldn't even say for certain why I was fixated on this one murder, out of all others that had occurred in the city. I guess I was desperate for some logical—and I use the word loosely—reason Mike was killed. Calvin would have already been going over the details, to see if there was a relation to any other unsolved—

And there it was. My clue.

The *look* Calvin had given me when I first started talking about Poe. I *knew* it.

"I fucking knew it!" I shouted triumphantly.

"Knew what?" Max called from somewhere in the shop.

"Uh...." I stared at one of the advertisements on the side of the webpage. The Garden was selling hockey tickets. "The Rangers are looking good for the play-offs this season!"

I could hear Max speaking to a customer on his way to the office. I shut the Internet tabs and turned the computer off just as he poked his head in the doorway.

"You don't follow hockey," he pointed out, as if I were losing my mind.

"I don't?"

Max snorted and laughed. "You're really starting anew. God, Neil must be in the doghouse."

I grunted while getting to my feet. "Is it busy?"

"A few people." Max turned and hurried to the counter as a posh-looking woman stepped up, holding a framed photo.

I paused in the doorway, holding my phone close to type a message. *Wwhat haopen on 13 btwn 2bd and 3rd ave?*

I'm really bad at texting. I'm a seventy-year-old man inside the body of one in his thirties. I don't know much slang past LOL and ASL—which I think is defunct anyway—and while apparently my phone has a massive library of emoji, I still have no idea how to access them.

I sent the message and tucked my phone into my back pocket before smoothing down my wrinkled shirt and making my way through the aisles of the Emporium. A familiar person stood along the back bookshelves, scouring the titles she'd seen a hundred times already. "Good afternoon, Beth."

Beth Harrison turned around. "Oh, hi, Sebby."

"Sebastian," I corrected. She never listened.

Beth ran the used bookshop next door. It had been in her family nearly as long as the Strand had been around, and while it had never been an official part of what was once Book Row, Beth was determined to keep her little shop going. She ran all sorts of weekly events and had an impressive amount of authors, both known and yet to be discovered, walking in and out of her doors. There were readers' circles, signings, release parties—she ate, slept, and breathed the book business.

She also had a habit of spending at least two or three lunch breaks a week in my shop, looking over my antique books. I honestly hoped there was nothing she wanted today. I wasn't ready to haggle prices.

"Nothing new?" she asked, looping gray hair behind one ear. Beth was a pretty, older woman in her late fifties who cared about fashion just as much as I did. She wore big, thick glasses that hung off a rhinestone chain. Her hair was twisted back with a pen sticking out of the bun, and she wore a cat-print skirt with a flannel button-up.

Yup, she gave no fucks.

"Not since yesterday." I paused. "Isn't that a line from *Beauty and the Beast*?"

"Princess," Beth mumbled as she turned back to the collection. "What about all those from the estate?"

"We're still cataloging," I answered.

Beth scoffed. "I can't pay you if you won't put the books on the shelf, Seb."

"You don't pay me anyway."

"I paid my account last week."

"And immediately bought my first edition of *The Hound of the Baskervilles*," I answered.

"You'd have gotten so much more for it if you'd had it in the shop when the second season of *Sherlock* aired," Beth added.

"You still owe me three grand."

"Next week," she said with a wave of her hand. "And I thought we agreed on twenty-eight?"

"Three," I said firmly. "It was in fine condition, and I know you charged more than enough to your customer."

Beth sighed and smiled. "Fine, fine, Sebby, but only because I like you."

"Thank God."

"You know that poor guy who passed away," she quickly started. "The estate sale gentleman—all those cheap books I won—"

"I know you won them," I managed to get in.

A few weeks back, several antique shops had been given the first chance to bid on an impressive library of antique books that a bank was trying to liquidate after the elderly owner passed. I had won and then told Beth the remaining books—paperbacks and the sort—were going to be on sale to the general public if no one bid on the lot. So she did, and Beth had been happy with the haul she won and took me out to lunch as a thank-you.

"Shh, listen," she chastised. "He had *so many* gay romance novels."

"Really?"

"Oh, tons, Sebastian," Beth laughed. "And you know, they've been flying off my shelves. Lots of mysteries too. He had very diverse tastes."

"Huh." I briefly considered switching it up and spending tomorrow's lunch next door. Maybe I could live my happily ever after vicariously through some cheap gay paperbacks. "Any with cops?"

Beth snorted. "Plenty with firemen."

"I prefer guns over hoses."

"Excuse me?" a quiet voice behind me asked, interrupting a conversation bound to lead down a rabbit hole full of bad puns.

Turning around, I was met by a man perhaps a few years younger than myself. He was very tall and lanky, with a large smile and big eyes. "Oh, hello. Can I help you find anything?"

The stranger beamed happily. "I was wondering if you had any American classics." He turned to wave at the bookshelves. "Hemingway, Fitzgerald, Dickinson, Poe?"

Beth patted my shoulder and leaned up to whisper, "Send him next door when you're done." She excused herself and hurried back to her shop, Good Books.

When Beth had departed, my new customer immediately reached a hand out. "My name is Duncan Andrews."

"Sebastian Snow," I said, shaking his hand.

"Are you the owner?"

"The bills are made out to me."

He chuckled. "I love your store. It's really nice. I came a few days ago. You have a lot of nice books."

"Oh, thank you," I said humbly. "Are you looking for a Christmas present?"

"Hmm… well, for myself," Duncan said with a sort of guilty smile.

"I think I have something from Emily Dickinson," I said, moving by Duncan to a bookcase farther down the wall.

He followed close behind. "I find Dickinson's work quite sad. Do you like her poetry?"

I paused beside the shelf nearest the front door and turned to look up at him. "Honestly, I've never been a huge fan, but I studied her work in college."

Duncan's face seemed to light up. "I majored in American Literature in college!"

"My dad taught it for a long time," I said. I looked at the books and leaned close to start scanning the spines. "I've come to appreciate the big names as I've gotten older," I continued. "But if I had to pick a poet who wrote about death—"

"Poe?" Duncan asked.

I looked sideways. "Er, yes. I'm a much bigger fan of Poe than Dickinson."

Duncan flashed another smile and ran a hand through his hair. "His work is really incredible. I think he's fascinating."

"Very mysterious," I agreed as images of pig hearts and dead cats entered my mind. I grabbed a small book and showed Duncan. "Here it is."

He took the offering. "I don't suppose you have any Poe too?"

"I don't," I answered. "But Good Books next door is sure to have something, albeit nothing antique."

Duncan nodded. "Okay. Thank you, Sebastian."

"Can I ring you up?" I motioned for him to follow me through the tangle of displays.

Dean Martin was serenading me over the speakers as we went to the brass register. If I held him tight, he'd be warm all the way home.

*I don't know, Dean. I've sort of got a thing for Frank Sinatra. You won't tell him if I do hold you, will you?*

"You don't have any Christmas decorations up," Duncan pointed out as he handed me back the book to wrap in tissue paper.

"Oh. Yeah, I guess I never got around to it. But I've got the tunes at least." I glanced up and smiled.

Duncan looked about to speak before the shop door banged open.

"Mr. Snow! Mr. Snow, I forgot one letter!" My energetic, lovely little mail lady spoke. If there ever was one USPS employee who took that "through rain and snow" shit seriously, it was my girl, Daphne.

"Thank you, Daphne," I said, reaching down to accept the envelope. "You could have dropped it off tomorrow."

She shushed me and waved. "Have a good afternoon, sweetheart!"

Duncan looked at the letter. "Secret admirer?"

I laughed and set the envelope aside. "Doubtful."

"Oh, don't think that." Duncan slid his credit card over for payment. "I think you're pretty... neat."

*Neat?*

I swiped his card and handed it back. "Oh."

Wait.

God, I'm bad at this.

"*Oh.*" I cleared my throat. "Uh, thanks."

Duncan lowered his head slightly, talking to his shoes. "Dinner?"

"What?"

"Lunch?" he quickly amended.

I fumbled with Duncan's purchase and quickly finished wrapping it. I hadn't been asked out on a date in a long time. I didn't even know this guy. Of course, isn't that really the point of going on a date, to get to know the person?

He was sort of cute too.

And the thing with Neil....

I put the book into a bag and pushed it across the counter. "Can I think about it? I don't mean to be rude," I continued. "It's only—I think I'm at the end of a long-term relationship and maybe should go slow."

Duncan looked back up. "You have a boyfriend?"

I shrugged. "Not so sure these days."

"I'll come see you again soon," Duncan promised as he took the bag.

I felt my face heat up as I smiled. I'll be honest, the attention was nice. "All right."

"Bye, Sebastian."

"Good-bye."

Duncan waved and offered another big lopsided smile before he left the shop.

I didn't notice Max until Duncan had left the counter.

"Dude," he said quickly. "Did you just get asked out?"

"Ah, yeah, I think so."

"Why are you blushing?"

"Am I?"

Max pointed an accusing finger. "What happened with Neil? Don't say, *nothing*, Seb."

I closed my mouth and considered an answer. "Very little."

"Smartass." He walked up to the counter and leaned over it. "Did you guys break up?" he whispered, for the sake of privacy since the shop wasn't empty.

"I think we should put up the holiday decorations."

"It's less than two weeks before Christmas."

"Better late than never."

"Don't change the subject," Max warned.

I let out an annoyed sigh and leaned down to whisper. "We had a fight. I don't know what's going to happen, okay?"

And I really didn't.

# CHAPTER SIX

CALVIN NEVER returned my text about that murder. Had I really expected him to? Sort of. Or at least I was hoping he would, which was stupid of me because he was a cop and wasn't going to divulge information via freaking *text*.

I planned on going to the bank and grocery store before seeing myself home but ended up diverting toward Thirteenth Street, the location of the East Village murder. Quiet, clean, lined with bare snow-covered trees, just like my street. There were a number of little restaurants and a few dry cleaners, but the buildings were multiuse and had three or four floors of apartments above the shops.

It was already dark, and the temperature was dropping fast. I stopped halfway down the block, looking up at the brightly lit windows of those already home. I must have looked out of sorts, standing in the middle of the sidewalk, shivering, and wearing sunglasses.

A woman walking a big golden retriever stopped nearby. "Are you lost?" she asked, maybe pegging me for a very confused tourist.

I glanced over at her and smiled awkwardly. "Oh, no. Actually, do you live around here?"

She looked me over, but I guess I appeared harmless enough, or she trusted her dog to guard her, because she nodded. "Yeah, sure. Why?"

"This might sound really, really strange," I warned, "but have you heard of any murders in this area?" You know—get right to the point.

She covered her mouth with a gloved hand. "Oh my God, yes, but you're not a reporter or anything, are you?"

I shook my head. "No, no. I live nearby. And am just a nosey jerk."

She laughed at that, but slowly put her hand to her chest. "It was about two weeks ago, I think. People around here know, but the police are keeping it really quiet. I heard it was *terribly* gruesome."

"Who'd you hear that from?"

She shrugged.

So, fifty-fifty on it being true. "Did it happen inside one of these restaurants?" When she hesitated, I could tell I might have been making her uncomfortable. *Shit, shit.* "I'll never be able to eat pasta again," I joked, glancing toward the closest shop.

She chuckled again and smiled. "It wasn't in a restaurant, but one of the chefs from 1-2-3 Sushi told a friend of mine that it happened in one of the apartments above his shop." She pointed with her free hand toward the building in question. "I guess the police had to close everything down for the day."

"That must have sucked."

She hummed and nodded in agreement.

"It's scary," I said quietly. "It's such a good neighborhood."

"Oh, I know," she agreed. "I made my boyfriend spend the night for a week. I was so freaked out." She sighed and switched the dog leash into her other hand. "Anyway, I better go."

"Yeah, sorry, have a good night." I smiled and stepped aside, letting her and the dog walk by.

I looked toward 1-2-3 Sushi, and a smile crossed my face. I felt—hell, like a detective, for lack of better description. I knew Mike's murder and the break-in at my shop had something to do with Edgar Allan Poe, and the look on Calvin's face had confirmed it. He seemed to have known a lot about the writer too, which could have been personal knowledge or something recently researched. And why? There had to be something afoot, and according to the NYPD crime statistics, there was only one murder in the neighborhood that wasn't all that far from both Mike and myself.

Serial literary murders? I had no idea what to expect, but there was no way I could quell my curiosity except to keep moving forward. I felt a surge of excitement as I ran across the street toward the restaurant and entered. It was tiny and busy, but luckily there was a seat open at the bar where the chefs worked. It was only after I sat and started looking around that I began to second-guess my plan. There were a few chefs working—how was I to know which one the woman was referring to? Were they even working tonight? What was I going to ask?

Had any murders lately?

*Shit.*

"Can I help you?" a woman behind the bar asked.

Good thing I liked sushi, because I guess I was having it for dinner too. "Uh, sushi dinner plate," I said, after quickly scanning the menu taped to the glass in front of me.

"Tamago or ebi?" Egg or shrimp for my cooked sushi option.

"Ebi is fine." I watched her nod and start expertly crafting my meal. I drummed my fingers absently and read her nametag. "Worked here a long time, Ann?"

"No, I don't want to go on a date," she replied.

"What?"

She looked up at me, narrowing her eyes and giving me a look that warned I was about to be dickless.

I quickly waved my hands. "Just making polite conversation. I'm gay. I don't want to date you." I winced and started to rephrase the statement so it didn't sound like I was insulting her.

To my surprise Ann laughed. "Oh thank God. I get asked at least once a week. I hate men sometimes."

I nodded. "So do I."

She held up a bare hand. "I can't wear my wedding ring when I cook, you know?" She sighed and shook her head while placing the completed sushi on a long narrow plate. "I'd rather have no tip than be hit on."

"Well, I promise not to make any moves, and I'll tip before I leave."

"Best customer all day."

"You flatter me," I replied.

She looked up as she started forming the next sushi in her hands. "So are you a secret agent or something?"

"The glasses? No, nothing cool. I have a light sensitivity."

She hummed quietly and nodded.

I watched as she finished the next sushi. She was liable to walk away and see to another customer once done with my meal. I didn't have a lot of time. "I heard what happened here," I said quietly. "What was it, like a week or two ago?"

Ann looked up, pausing from placing the ebi on the rice. "Here?"

"Well, upstairs."

"What happened—oh." She looked grave. "Yeah… God." She shook her head and made a funny sound while shivering in an exaggerated manner.

"That bad?"

"I didn't see anything exactly. I don't want you to lose your appetite."

"I'll be okay," I insisted.

She narrowed her eyes again, giving me a once-over like she would be able to tell if I were the squeamish sort. "Some lady upstairs was murdered," she whispered, leaning close. "I liked her. She got takeout here a lot."

"I heard from—er, my neighbor that it was pretty gruesome," I said, trying to get Ann to keep talking.

She nodded. "That's what I heard too. Hiro, the head chef here, said he saw the paramedics bring her down. That's how I know who she was." Ann finished the last pieces of sushi.

"But it was never in the papers, was it?"

"Hmm… I don't know. We had to stay closed for two days. I think the police are trying to keep it quiet." She picked up the plate and handed it over to me. "Don't tell anyone," she whispered while leaning close, "but Hiro told us he overheard one of the paramedics saying, 'They wrote on the walls in her blood.'"

I wasn't hungry anymore.


MAYBE I didn't have the stomach for this detective work.

I stood at one of my bank's branches after hours, depositing checks into the ATM and trying not to think too much about a murder where something had been *written* in the victim's blood.

I still had no way to know if I was chasing something even remotely connected to Mike's murder. I didn't know the woman, nor the details of her passing. All I knew was that hers and Mike's deaths were both terrible.

*Would you like another transaction?*

I reached into my pockets, checking to make sure I'd deposited all of my checks. My fingers brushed a folded envelope, and I pulled out the late letter that Daphne had dropped off. Max must have stuck it into the check pile for me, and I grabbed it without noticing.

I hastily tore the top open and pulled out a single sheet of paper. No check.

*I must not only punish, but punish with impunity.*

What the fuck?

I turned the paper over, but nothing else was written on it.

*This transaction will cancel in thirty seconds.*

I looked at the ATM screen and ended my deposit, took my receipt, and moved away. I stared at the slanted, scrawled words, reading it over and over.

Punish with impunity.

Punish who—*me*?

I took out the envelope. No return address, but it was addressed to the Emporium. Not me specifically, but I was the owner, so it was safe to assume it was meant for my eyes.

Now that my hands had been all over the letter, Neil and evidence collection came to mind, and I carefully folded the paper and gently stuck it into the envelope again. I tried not to handle it too much, like it would make a difference. It had already been through the USPS sorting facilities, Daphne, Max, and myself.

It was starting to snow again as I stepped out of the bank.

*I must not only punish, but punish with impunity.*

I ducked into a corner shop. I needed to buy food, but more importantly, I needed to be surrounded by other people. That note gave me worse heebie-jeebies than Ann's murder-mystery story. I looked around. Not many people—an elderly woman at the register, a stock boy putting away drinks, and one pregnant lady with an armful of chips.

The overhead lights were obnoxiously bright, and one flickered like an eye twitch. I grabbed one of the tiny baskets near the door and hastily tossed in a few cans of soup, granola bars, and several yogurt containers from the refrigerated area in the back. I grabbed a carton of chocolate ice cream while I weighed the pros and mostly cons of calling Neil.

Would he care that I was sufficiently freaked out and needed, well, *someone*? Would he come home if I asked him to? I knew if I asked, apologized, pleaded—of course he'd come back.

But did I want... *him*?

My gut rolled. It knew the answer, even if my mind wouldn't admit it.

Would I have said what I had to Duncan earlier in the day if I wanted Neil to come back?

Screw it. I grabbed a second container of ice cream and a frozen pizza for good measure. My basket looked like my diet from college. Guilt made me grab a few bananas from a box beside the loaves of bread before I brought my items over to the counter.

"Flowers?" the woman asked as she slowly counted up each item.

"What?"

"Half-off, all die soon," she said in broken English while pointing one gnarled hand at the flower display that had been brought back indoors.

"No thanks."

"Take, half-off," she insisted.

"I don't need flowers."

"For girlfriend."

"No."

"For boyfriend."

"No."

She gave me a look like I'd just insulted her parents. "Bad attitude. Thirty dollar."

"What, for ice cream and soup?" I asked defensively.

"Twenty-five with flowers."

"That makes no—fine." I turned around and grabbed a bouquet of carnations.

She gave me a cheeky smile and slowly bagged my purchases.

With my cardboard-tasting pizza and half-dead carnations that granny told me to "give to handsome boy, so get sex," I flagged down a stray taxi and got a lift home.

Up the rickety, creaking steps to the third floor, I glanced up over the rim of my sunglasses in time to see a big, dark mass standing at the top landing.

"Oh God—!"

"Hey."

Not Neil. That voice….

"Calvin?"

"Are we on a first-name basis now?"

"You scared the shit out of me."

"Sorry. Are you coming up?"

"Yeah, let me just pick my heart up off the floor first." I trudged up the last steps and stood beside him, looking up. "What are you doing here?"

"Waiting for you to get home."

"I can see that. I mean, how'd you get inside?"

He pulled out his wallet and flashed his badge at me in response.

"Oh good, which of my neighbors think I'm being arrested?" I asked, maneuvering both bags to one hand as I fished for my keys.

"The ones upstairs," he answered, taking my groceries for me.

"I—you don't need to hold those," I protested.

"I'd like to go inside sometime this century."

I scoffed and muttered what might have been *asshole* under my breath before unlocking the door. I pushed it open with my shoulder, the ever so slightly crooked doorframe always causing the door to stick.

"Make yourself at home."

"I take it Mr. Millett isn't coming home tonight," Calvin said, shutting the door behind himself.

The apartment had been dark before I turned a lamp on. Neil had certainly not been here. "Probably not," I agreed absently. I kicked my boots off and hung up my coat before taking back the bags. "Thanks." I hurried into the kitchen, turning on another lamp and setting my sunglasses aside for regular lenses. I could hear Calvin walking around the front room and tried to ignore his curious examination while I put away the ice cream and other junk I had bought.

"Nice flowers."

"What?" I turned suddenly to find Calvin leaning against the doorframe of the kitchen. I looked back at the carnations and laughed. "Oh. Yeah. Long story."

"You know what'll be shorter? You explaining why you're butting into another murder case of mine."

"Ah…."

"How did you know about the murder at that street address?"

I shut the freezer door. "Hey, that's public information."

"The hell it is."

"It's on NYPD's crime map, pal," I retorted.

Calvin stepped into the kitchen. "What are you doing getting yourself involved in this?"

"Someone killed Mike—"

"And that's for the police to investigate," he said sternly. "Not an antique dealer."

"But they're related, aren't they? Both murders and my prank." I moved forward to meet him. "I could see it, when I mentioned Poe. It got your attention."

Calvin crossed his arms and didn't respond.

"A woman above a sushi joint was murdered…," I started.

"I know that."

"Something was written in blood—"

"Where the hell did you hear that?" he retorted, voice low and dangerous.

"People talk," I answered quickly. "Maybe they find blind guys endearing and harmless and want to spill their secrets."

"Who did you talk to, Sebastian?"

"I went to the sushi bar. The chefs told me."

Calvin pushed his coat back to rest his hands on his hips, likely counting to ten to keep from killing me.

"What was written?" I dared to ask.

He shook his head.

I didn't expect him to share that ever so curious piece of information. Really. "Want a beer?"

"I'm on the clock."

"Water? Coffee?"

"No."

I looked back. "Well, you don't seem to be in a rush to leave. I know my personality is addictive but—"

"'She shall press, ah, nevermore.'"

I paused, considered the response, then asked, "Excuse me?"

"That's what was written," Calvin clarified, his voice quiet, as if he didn't want his partner or superiors hearing the confession of information.

"Nevermore. That's from 'The Raven,'" I said.

He nodded. "I know."

"So this is connected!" I exclaimed, feeling unreasonably triumphant despite there having already been two murders.

Calvin waved at me in an annoyed fashion. "Be quiet."

I rushed out of the kitchen, too excited to calm down. I fetched the copy of Poe's work that I had left on the table and flipped to the poetry section. "I remember that poem pretty well," I said while lifting a magnifying glass to the page and reading briefly. "Right, it's in regards to Lenore, the narrator's long lost love."

"I know," Calvin said again. "But I don't know why."

"Why that line?"

He nodded, staring at me.

I lowered the book. "Well, the narrator is sort of melodramatic. Everything around him reminds him of Lenore, specifically in that moment that she'd never rest her head on the cushion of the chair again. It's a realization that she is truly gone."

"Nevermore is also the name of the raven," Calvin added thoughtfully.

"Well, yes, technically," I agreed. "Who was the woman?"

"You mean, Lenore?"

"No." I shut the book. "The real woman who was murdered."

Calvin grew quiet again, but after a short pause, removed his coat and set it on the back of a chair at the table. "Merriam Byers. She worked for Northeast Unlimited Bank."

"That name sounds so familiar," I said, rubbing the back of my head as I thought.

"Please don't say that. If I can connect you to two murders—"

"Wait a minute," I said suddenly, holding a hand up. "I *do* know that name!" I looked around the apartment anxiously before opening the first box of estate books.

I could feel Calvin watching me from the table. "What?" he asked in growing curiosity.

"I've talked to her."

"How the hell do you know this woman?" he grumbled. "No friends or family in common, two different career paths…."

He was still talking as I put the top box on the floor and started digging through the next. "Northeast Unlimited. I did business briefly with them a few weeks ago."

"Sebastian."

"What?"

"Stop and look at me."

I looked over my shoulder. Calvin had one hand resting on his coat, the other on his hip. His dark suit hugged his gorgeous body, and the light from the kitchen made his left side shine, looking almost otherworldly.

Something angelic.

"I'm looking," I said quietly. You'd have to pay me to turn away from such a sight.

"You bank with National Trust."

"How do you know that?"

"It's my job to know," Calvin replied. "Explain to me your business with this particular bank."

"Let me show you." I pried my gaze away, and after digging through two more boxes, found the paperwork I knew existed somewhere in that general chaos. "Here, see? I made a bid a few weeks ago at an estate sale. Northeast was the bank handling the liquidation of property, and my contact was Merriam Byers."

Calvin reached out and accepted the folded, wrinkled records. "Do you know how this looks?" he asked.

"But I hardly even knew her, Calvin! I talked to her once or twice on the phone and met her for all of ten minutes when I went to collect the books."

"You're someone I can link to both victims," Calvin said, almost apologetically.

"But I didn't kill them! You know that, right? You believe me?" That panic I had felt at Mike's shop was starting to surface again.

And then suddenly Calvin's arms were wrapped tight around me, one strong hand on the back of my head.

Initially I froze. What the hell was he doing?

But nothing happened.

He was just hugging me.

And it was so... *nice.*

I felt the tension leave me entirely, and I slowly slid my arms under his, holding the back of his suit coat tightly. He smelled good. Really good. Neil wore some expensive name-brand cologne that always left me trying to guess exactly what it was supposed to smell like. Calvin wore some scent that was natural and simple and likely had a real name.

Spicy.

It made me think of traces of cinnamon and ginger.

It was masculine, and sexy.

He had no idea that this hug just got a lot more awkward for me.

"I believe you, baby," he whispered.

Whoa. Wait. Holy shit. Okay, I admit it, Calvin Winter was sexy as hell, and I wanted him, but what the fuck was he doing calling *me* baby? Did he *want* me? For God's sake, *why*?

"Want to repeat that last line again?" I muttered against his shoulder.

"You heard me," Calvin replied, not letting go.

"This is weird."

"Why?"

"Can we discuss this face to face?" I asked.

"Would rather not." Calvin didn't let go.

I almost laughed at how absurd this had just become. "Ah, are you—?"

"Are you really expecting Millett back tonight?" he interrupted.

"Er... I don't think so," I said quietly.

"Good." Calvin pulled back and kissed me hard.

I tripped backward and hit the wall behind me. Calvin moved close, his hands on either side of my head. He pressed up against me, hot and rough. He caught my mouth, his jaw scraping against mine as he bruised my lips with kisses. Calvin nudged a leg in between mine and pressed his erection against my hip.

I heard myself moan, and that was the end of it. No turning back.

I reached up and wrapped my arms around Calvin's neck, and then we were stumbling back into the kitchen, which seemed a decent enough place as any. He shoved me against the fridge, magnets and photos falling to the floor. I grabbed him by the back of the neck and pulled him into another searing hot kiss. His tongue pushed against my lips, and I opened my mouth to the warm invasion.

He tasted like coffee and cinnamon mints and male. The combination was erotic as hell.

My entire body was hot, ready to explode after just a few rough kisses. It was like I'd never been touched before, not really. Not like this—like how I needed it. Hard and fast, and still Calvin's only goal in mind seemed to be *my* pleasure.

I grabbed a handful of his hair as his hands started unbuttoning my trousers.

"Does Millett ever do this for you?" he whispered against my neck. I groaned pathetically as he bit down. "D-Do what?"

"Suck you?"

Oh good God. This couldn't be real.

"He doesn't really like it," I whispered, breath catching as he bit my neck again.

Calvin raised his head, looking down at me while he asked, "But do *you*? Do you want me to suck you?" He reached inside my pants and fondled me through my boxer briefs.

"God, yes."

That jerk smiled as he leaned closer. "Let me hear you beg."

"W-What?"

"Beg me," he ordered. Calvin slid his hand into my briefs next and gently gripped me with the hand I had imagined just the day before. He kissed my Adam's apple when I tilted my head back.

"P-Please," I whispered, pressing against him. "Please, suck me, oh God...!"

Somewhere in the recesses of my mind, I acknowledged Calvin was laughing at me, and I was about to knock him senseless, but then I opened my eyes and he was kneeling in front of me and sliding my pants off my hips.

A shiver ran over me as he freed my cock, hard and eager for attention. Calvin leaned forward and gave the head a good lick. I sighed and gently thrust my hips forward for more.

Calvin grabbed me firmly. "Don't hold back, baby. I want you to fuck my face."

"W-Who are you, and where is that jerk Calvin Winter?" I managed to ask.

He grinned, wrapped his mouth around me, and moved down my length until his nose pressed against trimmed hair.

I sucked in a sharp breath and looked down, watching as Calvin deep-throated.

It was true that Neil didn't like giving blowjobs. I don't think I'd had one in nearly a year. I'd almost forgotten how *incredible* it was, and even more so when your partner enjoyed giving it. Wet and tight and— and it was *Calvin*. Any moment I'd wake up from maybe slipping on ice. I'd be lying on the sidewalk, staring up at the stormy sky with a hard-on that refused to quit, because even that made more sense than a detective I had been certain was straight suddenly being on his knees in the kitchen, telling me to fuck his face.

Watching Calvin through half-hooded eyes, I reached down to grip his hair. He hummed in response and let go of my hips to unzip his pants. He freed his own cock, erect and huge, and stroked himself as he sucked.

I bit my lip and tentatively thrust into his mouth, gentle, but Calvin immediately groaned and sucked faster in response. I held his head still as I pushed in and out with more enthusiasm. It was an incredible turn-on to see him getting himself off, to be so aroused by giving me pleasure that he couldn't stand it.

I had no idea what was happening. One minute I'm accused of murder, the next I'm getting the best head of my life.

"Yes, yes," I heard myself cry out. I begged for more of *something*, never being able to finish the thought. I pulled back and then thrust into his mouth hard, thinking maybe I was being too rough, but Calvin groaned around my cock and egged me on.

And again, and again.

I wondered if he'd let me come in his mouth?

There was a sound I kept hearing, breaking my attention from my impending orgasm.

What the hell was that?

A phone.

Oh my God.

Calvin pulled off me, his breathing ragged and heavy. He wiped his lips on the back of one hand and let go of himself. "Goddamn it." He reached into his suit coat and pulled out his ringing cell, cleared his throat, and answered, "Detective Winter."

*You've got to be kidding me. I'm about to explode all over the kitchen floor, and he's got to take a phone call?*

One look at his face told me we weren't going to be finishing. I reached down and awkwardly tucked myself back into my pants. I closed my eyes to get the image of Calvin's hard cock out of my mind, replacing it with the thoughts of cold showers, watching a golf match, filing taxes—what else, what else? Those sloppy old lady kisses my grandmother's friends used to give me as a little boy.

"Something's come up."

I snorted and held back a laugh. When I opened my eyes, Calvin was standing and buttoning his pants. "I'll say."

He didn't reply.

"Do I get a rain check on the second half of the date, or are we done?" I stood away from the fridge, my legs feeling like they'd finally support my weight again.

Calvin finished tucking his dress shirt back into place before looking at me. "Sorry," he said quietly.

I shrugged, sort of at a loss. What was I supposed to say? "No pillow talk about our feelings, then?"

Calvin looked sideways and turned out of the kitchen, fetching his coat at the table.

*All right, then. We'll pretend that little episode didn't just happen.* "What about my connection to Byers?" I asked, walking out after him. "It's not going to be a problem, is it?"

Calvin pulled his arms through his coat as he turned around to look down at me. "Don't go talking about her to people. Give me a minute to figure this out."

I nodded. "Sure. Okay. Thanks for not arresting me."

He grunted while buttoning his jacket. "I'm taking this." He held up the documents from the estate sale.

"Fine."

"Good night."


IT WAS Friday, and Neil still hadn't called.

Granted, it was six in the morning and he was most likely asleep. Which was what I should have been doing, but after tossing restlessly for a frustrating three hours, I gave up. I braved the new storm coming down on the city full force now and went to set up the holiday decorations in the Emporium.

Because when I can't sleep, I deck the halls.

"Goddamn it." I stopped stretching out the garland and lights to untangle another section. Who put this away last year? I was going to kill them.

It had probably been me.

Hall-decking is a two-man job. Pop helped me the first year the Emporium opened, and last year Neil had helped me hang the garland and set up a small tree. It had been terribly domestic and—dare I say it—

*cute.* I missed that. Contrary to the evidence, I'm not always a cynical, crotchety old guy. I like the holidays. They're so festive and uplifting.

I liked spending them with Neil.

Or, I had. Because that was over. Right?

I walked across the floor with the string of lights and garland and stooped to plug in the end. I started to wrap the too-bright lights around the support beam beside the outlet.

Even if it wasn't over by some miracle and Neil came home, what had happened with Calvin? I had been trying to process our rushed, er— I'd been trying to process it all night. For me it was just pent-up nerves coupled with a crush on a really hot guy. That was it. Totally it.

But what the hell had been going through Calvin's mind?

I had to dump a mental bucket of ice-cold water over myself when the image of his mouth on me came back. That had been, without a doubt, the hottest and greatest blowjob I had ever received. And I didn't even get to finish.

I ended up right back at what had been gnawing at my gut all night. Had I cheated? Yes. I think so. Maybe. I had warned Neil if he walked out… but a threat to change the locks—which I hadn't done—was pretty far from just saying, *we're breaking up if you walk out.* What if Neil was just cooling down and didn't understand?

What if he came home? Apologized?

I could not tell him what happened. I was pretty sure Calvin wouldn't say a word either. Then I could go back to a happier relationship with Neil, and that would be that. Everything would be okay.

"Come on," I grumbled, tugging the strand of garland up with me as I climbed a ladder. It got tangled around the legs, and I cursed at length before managing it free.

Everything was not okay. The fact that I hadn't been able to sleep was enough.

What had happened with Calvin wasn't just fueled by a hot body and a hotter mouth. He believed me, knew I hadn't hurt anyone, despite what his growing pile of evidence said. He supported me when Neil hadn't. He told me himself, against all reason.

*I believe you, baby.*

Call it a hunch, but I was pretty certain he didn't make it a habit of calling his persons of interest *baby.* So—what? Did he like me? Should I pass him a note during class?

*Do u like me? Circle Y or N.*

One thing was certain. Calvin made me feel safe. Not only in regards to this case, but his presence was just so unbelievably comforting. Soothing, in a sense. It always felt like he had full control and would leave no man behind.

I tacked the garland in place at the top of the beam and started the long process of draping it around the shop overhead. I got past the counter and register and reached my collection of photos and maps when I had a curious thought about Calvin.

I knew nothing about him.

Good God, I'd let basically a stranger suck my dick.

All right, not a complete stranger. I knew his name was Calvin Winter, and he had fiery red hair. He was a homicide detective with NYPD and looked *so fine* in a suit. In comparison, he knew my boyfriend, my father, my assistant, where I banked, where I lived, and that I preferred boxer briefs. I could stand to learn a thing or two about him. Pretty much anything you want to research can be found on the Internet these days.

I wasn't climbing down from the ladder and going into my office to be a creep, of course.

I powered up the desktop computer and signed in.

He had that authoritative presence that intrigued me. If I had never met him in my life and just saw him standing in a crowded room, I'd have imagined him to be in charge. He gave off a natural aura of authority.

I liked it. It piqued my interest.

Besides, wasn't it fair to know basic information about one of the cops investigating you?

I typed "Calvin Winter NYPD" into Google and let it fly. The search brought up a ton of links to articles and several military sites. After glancing through a few, I realized exactly why Calvin was the way he was.

Twelve-year Army veteran. Four tours, three in Iraq and one in Afghanistan. Retired with the rank of major before returning to NYPD as a detective in major cases. Recently promoted to homicide.

I scrolled through an article listing Calvin's extensive achievements while in service before I came to a paragraph that covered his awards, and my jaw hit the desk.

Medal of Honor. Silver Star. Purple Heart.

At first, admittedly, I thought perhaps it was a different Calvin Winter, because what would a Medal of Honor recipient be doing in a stressful, shit job like homicide? What would he be doing with me? But there was a photo of Calvin in full military uniform. His hair was shorter and he looked a few years younger, but it was him.

His story was included in another article that covered recent recipients of the Medal of Honor. Apparently his patrol, while in Iraq, had been ambushed and outnumbered. Calvin had run from cover into the open to rescue his fallen comrades, all of them living because of his efforts. He was shot by insurgents while hauling the wounded soldiers to safety, but kept going and kept fighting with his own weapon and throwing back live grenades as they were lobbed at him.

*Holy fucking hell.*

This couldn't be—but no, this was real.

Calvin was a real-life hero.

A few of his fellow soldiers had been quoted in the article, saying they owed their lives to Calvin. One said every day that he looks at his daughter's face, he has Calvin to thank for it.

My chest got tight as I read.

His other awards had included saving civilians in Afghanistan who were being used as human shields. He had rescued one man, three women, and three children, then had been shot again and apparently was unable to save an elderly man and his grandson because of it.

I was at a loss for words.

His whole *walk into the room and immediately be given respect* thing made sense. Twelve years of military service. *Twelve.* And most of it not pretty. Active and dangerous combat, and a lot of it.

What I found interesting was that his authority didn't go to his head, at least not around me. He was in command, for sure, and even when he had been with his partner, he had been shown respect, but he never seemed to power trip. He was unreasonably quiet, actually. But maybe people knew. Maybe he didn't have to bark orders or throw around his rank because he had already earned everyone's respect.

I wondered why he had decided to leave the military, but I couldn't find anything about it. There weren't any interviews with him regarding his various awards, just a few photos of when he was given the Medal of Honor by the President of the United States.

Despite being loaded up with information on Calvin's last decade, he was more of a mystery to me than before, and as proven so far, I had a thing for mysteries.

As I sat in the quiet, reflecting on the retired major—now detective—the alarm system went off.

# CHAPTER SEVEN

IT WASN'T my alarm.

I jerked my head up and ran out of the office, looking around.

Next door, Good Books' security alarm was blaring. Our shops were connected around the back side. It looked like two separate buildings because of the small alleyway between us, but it was actually one large structure, and so if something was happening in Beth's store, chances were someone could run through the back door and into my shop.

It was too early for Beth to be at work, and the gate had been shut on the front of the store when I walked by. I ran through the Emporium and out the back. The alleyway was freezing, my breath visible in the chilled air. Wrapping my arms around myself, I walked down to the back entrance of Good Books.

I reached for the doorknob, ready to find it locked, but instead the door swung open.

I froze for a moment.

What was I doing? Someone broke in. They might still be in there, stealing what besides gay paperbacks, I had no idea, but I should get the hell out of Dodge.

I never listen to myself.

Instead, I got angry. I got really angry, because deep down, I just knew the same sick fuck who had killed that poor woman had killed Mike. That the same person broke into my shop, and now they were breaking into Beth's. Feeling invincible and ready for a battle of my own, I stormed inside.

The alarm was wailing and the shop phone was ringing—most likely the security company trying to get a hold of Beth. I put my hands to my ears, trying to gather my wits as the siren drilled into my brain.

Then the lights turned on and everything went white.

The sudden brightness, compared to the comfortable dim lighting of my shop and the darkness of the covered alley, was so intense, it nearly made me cry. It was like staring right at the sun. Unbearable and painful. Without my protective lenses, I was blinded.

Suddenly I was not so invincible.

My senses were completely overwhelmed, and for a minute, I just stood there in a panic. With my eyes shut, I could feel myself starting to walk toward the security panel by the door. I knew Beth's code—she'd given it to me a while back—and I could think of nothing else but getting that wailing alarm under control. I didn't get far, though, because someone hit me over the head.

At least it got quiet.


SOMEONE WAS holding my hand. It was warm and a little rough and nice.

"Neil?"

The hand loosened but remained.

"It's too bright," I whispered. My mouth felt thick and weird, like I was trying to talk around cotton balls. Even with my eyes closed, I could feel bright lights on me, penetrating my eyelids, making the throbbing in my head worse.

The hand left me suddenly, and I said... something, but then the room was dark and the hand returned and it was okay.

When I woke up for a second time, I was a little more aware of the world.

For one, I was lying down. It was not my bed because it felt too high and was definitely not as comfortable as a pillow-top mattress. Secondly, I was wearing significantly less clothing than how I had begun the day, which I found strange.

A wave of nausea hit me next, and I swallowed the sour taste and kept my eyes firmly shut. Something was wrong.

Where had Neil gone?

"Neil?" I asked, my own voice sounding far away.

"You awake, kiddo?"

"Dad?" I cracked open one eye. The room was dark and extremely fuzzy. I reached up to my face, but I wasn't wearing glasses. "Oh shit." I heard myself laugh dryly. "Help, I'm blind."

I could make out the blob shape of my father approaching the bed. He took my hand and patted it, but it wasn't the same as before. "You're all right, Sebastian," he said firmly. "Everything's all right."

"Where's Neil?" I asked again.

My father hesitated, but I had closed my eyes again and didn't know why. "He's not here."

"Where'd he go?"

"He hasn't been here, Sebastian."

"He was holding my hand."

Dad paused again, then just patted my arm once more.

"Do you think you can answer some questions, Sebastian?" another person asked.

"Whoa," I said quietly. "I know that voice. It's Mr. Medal of Honor."

"What?" That was Pop.

I opened my eyes again and raised my other hand slightly, pointing at the out-of-focus, standing figure. "Calvin is a hero." What the fuck was I talking about? I heard myself laugh again. "My head really hurts. What did I do?"

Calvin stepped closer to the bed and took a seat in the nearby chair. "What do you remember?"

That seemed an easy enough question.

"Let's see," I said slowly, licking my lips. "Garland...."

"Why were you at the Emporium so early?" His tone was calm and soothing. It made my head hurt less.

"Christmas," I muttered. "I didn't want to be a Grinch...."

"You were putting up decorations?" he asked, but sounded like he already knew that.

I started to nod and then winced and shut my eyes again.

"Then what?" he quietly pressed.

"I thought about you."

"Why?" he asked.

"I think you're hot," I answered, and even as I heard myself say it, I didn't censor myself. Was I on drugs? "I googled you."

Again, he asked, "Why?"

"Medal of Honor," I muttered. "Silver Star, Purple Heart...." I moved my hand to pat my dad's. "Army, Dad."

"So it seems," Pop answered.

I opened my eyes and glanced at my dad, but I think he was staring across the bed at Calvin. Shock? Impressed? I know, so was I. He was an action-movie hero, without the movie part.

Calvin cleared his throat. "Sebastian? Why were you next door?"

"Which next door?"

"Good Books."

"Oh shit, the security alarm," I muttered.

"It's taken care of," Calvin insisted.

"I heard it. I thought—Oh boy, it's sort of hard to remember."

"Try," he pressed.

"I went over there because I was angry. I wanted to kick that punk's ass, but then it got bright."

"I think he means someone turned the lights on," Dad said. "It's like whitewash to him. He can't see anything."

"It hurt," I added. "But my head hurts more. What happened?"

"Someone knocked you out," Calvin said.

"Whoa." I slowly turned my head to look at him. "Who?"

"Good question."

"Why are you here?" I asked next.

"You called me."

"Shut up."

He sounded slightly amused when he said, "You did."

"I don't remember."

"You weren't making much sense," he agreed quietly. "But I heard the alarm going off, and your speech was slurred. I knew something was wrong, so I got over there before the security company had a patrol stop by."

"You should get another medal."

Calvin was quiet for a beat. "I have enough," he finally said.

"Do I have a concussion?"

"Yes," Calvin answered. "Your doctor wants to keep you overnight for observation."

"I have to go home," I replied.

"You're staying, kiddo," my dad said.

"But I have to work."

"Work can wait," Pop said sternly. "I already called Max. If you want him to run the shop, let me know, but otherwise the Emporium can stay dark for a day." He stepped away from the bed. "I'm going to get your doctor now that you're awake. Detective Winter, could you stay for another moment and watch him?"

"Sure."

I closed my eyes, listening to my dad's footsteps leave the room. "Are you watching me?"

"Yes."

"I won't die, I don't think. You can leave."

"I'll stay," he said quietly.

I gripped the blankets lightly, taking deep breaths because the world still felt like it was spinning, even with my eyes closed.

"You scared me," Calvin said quietly.

"Hmm?"

"When you called."

I squeezed my eyes tighter, thinking about the bookstore. Then I added the wailing alarm to the memory and recalled walking toward the security panel. That's right. I was going to shut it off. Nine, nine, four, six was Beth's code.

But then I was hit.

I didn't remember pulling out my cell phone, nor calling Calvin. I didn't even remember him answering.

*"Sebastian? Where are you?"*

*"Surre—hurts. I can't turn ooooff."*

*"I'm on my way, sweetie. Please keep talking to me. Has someone hurt you?"*

*"Head—hurts a lot."*

*"Sebastian?"*

*"Isss loud—I—I'm sick."*

I remembered vomiting and then nothing.

"Did I pass out in my own barf?" I whispered.

"No one but the paramedics and me know," Calvin said, but I swore he spoke with a smile.

I opened my eyes again. "You like pet names."

"What?"

"Baby, sweetie. You're the romantic sort under that stern exterior."

"Why did you look up my military history?"

I waved one hand lightly. "Got curious. How do you have the highest military honor ever awarded and not talk about it?"

Calvin was silent for a long time.

"I can't see your face. Are you angry?"

"Do I sound angry?"

"No. You sound… weird."

"I don't like talking about it," he answered gently.

"Oh. Sorry."

"It's all right." Calvin was quiet for a beat. "Do you want me to call Millett for you?"

"W-What about you?" I asked. That whole, *baby* and *sweetie* thing was making me think….

"He's your partner. I'm sure he'd be worried," Calvin said. "I'll give him a ring."

That's how I ended up seeing Neil again.

My doctor was explaining to Pop and me that because of the bump on my head, and the fact that I had been sick and lost consciousness, it was a sign of a serious concussion that he felt was best monitored by authorized personnel for twenty-four hours. I had zero interest in staying in the hospital and running up a few grand for my brief and unpleasant stay, but Dad was having none of my bitching, so I promptly gave up.

I watched the blob standing against the wall near the door. Calvin had called Neil like some chivalrous knight and told me he was on his way. The doctor had hardly left the room before Neil burst in, breathless and anxious.

I thought his reaction should have been comforting—to see him upset over me—but instead it agitated me. Calvin had been upset, but he'd kept his calm the whole way through.

"Sebby?"

I let it go. "Hi."

Neil ignored Calvin as he stepped by him and dropped his coat on the chair Calvin had been sitting in before. He walked over to my side. "Jesus, they told me you have a concussion."

"Pretty hard head, though. I'm okay."

"Don't make jokes."

"I'm—" I took a deep breath. I was suddenly very tired. Did Neil always make me feel like this? "I'd like to sleep," I said while closing my eyes.

LINGERING LIGHT was coming in through the closed blinds when I woke up. I rubbed my eyes and yawned.

"How're you feeling?"

I glanced to my right. Neil had taken over the chair. I looked around. "Where's Dad and Calvin?"

"*Calvin?*"

I looked back at Neil. "What?"

"You called him and not me."

"I'd been hit over the head. I'm lucky I managed to call anyone, Neil. I probably just hit something at random." I didn't like that I couldn't see him. Without glasses, I couldn't even make out body posture well and needed to rely on his tone to understand his emotions.

Neil sighed heavily. "The weather is bad. I had a patrolman drive your dad home."

"Oh… thanks."

"Sure."

I pointed at the window. "What time is it?"

"Nearly four."

"What? I've been sleeping all day?"

Neil nodded, I think. "The nurses woke you up a few times, but you were a little loopy."

"I feel strange."

"That'd be the concussion."

Neil helped me with the bed remote once I started to complain of lying still too long. He got the bed into more of a sitting position for me before taking the chair once again. "How have you been? Besides this."

"I've been fine."

"Have you?"

I turned back to Neil. "Where have you been staying?"

"A hotel," he answered.

I looked down at my hands, rubbing them together absently. We were both tiptoeing around each other. Both wondering the same thing.

Where did we stand as a couple? I thought of Calvin. Should I just tell Neil then and there and—

"Sebby," he said. "I've been doing a lot of thinking."

I guess this was it.

"About the tension between us. You know I love you, right?"

I stopped rubbing my hands and looked up. "Neil," I protested.

"I think. If you can be patient with me, I can—become out about this."

"Patient?" I echoed. "Four years isn't long enough of a wait?"

"Seb," Neil said in his chastising tone. "It's different for me. You know that."

I pressed a hand gently to my forehead and shut my eyes. "I can't talk about this right now, Neil. It's only making me angry."

"Why angry?"

"I'm not waiting another four years to hold your hand in public," I replied firmly. "I can't. It's my fault, for not realizing so much sooner how difficult this actually was for you…. Neil, I—I still need some time to think about this."

"You don't want me to come home?" he asked, sounding surprised.

"You're the one who stormed out."

"Y-Yeah, but you need someone to take care of you."

"No, I don't." I turned my head a little to stare at him. "I'm sorry. I thought I was ready to discuss this, but honestly this wasn't the answer I expected from you."

"What did you expect?" When I didn't respond, Neil asked, "Do you want to break up?"

I swallowed the baseball lodged in my throat. "I… don't know."

I thought I had known the answer. Twelve hours ago I was sure of it. But maybe faced with Neil and no way to escape made me chicken out. Did I want to continue riding the rough waves of our relationship? I knew no pairing was perfect and the waters would always push you down, but shouldn't a healthy couple… not be struggling to break the surface all the time?

I just couldn't say that. The concussion must have knocked the courage out of me. Or maybe I just didn't know how to face saying good-bye to something that had been a part of me for so long.

"I can't do this now," I whispered.

"Sebby, if you don't know if you want to remain together, don't you think that speaks for itself?"

"Neil, please."

He let out one of his frustrated sighs. "Fine." He stood, leaned over, and kissed my forehead so gently, it felt like being touched by a feather. "Give me a call when they are ready to discharge you. I'll bring you home."

I didn't respond really, but squeezed his hand and waved when he left the room.

I needed another nap.

IT WAS completely dark when I woke again. My head still hurt like a bitch, but the heavy fog that had been making me feel disoriented and lost was starting to clear. It helped that I could see better in this darkness.

I looked around the tiny room. My glasses were sitting on the small table with a swinging arm so it could be moved in front of me. I reached over and missed once—twice—before snagging them and putting them on.

It felt better, being able to make out details.

Like Calvin asleep in the chair beside me. He looked uncomfortable. His arms were crossed firmly over his chest, and his suit jacket, which he'd been using as a blanket, was falling onto his lap. His head rested awkwardly on his shoulder.

It had to be the middle of the night. The hospital was quiet. Why had he come back? The precious few hours he had to sleep, he chose that uncomfortable chair at my side instead of his own bed?

My heart swelled and beat uncomfortably fast.

He looked cold too. I shivered myself and pulled the blanket up my chest.

I studied his sleeping face for another minute, wanting so badly to touch his hair, wrap my arms around him…. God, what was going on?

"Calvin?" I whispered.

He startled suddenly and sat straight up in the chair.

It caught me off guard. I didn't realize he had been awake.

"A-Are you okay?" I asked.

He looked over at me and let out a breath, like he'd been holding it. "Yeah. I'm fine. Are you? Do you need me to get a nurse?"

"No." I fiddled with the blanket. "Why are you here? It must be late."

Calvin raised his watch, squinting and frowning before pulling his cell out and checking the time. "It's three."

"Yeah, I figured."

He looked back at me. "I didn't want you here alone."

"You look tired," I said in response.

He smiled, and that chiseled, handsome face seemed to light up. "A little. I'm okay, though."

"You can lay with me," I said, not even processing the offer.

"What?"

I refused to back out. What did I want with Neil? Nothing, maybe. He deserved to know *that*—that I was done fighting to right a capsized ship. But what did I want with Calvin? Right now, in that moment, I just wanted to hold him.

I carefully moved closer to the edge of the bed, freeing the space nearest his chair and pulling the blankets back. "Hurry up. This gown isn't exactly keeping me warm," I said with a quiet chuckle.

Calvin turned his head to the closed door, eyeing it a moment before standing. He dropped his coat on the chair, wordlessly climbed onto the bed, and stretched out on his side next to me.

"Come closer," I said, moving my arm to accommodate him.

Calvin put his head on my chest and rested his hand on my neck, rubbing his thumb against my stubble. I put mine in his hair, combing my fingers through the thick, fiery redness and wishing more than ever that I could experience the color.

"I can't stay here," he whispered.

"It's okay," I murmured. "Just relax."

That made him laugh, but I didn't know why.

"How's your head?"

"Better than earlier."

He hummed in response, moving his hand down to take my other. He slid his fingers through mine and squeezed lightly.

"That hand feels awfully familiar."

He snorted. "You kept asking for Millett."

"What did you expect?"

Calvin shrugged a shoulder. "Nothing less."

"You smell good."

"Yeah? It's called forty-eight-hour shift."

"I take it back. You need a shower."

He chuckled, and it really was a nice laugh. "I forgot to compliment your dress. It really brings out the color of your eyes."

"Ass."

"No, but several people saw yours."

I grumbled.

"I saw," Calvin continued.

"Oh? Acceptable?"

"Very," he purred.

It was my turn to laugh, and I tightened my hold on him. I looked down, staring at our locked hands and studying the splatter of freckles across his skin. "I love your freckles."

"Funny."

"I'm not teasing," I answered.

Calvin raised his head, and with his face so close to mine, I could make out all of his rugged beauty. Handsome, classic-looking—a study of monochromatic artwork.

I freed my hand from his to touch his cheek, tracing the spots with my fingertip. "I think you're one of the most gorgeous men I've ever seen," I whispered. I carefully moved my finger to his lips. "Freckles on your lips too."

Calvin smiled lopsidedly. "Everywhere," he agreed.

"I hoped so."

He stared at me a moment longer before leaning in and gently pressing his mouth to mine. Our tongues met and caressed while his fingers toyed with my nipple through the hospital gown. My breathing hitched, and he tenderly nipped my lower lip.

I moaned.

"Like that?" he whispered, pinching the nipple.

I sucked in a breath. "Yeah."

Calvin kissed me again, taking his time as he explored my mouth. His hand left my chest and moved down to rub my stiffening cock. "Want me to finish?"

"Y-You don't need to," I managed, fighting every screaming nerve in my body.

He grinned and pushed the blankets aside. Calvin moved down the hospital bed enough to tug my gown up and take my entire length into his hot, perfect mouth. He bobbed up and down, finding just the right speed and pressure I needed.

It didn't take long. I was tired and pent up and halfway to coming before he even put his mouth on me. I bit my knuckles to keep from crying out, weakly thrusting up and pushing his head down at the same time.

"Cal," I whispered. "Oh God…." My stomach muscles tightened, and my skin prickled with sweat all over. I was standing on the ledge, closer, closer, ready to fall off, waiting for the final push—and then there was an explosion and I was tumbling, screaming all the way down.

Calvin had his hand over my mouth as he milked the last of my orgasm. He raised his lips from my softening erection, licking them. "No crying out," he said with a twinkle of amusement in his eyes. "Not here, anyway." He pulled my gown back down and put the blankets back over us.

I grabbed his shirt, tugged him back to me, and kissed him, tasting myself on him. "What about you?" I asked against his lips.

"I'm fine." He smiled and stroked my hair gently before lying down against my chest again.

I was dimly aware of the press of his erection against my leg, but I was sated and tired and so was he, and I fell into one of the most comfortable sleeps I've had in a long time.

# CHAPTER EIGHT

"YEAH, POP," I said, talking on the phone the next morning. I sat in the chair beside the hospital bed, tugging my shoes on. "Cal—er, Detective Winter was already here. He's driving me home." I glanced up.

Calvin stood patiently by the door, winter coat on and his hands in his pockets.

"I'm feeling a lot better. All right. I'll call you after I get some rest at home. Thanks, Dad." I hung up and slid the phone into my pocket. "Sorry about that."

"No trouble."

When I had woken up, Calvin wasn't in the hospital bed with me anymore, which was surprisingly depressing. I was beginning to worry about what we had done when Calvin appeared in the doorway. He looked awake and refreshed and was wearing different clothes.

"Hey," he had said, smiling. "I spoke with your doctor. He's on his way to check on you. Want a ride home?"

I had been given a clean bill of health early that morning and insisted on leaving right away. Dressed in yesterday's clothes, I went to the door with Calvin.

He handed me my sunglasses. "I got these from your store yesterday."

"Thank you." I put them on. "Hospital lighting is the worst." I followed Calvin out into the hallway. "Where did you go this morning?"

"Oh. Home. Shower and shave." He rubbed his cheek to stress his point.

"You didn't have to come back," I protested. "Don't you have to get to work anyway?"

"Don't worry." Calvin put a hand on my shoulder and steered me down another turn toward the exits.

"I appreciate it. Neil was going to drive me, but…."

"What?"

"I don't know if I can deal with seeing him right now."

"I see." He didn't push the subject, and I was grateful.

It was still snowing when the hospital doors slid open and we walked out. Cars parked overnight were buried. The driveway had been plowed and salted for the arriving ambulances, and bless those poor guys who were driving in this weather.

"Over here," Calvin called, leading the way to a Ford Fusion in some dark color.

"I like this car," I said, opening the passenger door.

"Do you?" He climbed in behind the wheel.

"Affordable," I said as I got in.

"Yeah." He turned the heat on and adjusted it for a moment before cranking on the windshield wipers. "Warm enough?"

"Getting there. Are you able to drive? I mean, the mayor banned driving the other day."

"Yeah, it's likely to be in effect again by tonight." Calvin pulled out and exited the hospital. "These storms aren't giving us a break." He glanced at me. "But yeah, I've got a badge and a gun. I can do a lot of things."

I snorted. "Jerk."

He grinned.

I settled back in my seat, watching the frozen, buried city pass by. "Hey," I said suddenly. "I meant to tell you something the other day."

"Why didn't you?"

"You started sucking my cock."

"Oh."

I patted my coat, reached inside, and removed the envelope that I'd gotten in the mail. "I got this letter Wed—no, Thursday. In the mail. No return address or anything, but it's addressed to the Emporium."

"What does it say?" Calvin asked, not looking away from the road.

I gingerly opened the letter once more. "'I must not only punish, but punish with impunity.'" I looked at Calvin. "I don't know if this means anything about… *anything*, but it's strange."

"Is that all?"

"Yeah." I put the letter away. "Does it mean something to you?"

He was reluctant, but eventually nodded. "Yes."

"Really? What?"

"'The Cask of Amontillado.'"

"The Cask—that's another Poe story." I swore under my breath. "I should have realized."

"Have you read that one? I had to search the phrase."

"I think I have. Isn't that the one where a man walls up his enemy?"

"Yes," Calvin answered.

I hesitated over my next question. "Did Mike get the same letter?"

Again, Calvin just said, "Yes."

"Jesus." I looked out the side window. "He's going to kill me." The statement was some sort of terrifying revelation. "He actually tried yesterday."

"No one is going to kill you," Calvin said sternly. "And yesterday he failed."

"Yeah, but—"

"Don't argue with me, baby." Calvin glanced sideways briefly. "No one is going to hurt you again."

It was difficult to not fight him, to point out that he couldn't be around 24/7, but I didn't have the energy to complain. And besides, having him be so defensive of me was sort of nice.

"Sebastian?"

"Hmm?"

"Do you know anything about African greys?"

"Come again?"

"The parrot."

I turned to Calvin and sort of laughed. "No, should I?"

"Just curious."

"Why?" When he didn't answer, I kept pressing. "Does this have to do with *the case*?"

"I can't discuss it."

"You've discussed other points with me."

"And I shouldn't have."

That irked me. "Yeah well, I don't know anything about parrots."

"All right."

I let out an annoyed sigh and looked at him again. How unlike Neil. No fighting, no bitching, and he didn't give me fuel to continue being an asshole. "My dad," I said reluctantly. "He volunteers at a lot of pet shelters. I know one deals in exotic animals. I could ask him for the contact information. Maybe they can help."

He smiled. "I'd like that. Thank you."

I was home not much later, shoving open the front door and ushering Calvin in. "I need to take a shower," I said while locking the door. "Uh, but if you need to go…." I glanced back at the door.

Why would he stay? He'd been with me all night, drove me home, and the man didn't—

"I can stay for a bit." Calvin unbuttoned his coat. "Go freshen up."

One hot shower, a shave, and brushing of the awful taste out of my mouth later, I felt practically human. I popped in my red-tinted contacts and pulled on a pair of loose old Levi's and a dark-colored long-sleeve shirt.

Opening the bedroom door, I stepped into the front room. "Look at me, good as new."

Calvin was standing among the boxes of estate books, looking over my bookcase. His jacket was neatly draped over a chair at the table. "How do you feel?" he asked, turning my way.

"Like a crisp twenty-dollar bill."

He shook his head, and I think he was laughing quietly. "You hungry?"

I shrugged, rubbing my stomach as it perked up at the mention of food. "I'll get something later."

"I can make breakfast."

"What? No. Come on. You don't need to do that."

"I'm hungry too." Before I could protest, Calvin was walking into the kitchen. He opened the fridge and leaned down to rummage around. "You should go shopping."

"I did the other day, remember?"

"I recall frozen pizza and ice cream."

"That's right. I was having a crisis of the heart," I said, standing in the doorway.

Calvin looked at me and smiled. "How's the heart now?"

It actually was beating hard and making nervous flips all the way down to my gut. "O-Okay," I managed.

He grabbed a carton of eggs and some onion and potatoes. "Scrambled eggs and home fries good?"

"Toast too."

Calvin nodded and set the ingredients on the counter. He opened the cupboards, moving around like he knew my kitchen. He poured some oil into a pan and began chopping the potatoes.

I walked in and grabbed the bread off the top of the fridge. "So you can cook too?"

"You say that like you're impressed."

"I am." I looked at him and grinned. "I never have guys cook me breakfast."

"Millett doesn't cook?"

"Ah, no, he doesn't."

Calvin nodded. "I like cooking." He dropped the diced potato into the pan and added some spices.

I stupidly did nothing but put two slices of bread in the toaster before realizing coffee would be a good idea and started a pot. Watching Calvin was far too great a pleasure over offering to help. He had his sleeves rolled back, showing off the cords of muscles in his arms. He hummed quietly while he worked.

It was relaxing.

And honestly a little upsetting at the same time.

I was falling for him hard and fast. I liked Calvin. A lot. He was hot and smart and quickly becoming everything I'd wanted in a partner. But I had no idea how deep it went for him, and talking about it only felt like it would shatter the precious moment.

"Sebastian?"

I shook my head and glanced up to see him watching me. "What?"

He smiled in that cute, lopsided way. "Do you like onions, I asked."

"Oh, sure."

He added the chopped onion to the eggs. I grabbed jam from the fridge when the toast popped. If I wasn't careful, I was going to fall in love with this little domestic moment. I'd always wanted this. Maybe it was stupid, but sharing the chores and cooking together, spending time with someone in a comfortable, understanding silence—that was what I wanted in life.

Toast sufficiently jammed, coffee perked, and eggs hot, we sat down to eat.

"How is it?" he asked, taking a bite.

"Really good. You want to come by and cook more often?"

Calvin smiled at that. "I find cooking to be relaxing. I need that sometimes."

"I can imagine."

He made a face and nodded, taking another bite.

I watched him for a moment. He seemed to have tensed up. "I thought you were an asshole when we first met."

Calvin laughed. "And now?"

"You're still an ass. But you're a great cook, so you can see how I'm torn," I teased.

"I thought you were a sarcastic shit and your mouth was going to get you in serious trouble."

I arched a brow. "Oh boy. And how about now for me?"

"It's still early."

"What?"

Calvin took a sip of coffee. "Plenty of time left in the day to still get in trouble."

I snorted and took another bite. "Have something planned for me?"

"I can think of a thing or two," Calvin said.

I didn't know how to respond to that. Would he think me dramatic if I asked about his feelings before sex? Because for sure I knew we were going to be fucking. It was only a matter of finishing toast and eggs. But were there any feelings to even be discussed?

I thought about the phone call I had made after being hit.

*Sweetie.*

Neil never called me sweetie. Or baby, for that matter.

I liked the names quite a bit. To me, though, they indicated some form of affection deeper than just lust.

I looked at Calvin again. What was I expecting from him? Passionate, mind-blowing sex? Yes. Absolutely, 100 percent, God please, yes. But my gut told me I wanted more. My heart told me I wanted more. My brain told me I was insane for even thinking it.

*Dump Neil for Calvin.*

Oh boy. Jumping out of a long-term relationship and immediately into a new one was a bad idea. Assuming Calvin even wanted a relationship. It was even more of a bad idea to get tangled up with the cop who's investigating you—sort of. Was this a conflict of interest? Calvin didn't seem to think so. At least, not conflict enough for sex.

I had no less than a million thoughts bouncing around in my head as breakfast was finished and cleared away. I went to the bathroom, grabbed a painkiller from the medicine cabinet, and downed it with cold tap water. When I exited, Calvin was standing in the front room, staring out the window that overlooked the street below.

"How're you feeling?" he asked, glancing up.

"A lot better," I replied. "Thanks for breakfast."

"Of course. Thank you for letting me cook."

I slowly stepped up to his side, glancing up at him. "So."

"So?" he repeated.

"I'm ready to jump you, but I guess I'm nervous over whether I read the signs right." I laughed.

Calvin turned fully to me and smiled. He reached out, cupped my face with his big hands, and kissed my mouth. He pressed his tongue against my lips, and I opened up to it, groaning when the touch sent electricity down my spine.

"Are you sure you're up for this?" he whispered against my mouth.

"Yeah."

"Promise to tell me if you need to stop?"

"I promise," I answered.

I wrapped my arms around his neck, and he walked us back toward the bedroom door. Calvin's hand was under my shirt and pinching a nipple while I yanked his tie loose. A trail of clothes soon led into the dim room.

"Is your head okay?" Calvin asked again.

"Okay," I confirmed breathlessly.

"Can I fuck you?" Calvin asked quietly between kisses.

What a goddamn gentleman. "Yes," I begged. "I need you inside me."

Once I was naked, Calvin helped me down onto the bed and finished tugging off his unbuckled trousers. His massive cock jumped to attention as it was freed, and I was both thrilled and intimidated. Definitely bigger and thicker than Neil. Fully naked himself, Calvin climbed onto the bed and leaned over me, his muscled frame pushing me down into the mattress.

He was so hot, so unbelievably sexy.

Calvin kissed me and briefly rolled his hips against mine. A shudder went through my body as our erections touched and rubbed. "Yeah, you like that, baby?" he whispered.

"Yes! Cal, please."

"Please what?" he murmured before kissing gently along my neck.

"Please fuck me!"

He bit my chest, and I bucked up against him. "I will," he promised. Calvin reached down to stroke me slowly, teasingly. "I'm going to shove every inch of myself into that perfect ass of yours. You want that?"

My mind was trying to stay afloat during a hurricane. Yes, I wanted that! All of it, every little bit of Calvin I wanted inside me. I wanted him to stretch me and fill me in ways I never had been. I wanted him to keep talking, to keep saying all of these dirty things to me because I found it to be an incredible turn-on that I had always been embarrassed to ask for.

Calvin was either psychic or a gifted sex partner.

He nuzzled his nose briefly against mine. "You like being talked to this way, don't you?"

I nodded.

"I thought so." He kissed me once again and gave my cock another few tugs. "Where's your lube?"

He sat back as I moved to the side of the bed to rummage around briefly in the nightstand. I handed over the small bottle and a condom. "Condom or no sex," I said firmly.

"Of course, a condom, baby. Don't worry." Calvin took the lube in one hand and wrapped his other around my neck. He squeezed lightly, just enough to make me gasp as he kissed me. "Raise your legs up."

"Do you want me on my stomach?"

"No. You need to take it easy, and I want to see your face."

If it were possible to be harder than I was, I managed it.

I moved my legs as told, holding my knees.

Calvin smiled widely and stroked himself briefly. "Jesus, you are so fucking beautiful." He squirted some lube onto his fingers and reached down to press the first into me. He thrust his finger in and out gently, grinning when I groaned. "Look at you, getting so worked up over a finger." He added another and began to stretch me with extreme care and precision.

"Oh God. Cal, please… don't stop."

He kissed me again, finger searching until it found the spot that made me buck. Calvin laughed quietly. "Like that?" He pressed again a few more times, reducing me to a quivering mess.

After having spent longer than I was used to being prepared—not that I'm complaining, because fingers have never felt so good—Calvin tore open the condom and tugged it down over himself.

"Does that fit you?"

He chuckled. "What a compliment. Yeah, of course." He squirted more lube and got himself slick before taking my hips and lining up. He pressed the head of his cock against me and pushed slowly.

Calvin took a lot more time to make sure I was ready, and I found myself oddly touched. Neil had a tendency to rush, to make it a task instead of pleasure. Sometimes it wasn't great for me, and sex ended up being uncomfortable, but Calvin had made it feel good from the start.

Really good. And he seemed to have enjoyed doing that for me.

But even still, he was bigger than what I was accustomed to, and the head of his cock was enormous. I shook as he pushed against the ring of muscles, groaning as he filled me. I wanted—loved—rough sex, but this part needed to be gentle. As fast and as frantic as I desired to be fucked, the initial moments I had to have slow.

Calvin read that request from my body language. He leaned over me, pressing our foreheads together as he paused to let me adjust. He leaned on his forearms on either side of my chest. He kissed my lips, cheeks, nose, and down my neck.

"Are you okay?" he whispered.

I nodded and let out a breath. "Y-Yeah."

"Want me to move again?"

I gripped his biceps hard. "Just a little slow," I said with a shaky voice.

Calvin gently thrust forward, easing a bit more of himself into me. I knew he wanted to move, but God, his patience was that of a saint as he calmly waited for my grip on his arms to loosen.

"*Fuck*," he groaned. "Sebastian."

"Good?" I asked.

He laughed quietly and kissed me again. "*So* good. So tight."

I carefully wrapped my legs around Calvin's hips, urging him forward. "You can move more."

"Sure?"

I nodded.

Calvin took me for my word and pressed in until his balls touched my ass. Those moments with him made me feel like I was new to sex all over again. I wasn't a virgin, of course not. I'd had three boyfriends and sex with each of them. The first, we'd both been inexperienced, so it wasn't that good in retrospect. The second was better but too demanding of me. And Neil... let's just say Neil and I had never had chemistry like what I was feeling with Calvin.

Every touch seemed to light a fire under my skin. His kisses were intoxicating, his taste something I found myself craving. He pressed his powerful frame against mine, pinning me into place. I loved being able to dig my fingers into his muscles, which only seemed to spur him on. He spoke rough to me, but was exceptionally mindful of my needs and well-being.

I'd never felt so cared for.

"Still okay?" he asked, voice gruff.

"Y-Yeah."

His cock shoved in and out, the burning scrape so good, it made my toes curl. Calvin's hips moved fast as he thrust into me. "Goddamn, Sebastian. You're so fucking *good*," he growled, pounding the last word in hard.

I cried out and arched my back, meeting each of his movements with my own half-assed attempts. "M-More! Calvin!"

"More?" Calvin repeated, a grin spreading across his face. "You've already got my whole cock, baby." He stopped suddenly, remaining inside but motionless.

I looked at him and grabbed at his arms. "Don't stop now!"

"Beg," he ordered.

I was a little embarrassed, but the order was so sexy, just like with the blowjob. "I need it!" I moved my hands down to Calvin's ass and squeezed hard.

He grunted but didn't move. "You need what?" he asked instead.

"Calvin! Come on!"

He wrapped his big hand around my neck again, squeezing gently and making me groan. He repeated the question.

"I need you—to—to fuck me. Please, please, I'm so close!"

"Hungry for my cock?" he asked, lips ghosting over mine.

I moaned in response and pushed back against him again. "Yes, you're so good, so big!"

He kissed me while reaching between us to stroke me. "Want to come with me inside you?" he murmured.

I bucked up into his hand while trying to move my hips against his at the same time. "Yes!"

And then Calvin was thrusting into me again, his mouth on mine. He stroked me in time with his movements. Every sensation, from his tongue to his cock, was overwhelming, and I barely had a chance to cry out before I started coming in his hand. He groaned and swore while burying his face into my neck, shoving into my clenching muscles.

"Yeah, you love this, don't you? You love my cock." Calvin groaned.

My body shook as I spent myself, and I wrapped my arms around Calvin's neck. I could barely stand him inside me now, only because my nerves were so strung out on pleasure, but he was nearly there.

"Come inside me," I moaned.

Calvin took the side of my face with one hand and kissed me again. His tongue faltered, and he muffled his voice against my mouth when he started coming. He was breathing heavy and kissing me much more gently before pulling his face away.

"You okay?" he whispered, stroking my cheek.

I smiled, looking at him through askew glasses. "I'm fantastic," I clarified.

He laughed. "Good." Calvin pulled out as he sat up. "One minute." He rose and tugged off the condom while walking out of the room and into the bathroom.

I grabbed a few tissues from the box beside the bed to wipe myself clean. I tossed them into the wastebasket and set my glasses aside before getting comfortable. I was waiting for Calvin to come back, to climb into bed with me and fall into an exhausted, sated nap before reality dawned.

It was morning, and he had to work.

This was sex. No indication of anything more. He wasn't going to *cuddle*.

"How does your head feel?" Calvin asked, walking back into the bedroom.

"Which one?"

"Ha-ha."

I laughed and tilted my head to look in his direction. "Blood is leaving one in favor of another. I'm good."

"Move over."

"You're staying?" I asked in surprise.

Calvin paused as he started to pull the blankets back. "Should I go?" he asked.

"N-No, I just figured you had places to be."

He grunted and got into bed, stretched out beside me, and draped an arm across my chest. After a minute of shifting about to get comfortable, Calvin once again used my chest as a pillow and snaked a leg between mine. I liked this, liked him finding relief in my arms. I ran one hand down his side and hip to his thigh, where I felt the skin texture change.

Scar tissue, maybe?

Calvin hummed sleepily. "Bullet," he mumbled.

"What?"

"I was shot there."

"In the Army?"

He nodded against me. "Missed my femoral artery just barely."

"Jesus," I whispered. "But you were shot twice, weren't you?"

He tilted his head up, staring at me. "Yes," he said after a pause. He took my hand, moved it to his shoulder, and pressed a finger against a spot. "Not as bad as the leg."

"Were you scared?"

"I really don't like talking about my time in the military, Sebastian." It wasn't rude or angry, the way he spoke, but it was wary. Tired, almost.

"Sorry." I had to hold the questions at bay.

Calvin put his head back down.

I closed my eyes, losing myself in the gentle touches against my body that Calvin made with his firm, callused hands. "Is Beth okay?" I murmured at length.

"Beth Harrison?" Calvin sounded half-asleep.

"Yeah, bookshop Beth."

"She's fine. No one was in the store when it was broken into."

"Was anything stolen?"

"I'm not sure. I don't believe so," Calvin replied. He pinched my nipple, and I felt him grin against my chest when I yelped. "Go to sleep."

"Yes, Officer."

"Smartass."

I SLEPT harder than I ever remembered doing. I guess a concussion coupled with the fiercest sex you've had in years will knock you out a good few hours. Or half of the day. I had no idea what time it was, what day it was, and I was really, perfectly okay with that.

I awoke to having shifted around in bed, pressed up against Calvin's back with an arm around his waist. Minus the annoyance of having slept with my contacts in again, I sighed comfortably and curled up tighter against him. Calvin was awake. He pulled my arm up to his chest and covered my hand with his. I was cognizant enough to register my erection pressing against the curve of his ass.

I hoped he didn't mind.

I usually preferred playing catcher, so to speak. I loved the overwhelming sensations that came with being fucked. I liked to submit a little, to have someone else take control and lead me along. That being said, I enjoyed the occasional switch in roles. It was healthy, I thought, but Neil had only let me do it once before putting his foot down.

I was horrified by the thought. *Let* me?

Calvin's husky chuckle scattered the dark thoughts. "Sleep okay?" he murmured.

"Better than okay," I said around a yawn.

"Always wake up like this?" He pressed back slightly.

"You can hardly blame me. Have you looked at yourself in a mirror recently?"

"Yes." Calvin rolled over, his face close to mine. "Have you?"

"Yep. Old and gray, and I do mean that literally."

"You're thirty-three. Not old." Calvin shook his head.

"You know way too much about me," I replied. "How old are you?"

Calvin looked sheepish. "Forty-two."

"Wow, really?"

"What?" he asked, sounding a bit defensive.

"No, no. I mean, wow, I can't believe that. You look fantastic."

"I'd like to be thirty-three again," he countered.

"It's not all it's cracked up to be."

Calvin grumbled, cupped my face, and kissed me. "I should get going."

"But look at me," I said, glancing down meaningfully. "What am I supposed to do with this?"

"Am I supposed to take care of you every time you get hard?"

"It'd be nice. Can I put you on speed dial?"

Calvin laughed and kissed me again. "I don't think I have time. I would hate to rush how good you are."

The compliment made my cheeks heat up.

"How about I jerk us off together?" he asked, reaching down to wrap his hand briefly around me and tug.

I immediately pressed my hips forward into the touch. "I want that," I whispered.

"Need me to put a condom on?"

I considered the question for a moment. He was so thoughtful in bed. I really didn't know what to make of it. Were most guys like Calvin, or was I simply used to attracting the kind that didn't care so much? I kissed him, putting a hand on the back of his head to deepen the touch.

"No?" he muttered against my mouth.

"No," I agreed.

He pulled me flush against his own body, wrapped his hand around both of our cocks, and stroked them slowly. Calvin kissed me some more, nibbled on my bottom lip, and moved along my chin and jaw.

"I wanted to fuck you from the minute we met," Calvin whispered.

I moaned quietly, pushing against his hand eagerly. "R-Really?"

"Really." He kissed me again. "But I knew something was going on between you and Millett."

"How did you know?"

"Because I didn't buy his 'friend' bullshit. Not when you looked like a lover scorned."

Jesus, had I looked that pissed at Neil the day I found the pig heart? But thinking about Neil in that moment of time wasn't what I wanted.

"Faster," I muttered, wrapping my arm around Calvin's neck.

"Yeah, baby." He kissed me and did as told, moving his hand with greater urgency.

I closed my eyes and focused on Calvin. The warmth and pressure of his hand, the fullness of his cock pressing against mine. The deep, urgent breaths that ghosted against my lips before I grabbed him in another long, exploring kiss. Calvin sped up, and my muscles tightened as I got closer.

"Cal?" I whispered.

"Hmm?"

"Would you let me fuck you, if I wanted it the other way?"

"Sure, sweetie." He kissed me, tongue pressing against mine briefly. God, it was that simple?

"Shit," Calvin groaned. "I'm almost there."

"On my stomach," I said, gently tugging free and rolling onto my back. I pushed the blankets down and continued jerking myself.

Calvin sat up on his knees, moving onto either side of one of my legs. "God, look at you," he said, half talking to himself. "You're so fucking hot. Yeah, keep touching yourself."

I think I would have been a lot more self-conscious with any other guy, feeling sort of stupid while he watched me get off, but Calvin was staring like it was the single greatest experience of his life and that— made me feel really attractive.

Like not an old man. But a sexy, young guy.

I wanted to be that for him.

I reached up and touched his firm stomach, fingers gripping his warm skin when everything tensed. I closed my eyes and moaned as I came, the wet and sticky aftermath making a mess on my body. I had barely finished stroking the last of my orgasm out when I felt another spurt hit me. I looked up, watching Calvin coming on me, his mouth swollen from kisses and eyes dark with lust.

"Fuck," he groaned loudly as he finished, letting go of himself. "That face you make when you come," he growled while leaning over to give me a hard, possessive kiss. "You're going to keep me in an endless loop of screwing."

"Do you hear me complaining?" I laughed.

Calvin moved, trailing his tongue down my sweaty chest before he started to lick my stomach clean. He lapped up every drop before sitting back with a content sigh.

"You like that?"

"The taste?"

"Yeah."

He nodded. "Do you not want me to do that?"

I waved a hand lazily. "Oh no. I don't mind."

Calvin smiled. "You want to suck me next time?"

"God yes, but please don't tease me now," I murmured. "I don't know if I can manage a third round."

He laughed again in that airy, carefree manner that one often has after fantastic orgasms. "I really have to go now." Calvin climbed off the bed and started gathering his clothes and dressing.

I rolled onto my stomach, watching him tug his trousers back on and button his shirt. "Thank you," I said at length.

"For what?" Calvin turned around.

"Everything. In the course of one day, you've come to my rescue, kept me company, driven me home, cooked me breakfast, and gave me two—no, three amazing orgasms." I grinned. "Is this all part of being a public servant?"

Calvin grew quiet, turned away to grab his tie off the floor, and put the knot into place at his neck.

I raised my head. "Hey, I was teasing," I said quickly.

Calvin buttoned the cuffs of his shirt and finished getting himself presentable before he leaned over the bed and kissed my mouth. "I know," he murmured. "Stay in bed and relax today, okay?"

"Are you ordering me?"

"I will if I find you've gotten up from this exact spot," he said with a small smile.

"What if I have to piss?"

"All right, that's allowed, but nothing else. Concussions are serious."

"Yes, I'm aware."

He combed his fingers briefly through my hair. "You've got my number."

"What would I need it for?" I asked, tilting my head into his touch.

He shrugged. "Anything."

"When will I see you again?"

Calvin hesitated. "Maybe you should consider this a done thing."

"What?" I sat up abruptly.

"You're dating Millett, Sebastian," Calvin said as he let go. "Aren't you?"

My gut rolled and made me feel sick. "I don't know," I said.

"You should tell him."

"That we fucked? Are you serious?"

"Yes," Calvin replied calmly. "I admit it's partially my fault, but I know you're not the sort of man to deceive someone."

"Jesus Christ, Calvin. Has anyone told you that you need to work on your pillow talk?" I stared at him, wanting to stand up and argue, but I felt I wouldn't be as intimidating stark-ass naked. "I mean, not to get all teenage mushy, but was this anything more to you than sex? I'll be honest, you send some fairly conflicting signals."

"I know I do," he said simply.

"That's not helpful," I retorted. "God... *damn it.* I want you, Calvin."

"Millett—"

"Neil and I have been circling the fucking drain for six months," I said, now angry. "I've just been too afraid to admit it. And—and now you're here and I've never felt anything like this before."

Calvin was silent for too long. Eventually, he said, "I shouldn't have initiated anything. I'm sorry."

"You can't just apologize after all of this! Are you fucking nuts?"

I watched the muscle in his jaw tighten. "I need to go, Sebastian."

"Screw you," I answered.

He didn't respond, which was nice, because I might have throttled him if he had.

# CHAPTER NINE

NEIL CALLED me in the afternoon, waking me up from an anger-, contempt-, and painkiller-induced sleep. "Seb?"

"What?" I grumbled, pulling the blankets up over my head.

"Are you still at the hospital?"

"No, I'm home."

"Why didn't you call me?"

I was quiet.

Neil deserved to know. Calvin was right. I couldn't forgive him for the fight we had had and fail to mention I had sex with another man in the bed we shared together. I covered my eyes with my hand, taking a deep breath. I had to man up and be honest about this—*us*. Dragging us both along in a relationship that my heart and mind could no longer commit to wasn't fair to Neil, and it wasn't fair to myself.

And it wasn't so I could have Calvin. It was stupid to want to be with him before I'd even nailed the coffin lid closed on this dead romance with Neil. I'd been with him for four years. I needed to breathe afterward.

Besides, Calvin didn't want to date me. That was obvious.

It was just sex. Really, really incredible sex. Nothing more.

"Seb? Are you there?"

"Neil?" I asked, my voice surprisingly thick. "Can you come home? I—we need to talk."

The silence on his end was overwhelming. He knew what I was thinking. "Yeah," he said quietly. "I'll be there soon."

While I waited for Neil, I got dressed and heated a frozen pizza for lunch. Or dinner.

What time was it?

Screw it, I didn't care.

I was on my third slice, sitting in front of the television, when the front door unlocked and Neil stepped inside.

"You didn't change the locks" was the first thing he said, shutting the door.

"No."

He pocketed his keys, glancing around. He was nervous.

So was I.

I set the plate on the couch and shut the television off, got up, and walked over to the table. "Can we sit and talk?"

Neil nodded, setting his bag and coat aside before joining me. "Seb," he said quietly, reaching out for my hands.

It felt wrong to be touching Neil intimately, and I pulled my hands away. I had broken his trust by sleeping with Calvin, which, believe me, now that the lust had waned, I felt like utter shit about. Even more, though, it felt wrong for it to not be Calvin touching me.

And that thought just made me… sad.

"I know what's on your mind."

I shook my head. "No, you don't. Believe me."

"Try me," he said gently.

"I slept with Calvin."

An awkward moment of silence.

"Calvin Winter?" he hesitated.

I nodded and looked up. "Yes."

"You had sex with that shithead? He's not even gay!"

"Yes, I think he is, and don't call him that, Neil."

"Are you—what the—Sebastian, what the hell!" he stood quickly. "When?"

"Today."

"Today?" he echoed. "Where? Here? You fucked in our bed?"

"It's technically my bed."

"Oh, shut up! Don't start being a smartass with me!"

I leaned back in my chair, looking up at Neil. "I'm sorry."

"You think you can just apologize for letting some other guy slip his dick in you and I'm going to magically be okay with that?"

"No… I just wanted you to know. You have a right to."

"And now what?" Neil asked. "You're breaking up with me for him?"

I shook my head. I wasn't going to start crying over this. Not now. *Just get through it.* "I think we should break up," I agreed. "But I'm not going to date Calvin."

"Oh thank God," Neil retorted, loud and sarcastically.

"Neil, we've been a train wreck for six months. This isn't all my fault."

"You fucked around behind my back, Sebastian!"

"While we were on the verge of already ending it, Neil. Come on. I would have told you this yesterday at the hospital, but I couldn't. I was just too out of it."

"That doesn't make it better!"

"I know, and I'm not looking to be excused for what I did. But this relationship has been dying for months." I swallowed the lump in my throat, and it hurt like hell. "Neil, I don't want us to force ourselves to stay together for the sake of having already managed four years. It's not… the way it should be. I'm not happy. And I know, even if you don't want to admit it, you're not happy either."

Neil was shaking his head as he eventually took a seat again. He rubbed his face and muttered around his hands, "You really want to end this?"

"Yes," I said simply.

Neil was pissed. But he was also heartbroken.

So was I. It's not easy saying good-bye to something like this, never easy to say farewell to years of commitment, but as I answered him, I felt a wave of relief.

It was done. Over.

No more of Max asking me what last night's fight was about. No more of my dad's concerned looks and questions. It was over with Neil, and I couldn't have Calvin, but I at least could work on finding happiness within myself.

Somewhere along this troubled path, I'd lost it.

Neil was nodding, staring at his hands. "All right," he whispered. "I'll… stay at my brother's or something. Give me a day or two to get my things."

"Take the time you need," I replied.

Neil looked back up. "I didn't fuck up all the time, did I?"

"No, of course not, Neil."

I don't know if that's what he wanted to hear or not, but he nodded. "I'm going to pack my clothes."

I watched him stand and head into the bedroom. I pulled my phone from my pocket and set it down on the tabletop, leaned over it, and pecked at the keypad with one finger like a chicken. I sent my dad a text and immediately received a response.

*Do you need me to come over?*

Yeah, I kind of did. Was it stupid to want my parent? I was a grown man, but my dad was my world. I listened to Neil quietly moving around the bedroom, collecting what he could stuff into a bag.

*Baad weathr pop. It's OK.*

*Sebastian I live 15 minutes away.*

William Snow was being serious if he took the time to text my name.

*Pleaase come.*

*I'll be there soon.*

"That isn't... Winter, is it?"

I looked up from my phone to see Neil standing awkwardly in the bedroom doorway. "No. My dad."

His shoulders visibly relaxed, and he walked into the bathroom to gather more items. He set his bag near the front door after, then went back into the bedroom, muttering, "At least you used a condom."

I guess I should have taken the trash out.

Ten minutes later, Neil had enough of his belongings that I could see a difference in the apartment. He brought most of it out to his car in one trip before returning for the last bag. I stood from the table as he walked back inside, fiddling with the keys on his ring.

"Keep the key. It's not a rush to vacate. When you have the time."

Neil paused, weighing his words before simply nodding and pocketing the keys. "Thanks."

"Yeah."

He picked up his bag. "I'll let you know when I'm coming by for the rest."

"Sure."

"Okay." He hesitated. "Be good."

God, even now, that still bothered me. It'd probably be the last time I heard it, though.

I watched him step out and quietly walk down the rickety stairs, vanishing around the corner. Knowing Neil, he'd arrange to pick up the rest of his belongings when I wasn't home and then would mail me the key.

I shut the door and sat on the couch. It was quiet.

I didn't move until the door buzzer sounded about thirty minutes later. My dad was at my landing, Maggie too, grinning her big silly dog smile with her tongue hanging to one side.

"Hey, Pop."

Dad walked inside and pulled me into a hug immediately. "How are you?"

I wrapped both of my arms tight around him and shrugged, not trusting my voice.

"Did Neil leave already?" he asked next, patting my back.

I nodded against him. "Yeah," I croaked. I reluctantly let him go, took his jacket, and hung it up.

"Was this your dinner?" Dad asked, picking up the plate of half-eaten pizza. "I'll make something."

"I'm not that hungry, Dad," I said, following him.

"Hey." He stopped and turned around. "Kiddo, believe me, I know what you're going through." He smiled and squeezed my arm. "Let's see what you have to cook."

Maggie followed us into the kitchen, her tail wagging happily. She sat, watching my dad toss out the shitty pizza, and then looked up at me, like she couldn't believe he'd let that go to waste.

I scratched behind her ears and asked, much to my own horror, "Why can't I keep a boyfriend?"

My dad turned from the fridge, giving me a critical look.

"Dad, I've just ended my third disaster of an attempt."

"Can you even count Marcus as a boyfriend? It was your first year of college."

"He counted," I insisted. "And Brian was a jerk, and Neil—"

"Wasn't healthy for you, Seb," he offered quietly. "A man who can't love himself can't love another person."

That was the thing about Pop. Didn't matter if you were gay, straight, bi, whatever your flavor was, there was nothing he cared more about than making sure you were content with yourself above all else. Sometimes I wondered if he considered me a failure in that respect. I always ended up being tossed aside or committing to something less than what I was worth, according to him.

I looked down at Maggie. She was mesmerized by my ear-scratching. "I fucked up so hard, Pop."

Realizing I had nothing remotely decent for dinner, my dad went to his go-to: grilled cheese and tomato soup. He pulled that card whenever I was down, and throughout my childhood, it had always worked to perk me up. But now, thinking about the fact that he had to resort to it—depressed me.

"You didn't do anything wrong, Sebastian."

"Yes, I did." I kept staring at Maggie, ashamed to look up. "I… want Calvin." When I heard him stop moving around, I dared a look up.

Pop was watching me. Eventually he said, "Yeah. I figured."

"What?"

"Seb. I've seen you go through a few relationships now." He turned the burners on and set the buttered bread down. "I've never seen you in love."

"I loved Neil."

"Maybe the concept of Neil, but I don't think you really, deeply loved him," Pop answered. He put some slices of cheese down and completed the sandwiches before pouring some soup into a pot. "But I saw your face when Calvin was at the hospital yesterday, and I saw how he looked at you."

My heart started beating hard and fast, making me feel a little sick. "Dad, I'm not, God no. I'm not in love with Calvin. I've only known him a few days."

"I'm aware."

"Then you know how stupid—*silly*, that sounds," I corrected.

Pop looked at me. "Tell me to my face that I'm wrong."


My SLEEP cycle was starting to take on a terrible new pattern. Worst, best, worst—that meant tonight everything would be puppies and sunshine and I'd fall asleep without a care in the world, right?

Yeah, sure.

"Good morning," Max called, trudging down the sidewalk toward me.

"Morning," I muttered while unlocking the front door to the Emporium and punching in the security code.

It wasn't snowing that Sunday, but it was dark and overcast, and the wind was biting, dropping the temperature below freezing. It was expected to be this cold for the next several days. People were calling this one of the worst storms the city had experienced in over one hundred years.

"How're you doing?" he asked as we stepped out of the gale-force winds. "Should you be back to work so soon?"

"I'll keep the workload light," I assured, turning on the nearest lamp.

"Yeah right," Max said with a smile. "I'm really glad you're okay, Seb," he continued as we both hung up our winter clothes on the coatrack.

"Me too," I agreed.

"Beth feels terrible about what happened."

"Why? Did she clobber me?"

Max laughed lightly. "No, but you went to defend her shop, she said."

"I just wanted to turn the wailing alarm off."

Max rolled his eyes. "Anyway, she said she wanted to talk to you, first chance you had."

"All right, thanks." I could already sense Max knew something else was up, so I walked away before he had a chance to say anything. I stopped at the steps up to the register, glancing around a bit hesitantly before calling, "Max?"

"Yeah?" He was turning on a few more lamps behind me.

"Did you leave these?"

"Leave what?" He came up behind me to see I was pointing at a bouquet of flowers sitting beside the register. "Whoa, no way. Your dad and I were here for a little while in the morning, but just to take care of the place. We didn't stay open for business." He looked at me warily. "Is this like the pig heart thing?"

"I don't know," I admitted.

Max looked back at the flowers and then nodded to himself, suddenly understanding. "Neil."

"What?"

"Neil had to have brought them."

"I... don't think so."

"Why not?"

"We... broke up, last night."

"Oh shit." Max put a hand on my shoulder. "Man, I'm so sorry, Seb."

I cleared my throat. "Thanks. Still doesn't explain the flowers."

"Want me to see if there's a note?"

"No, I'm not afraid of roses," I muttered.

I walked up the steps and stood at the counter, staring at the bouquet. They were wrapped in cheap plastic to hold them together, but they looked wilted, as if they'd been out of water for too long. I took a picture of their position beside the register with my phone before moving them.

Paranoid? I was starting to get there.

"Well?" Max asked expectantly.

I lifted the flowers with a tissue and found a slip of paper sitting underneath. "'We grew in age—and love—together—Roaming the forest, and the wild; My breast her shield in wintry weather—And, when the friendly sunshine smil'd, And she would mark the opening skies, *I* saw no Heaven—but in her eyes.'"

"Shakespeare?" Max asked.

"No." I put the flowers down. "Poe. This is from his poem 'Tamerlane.'"

"I don't think I read it," Max answered. He sounded a little nervous.

"I wrote a paper on this poem in college," I said, bending down and grabbing a big paper bag. I gently slipped the note and bouquet inside. "I need to bring this to Calvin."

"Ginger cop?"

"Yeah, that one," I answered, standing. "Will you be okay here alone for a bit?"

"Sure, but if I have to call 911, at a certain point, the police will be convinced this address is cursed and will stop coming by."

"Very funny."

"Poe died under mysterious circumstances, didn't he?" Max asked as he walked up to the counter beside me, taking the moneybag and putting the change into the register.

"Yes, why?"

"Maybe a curse killed him."

"Oh, don't start, Max." I shook my head and walked down the steps.

"Hey," he called, leaning over the counter to watch me go toward the door. "Since when do you call that detective by his first name?"

I paused and turned around. "I don't know. Does it matter?"

I couldn't see Max's expression all that well from afar, but I figured he had to be grinning when he said, "You slept with him."

"W-What!"

"Damn, Seb. The sheets from Neil aren't even cool yet."

"Don't joke about that."

"But it's true, isn't it?"

"I… may… have," I muttered. "A little."

"How was he?"

"Max, keep it in your pants and cover the shop. I'll be back in an hour." I stopped by the front door, rushing to put my coat and scarf back on.

"I wish you weren't colorblind!" Max called. "I need to know if the carpet matches the drapes!"

"For the love of God, Max!"

I TOOK a taxi to the address on Calvin's business card, which I now carried in my wallet. I had thought I'd be doing him a favor, coming to drop off suspicious evidence so he wouldn't need to drive over to me, but once I walked into the precinct, I wasn't so sure. Like so many of my ideas, I hadn't thought this one through. Would he even want to see me after yesterday? Could he separate professional and private life enough to be gentle with me as the officer involved in my—this—case?

The lights of the building were excruciatingly bright, and I had to keep my sunglasses on.

"Can I help you?" a woman at the front desk asked in an already-impatient tone. She was destined to have a shitty rest of the day with that attitude.

"Is Detective Winter in?"

"He's always in. Who's asking?" She picked up the desk phone and stared expectantly.

"Uh, Snow. Sebastian Snow."

"Hold on." She dialed an extension, waited a beat, then said, "Sebastian Snow at the front desk. Fine, sure." She hung up and motioned down the hall. "Elevator."

I looked over there. "To where?"

She waved impatiently at a billboard beside the elevator.

"Appreciate the help," I muttered, walking away.

I scanned the list of names and departments, finding "Winter, Calvin, Homicide" on the third floor. I stepped into the elevator and was joined by several other men in suits before the doors closed. I kept my head ducked, staring at the dying flowers in the bag.

"Mr. Snow?"

I knew that voice. That was Calvin's partner. I looked up, then down. "Good morning, Detective Lancaster."

She gave me a grin. "This is a pleasant surprise."

"For me or you?"

Lancaster chuckled quietly, like the idea that I was happy to see her in particular really just teased her funny bone. "Smooth."

I glanced at the other men in the elevator. None of them were smiling.

"Can't say I expected to see you step into a police precinct," Lancaster continued.

"Er—me neither." I gripped the bag tighter.

"You're going up to see Calvin, I presume?" she asked.

I caught one of the other guys look at us. He gave me a once-over and sneered while looking away. Huh. That was probably not good. Did Lancaster know Calvin was gay? Did these other detectives?

"Desperate times call for desperate measures," I told her.

When the elevator doors slid open on the third floor, Lancaster walked out with me and pointed across an open area at several desks with detectives seated at them. "Across the room, down that hall. It's the first office on the left."

"Do you... share an office?"

"Yeah." She gave me a sort of friendly slap on the shoulder, but Lancaster was stronger than she looked and it shoved me forward. "Not my destination, though. You're safe."

"Uh."

"Speak of the devil." Lancaster motioned across the room at a figure who exited a door and stood in the hallway. It couldn't be anyone but Calvin.

Oh boy.

I said good-bye to Lancaster and took a breath before walking across the room. I watched Calvin slowly come into focus as I approached. He was leaning against the wall, strong arms crossed firmly over his chest. He wore a tie but no suit coat, and I was able to get a good look at the shoulder holster he wore.

Man, he was probably going to shoot me for coming here.

"Hi," I said quietly as I reached the hallway.

Calvin didn't say anything. He straightened and took a step back, motioning me into a room.

It was tiny, mostly taken up with two cramped desks, chairs, and filing cabinet. Despite the lack of space, it was clean and orderly, to the point of it being near ridiculous. The lights snapped off from overhead and the only light was the gray overcast coming in through the window behind the computer chair.

"Oh, thanks," I said, starting to turn around.

"Thanks," someone mimicked nearly the same time as me.

Beside the door was a massive gray bird on a perch. "What the hell?"

Calvin shut the door behind him as he entered. "What are you doing here?" he asked forcefully.

I glanced back at him, then to the bird once or twice. "Nice parrot. Yours?"

"Answer the question."

"Jesus, am I being interrogated?" I asked, looking up and pushing back my sunglasses.

Calvin didn't appear to be in a good mood. "I asked what you're doing here, Sebastian."

"I heard you already," I remarked while pulling my regular glasses from my coat and putting them on. "I have something to show you."

"And you decided it would be wise to come here?"

"I… thought it would save you time," I replied slowly. I took a breath, steadying myself. "I know you're angry about yesterday."

"This isn't about yesterday."

"Not about that part when I told you to screw yourself?"

Calvin narrowed his eyes. "What do you need to show me?"

I handed over the bag. "Your bird looks sick," I commented when Calvin had taken the offering and I looked back at the parrot.

"It's not mine. And he keeps pulling his feathers out."

I made a face. "Poor bird."

The parrot cocked his head to the side and stared at me.

"Whose is it?"

Calvin looked up from the bag's contents. "What?" He sounded on the verge of exasperation, which was a complete turnaround from his bedroom demeanor.

"Wrong side of the bed this morning or what?"

Calvin cleared his throat. "Sebastian, you came to my place of work unannounced."

"You do the same with me."

"I'm a cop. It's different."

"What the hell? If you'd rather not investigate the ongoing harassment I've been receiving, I'll deal with it myself." I grabbed for the bag, but he held it out of reach. "Why are you being such an asshole this morning?"

"I'm not."

I snorted. "Then this is just your attitude prior to coffee?"

Neither of us moved, but the sudden tension coming off Calvin was palpable. It was as if he were building a brick wall right in front of me. Keeping me at a distance. A safe distance.

It was like a lightbulb turning on. "You're afraid someone will peg you as gay for just being around me, aren't you?"

"That's not true."

"Yes, it is," I retorted. "Does Lancaster know?"

"No."

"Don't be so sure."

Calvin ignored the jab and raised the bag. "What is this?"

"The fuck does it look like?"

"Don't get uppity with me," he demanded.

The bird suddenly squawked loudly. Calvin jumped at the noise, glaring at the bird as it proceeded to make sounds similar to words, but not quite understandable. I'd seen him jump like that a few times now.

Stress from the case? I knew he wasn't sleeping a lot.

I didn't ask, though. He was already angry and defensive. I pointed at the bird. "Really, why is there a bird in here?"

"Ben belonged to Merriam Byers."

"The banker?"

Calvin nodded. "Whatever garbled sentence that is, he's been screeching it nonstop. Now tell me about these flowers."

"There's a note in there too."

"Sebastian."

I was staring at Ben the African grey while saying, "They were on my register this morning when I unlocked the shop. And no, before you ask, it definitely wasn't Max."

"Can his movements be accounted for yesterday?" Calvin asked.

"His movements?" I echoed before laughing sarcastically. "Is he a suspect? Yes, my dad was with him yesterday at the Emporium."

Calvin paused for an extra beat before asking, "And Millett?"

My heart thumped hard once against my chest and then fell into my stomach. I looked up. "What about him?"

"These aren't from him? You said you've been fighting."

"Neil would never apologize with flowers."

In the silence that followed, I couldn't figure out why I just didn't tell him we had broken up. It felt important that Calvin know—that his assessment of me was correct and that I wasn't a man who screwed around behind his loved ones' backs. That I had had the courage to do the right thing. That I was *available*.

Except that being single again wasn't vital knowledge to share with Calvin, because he still hadn't indicated an interest in dating, and I'm really not the sort to just "have fun" together. Besides, how many times already had I told myself to commit to *me* for a change? Be happy with myself for a while, and don't jump immediately at a new boyfriend, especially another cop.

Another terrified-to-be-out cop.

Calvin was talking again, but I spoke over him and asked, "How deep in the closet are you?"

He blinked and raised an eyebrow. "Come again?"

"I mean, are you hanging out with the shoes, or are you so far in the back, you're with your tuxedo from junior prom and you stink of moth balls?"

"How very literal of you, Sebastian," he stated dryly.

"I'm being serious."

"It's none of your business."

"I think it's a little my business, considering the sex we had."

Ben started screeching again.

I could now see why Calvin was at wit's end. I glared at the bird myself before catching the word it kept repeating. "Book."

"What?"

I held my hand up and listened as Ben repeated the phrase before scrubbing in an agitated manner at its feathers. "Three words, I think. *Dun, dun*, book. Who's the—Where's the book?"

"How can you tell?" Calvin asked.

"You know, one sense is weak, so the others compensate," I replied. "I've got excellent hearing."

"You don't say?" he asked. "Then which book are we talking about?"

"I don't know."

"Exceptional detective work, Sherlock," Calvin concluded.

"Wow, you're such an asshole today."

"Someone has access to your shop's security code," Calvin said, ignoring the comment as he raised the bag up to stress his point. "You said only you had it."

"Okay, I lied."

"Who else knows it, Sebastian?"

"Neil and my dad. Oh, and the crazed Edgar Allan Poe killer, of course. Did I not mention that one?" I tapped my chin thoughtfully.

Calvin dumped the bag onto his desk, turning the note over carefully by the corner. He read the scrawled message in silence. "Threats and love notes."

"Sounds like my second boyfriend," I joked.

"You're a riot, Sebastian."

"Remember to tip your waitress."

Calvin crossed his arms and looked back at me. "What do you know about this note?"

I shrugged. "It's a line from Poe's poem 'Tamerlane.'" When Calvin failed to respond, I asked, "What?"

"Is 'Tamerlane' a book by him too?"

"No, it's just a poem," I said. "Well, if memory serves me correct, he released it and a few other poems on their own and it was called *Tamerlane*, so yeah, technically you're right."

Calvin moved around me, went to his filing cabinet, pulled out a large folder, and flipped through the hefty contents.

"What did I say?"

"Do you know a Gregory Thompson?"

"Should I?"

"He's a member of the antiquing community."

"Well, it's not like we all get together for drinks on Tuesday evenings," I replied. "He's in the city?"

"Marshall's Oddities," Calvin answered as he turned to stare at me, folder still in hand.

"Oddities. Yeah, I know that shop. I've met the guy once before, then."

"And?"

I raised my hands. "And what? If I recall, he was a bit of a jerk."

"Seems other antique shops have a problem with you."

"Oh no, Oddities just opened. He's new to the scene," I said. "He gave me grief because of some deal I offered a client for whatever silly trinket they were selling. I hardly remember the details. It was early this year."

"It seemed to me he deals in similar items as you."

"He does. Or tries, anyway."

"What does that mean?"

"It means, my clientele is growing every year, that's all. Take from that what you will. What does this have to do with anything?"

Calvin shut the folder and set it carefully on his desk. "Mr. Thompson claims to have received a disturbing phone call, demanding to hand over 'Tamerlane.'"

I considered this information carefully, knowing Calvin shouldn't have been sharing it, and I wanted to learn more. "When did he get the phone call?"

"Yesterday."

"And?"

Calvin looked at me. "And what?"

"You think something is off about it, don't you?"

"How did you guess?"

"I don't know. I never received any phone call. Mike neither, right?"

Calvin shook his head. "But you both received letters in the mail. I'm trying to get records of Mr. Thompson's phone."

"Do you think this psycho is escalating?"

"Maybe," Calvin admitted. "But it doesn't seem right. He's always kept himself hidden behind Poe's work. His threats—*love notes*—it's all to do with Poe. He's never admitted to being himself, never disengaged from the writing."

"Do you think Mr. Oddities is making it up?"

"I've considered it, but we've kept this pretty wrapped up. I don't know how he would have gotten these details."

"This guy seems to be striking at all of the antique shops in the city, then. Maybe—wait, did Gregory tell you exactly what the man said on the phone?"

Calvin stared at me for a moment before opening the folder again and flipping through several pages. "Where's the book," he read. "He said the voice was distorted and difficult to make out, sounded like there was some weeping, then it ended with the man screaming for 'Tamerlane' and hanging up."

And then it hit me like a bullet train going full speed.

"Jesus," I heard myself say. "That's why... that's why he went to Merriam."

Calvin narrowed his eyes. "What do you mean?"

"Merriam—I told you, she was the woman I worked with on the estate sale. Holy shit. Cal, the lot I won from the bid was for all of the antique books. He had to have known her connection with the sale and tried to pry from her who the store owners were that purchased all of the belongings.

"And the bird," I continued, pointing at Ben. "That—*where's the book? Tamerlane*. He's asking about *Tamerlane* the book. She must not have told him which antique shops bid on the books, so he's just been harassing all of us. And Beth's bookshop—she put in a bid and won all of the paperbacks."

I could see Calvin's mind running a mile a minute now. "Do you have this book in your possession?"

I shook my head. "No. Max has been cataloging the books in the shop. He hasn't come across anything by Poe."

"Then Beth got it."

"No, she got romance novels. *Gay* romance novels."

Calvin put a firm hand on my shoulder and pushed me to the door. "I need you to go."

"What? But—"

"Sebastian, I need to get on this right now."

"You wouldn't have put two and two together without me."

"I'm the cop. I appreciate your help, but let me do my job."

"What about the message from this morning?" I pointed at his desk.

"I'll deal with it."

"*Calvin.*"

"Baby, *leave.*"

To say I felt slighted was an understatement. I stormed out of the precinct while putting my sunglasses on. I shoved my hands into my pockets and walked toward the end of the block, away from the parked police cruisers and uniformed officers on break.

"Snow!"

I halted from crossing the street and turned around. Lancaster was leaning against the wall of a bakery, smoking a cigarillo away from where other officers would bother her. "Detective?"

"Where you off to in such a rush?"

I shrugged lamely.

She pushed away from the wall and walked toward me. "Mind walking around the block with me?" Lancaster didn't give me a real choice because she put a firm hand on my elbow and directed me away from the street. "I guess I should have warned you."

"About what, ma'am?"

She snorted and put the cigarillo to her lips briefly. "Calvin. He's in a mood today."

"I'll say," I muttered.

"He works hard," she said, and I could hear the defense in her tone. "Sometimes he forgets to sleep, gets cranky is all."

That wasn't all. I knew it was more, but it would be selfish to think it was about me. It was something just out of my reach of understanding.

"Sure."

Lancaster looked up and stopped walking. She puffed out smoke, and it smelled sort of like vanilla. "I know you're interested in him," she said, pointing at me with the cigarillo.

"Yes, apparently I keep a sign around my neck," I answered shortly.

Lancaster shook her head and let the attitude slide. "And I think he's got a hang-up about you too."

*Hang-up.*

Lancaster wasn't done, just sucking on the cigarillo again. "Seeing you in Mr. Rodriguez's shop, covered in blood, I was ready to read you your rights then and there, but Calvin said no. It's *not* you, and he *knows* it. He's the senior detective—he calls the shots."

"You think I killed Mike?" I asked quietly, sort of horrified.

She paused again, blew smoke, and shook her head. "Not anymore. I'm not sure. I can't figure you out, Snow."

"Sebastian."

"Quinn."

"Pleasure," I finished.

"Yeah, well," Quinn continued. "This case is ready to rip open at the seams, and we can't afford to have superiors or the media looking at the two of you."

I cleared my throat. "I'm a discreet person."

"Doesn't fucking matter," she replied, and I shut up.

I'll be honest, Quinn sort of scared me. But she had an authoritative air about her like she had to fight tooth and nail for respect—polar opposite of Calvin. And I'm sure she did. She was partnered with a real-life hero, and that might have made it easy for her at times, but I hadn't seen any other female detectives upstairs. Boys' club.

"Don't sniff around Calvin."

"Does... Calvin get this same speech?" I slowly asked.

"He already did."

I bit my tongue. She needed to give it to him again.

Quinn looked down at her cigarillo. "A police officer can't be seen fraternizing with a person of interest. Even someone like you."

"What does that mean? Although I'm honestly not sure I want to know."

"I've only been working with Calvin for a few months," Quinn said quietly. "And... if the situation had been different, I'd think you'd maybe be a good speed for him."

So did she know, or was she assuming about Calvin? "Look," I said. "I won't lie to you. I'm gay."

"I know."

"Swell."

"No straight guy stares at Calvin like you do," Quinn said.

"Okay, well, point to you, but—"

"Calvin doesn't have to say anything to me," she said, finishing my thought. "If he wants to be quiet about it—and he should be—it's for the best in our line of work. But I know."

As if there weren't enough red lights and sirens now telling me to back away from Calvin. The sex was fucking amazing and so was he, but it was clearly a bad idea.

I pushed my sunglasses up. "I understand."

# CHAPTER TEN

ELLA FITZGERALD and Louis Armstrong were singing to my soul as I entered Exotic Animal Haven on the Upper West Side after being shoved out of the police precinct by Calvin and cornered by his rightfully concerned partner.

I lingered in the doorway, letting Ella's beautiful voice soothe my nerves. I owned quite a bit of her work on 78 records, but hadn't been able to play them since my antique gramophone fell into disrepair. Neil had just told me to buy a replica turntable for two hundred bucks if I liked the aesthetic look so much, but that wasn't the point.

I didn't want a Bluetooth, USB-enabled gramophone. I wanted *mine*. The real McCoy that had the wear and tear from use and love. The one that needed to have needles constantly replaced to keep the records in mint condition.

Antiques speak to me. It's not just a job.

Every little item had a story, a past. The gramophone now in a closet had seen how many owners in the last century? How many different records had it spun? What was the music that moved that person? It was all just another aspect of my life that Neil hadn't understood.

Louis was still craving her kiss when a spunky girl walked out of a side door and waved at me. "Good morning!"

"Hi," I said, forcing a smile. "Is William Snow here?"

"Sure, but he's actually with two dogs right now, doing behavioral lessons. Can I help you instead?"

"I'm his son."

"Oh…. You're Sebastian!" She pointed at the stairs that led up to where Pop most likely was. "Your dad and Maggie are the best. We have a lot of volunteers, but everyone here loves William the most."

"I know it means a lot to him," I agreed.

"I'm Charlotte."

I shook her hand.

"Want to adopt a lizard?" she asked with a hopeful smile.

"Uh, not really in the market," I said. "Actually, you *do* deal with parrots, right?"

"Sure!" she said excitedly, and I felt bad because I think she thought I would take one home.

"Can I ask you a question about African greys?"

"Oh yeah. What do you want to know?"

"Why would one pull its feathers out?"

She frowned and tapped her chin. "Sounds like a behavioral problem. If they become agitated or are uncomfortable with their environment, they could harm themselves from the stress."

"What if one lost their owner very suddenly? Would that freak a bird out?"

"Sure. All animals have a bond with their owners. It isn't yours, is it?"

"Er… no, a friend of mine suddenly ended up with it when the owner… died."

"I'm sorry to hear that," Charlotte answered.

I glanced to the stairs when I heard dogs barking and someone laugh. "One last question? This grey can speak. Is that common?"

"Yeah, they all can learn. African greys are extremely intelligent."

"Could they learn a word after hearing it only once or twice, though?"

She shrugged, turning to watch the first dog on a leash coming down, tugging an employee along. "They could. If they like the sound or it's easy to mimic. We actually have a grey here, and after hearing a customer cough, it started to imitate it the next day."

*Huh.*

I thanked Charlotte just as a big pit bull hurried down the stairs. Maggie jumped on her hind legs, slobbering my face. "*Maggie!*"

"Down, girl! Oh, Sebastian!"

I pushed Maggie down and took off my sunglasses. "Hey, Pop."
I kept my eyes closed while wiping the lenses on my shirt under my
jacket, then put them back on.

My dad reached out and gave me a quick hug. "How're you?"

"Okay."

"Yeah?" The question held significant weight.

"I'm okay," I said again with a nod. "Hey, Pop, can I ask you a
question if you have a minute?"

"Sure." He turned to Charlotte and said, "Those pups are going out
on their walk now."

"I saw Teddy come down with one already," Charlotte answered.
She perked up when a customer walked into the shop and excused herself
to hurry over.

Pop turned back to me. "You could have just called, kiddo."

I shrugged, moved toward a side counter, and flipped through
a binder of adoptable animals. "Dad, do you know a lot about Poe's
'Tamerlane'?"

"Yeah, what did you want to know?"

"He released that and some other poems in a book and called it
*Tamerlane*, didn't he?" I asked.

"It was Poe's first publication."

"That's right," I agreed, the old information slowly coming back
to memory.

"It wasn't credited to him, though. Only, *a Bostonian.*"

I had been considering my next question on the subway ride over.
Maybe we—that being, the police and myself—didn't know *who* would
kill and assault several people on behalf of *Tamerlane*, so perhaps we
should focus on *why* and follow those clues.

I knew this case was becoming high profile within the NYPD,
and everything Calvin did was scrutinized. And he was overworked and
stressed. Quinn had said so herself. So it wouldn't hurt for me to look
into what I felt wasn't being given ample consideration, right? Fuck it. I
was helping.

Why would someone kill for this book?

Value.

Literary and historical value—sure, it had that—but I've read about
people who have killed for twenty bucks. It's always about money.

"Pop, do you know if the book is worth a lot?"

He smiled and patted Maggie's head. "You're the antique dealer, Sebastian."

"And you know more about Poe," I answered while shutting the adoption folder.

"It's worth a lot," he agreed, nodding. "There are only twelve copies known to exist. It's one of the rarest first editions to be had when it comes to American literature."

"How much is it worth?"

"I don't know, but a lot I bet."

"Where are the twelve copies these days?"

Pop looked thoughtful for a moment. "I know some are privately owned. Oh, the New York Public Library has one in their rare books vault."

"What, really? Can the public view it?" I asked quickly.

My dad cocked his head to the side. "What's with the twenty questions, Sebastian?"

"It's—"

"*Nothing*?" he finished for me. He shook his head and checked his watch. "Want to get some brunch?"


WE LEFT Maggie at the shelter and hopped over to a little restaurant across the street. He sipped at a glass of orange juice, and I ordered an Irish coffee.

"Whiskey before eleven?" my dad asked curiously.

"It's the least I can do for myself." I took a drink of the whipped cream and spiked coffee.

"Drinking isn't going to make this better."

"I'm not drinking because of Neil," I insisted, though without knowledge of the case Calvin was working, I could understand why my dad thought it was only about Neil.

Pop didn't speak much more until our meals arrived. I was poking at my eggs when he asked, "Why are you not at the Emporium?"

"I had some chores to do."

"Sebastian."

I glanced up. My dad was staring sternly at me, and I felt like I should ask for a second drink, hold the coffee. I knew he was worried. I had been attacked by an unknown assailant and then broke up with my long-term boyfriend the next day. I guess if I were a father, I'd be worried too, but I couldn't explain to him that I thought the man who attacked me had killed two people and would undoubtedly strike again if he didn't get what he wanted soon.

So I lied. Sort of.

"I'm just a little preoccupied."

"Keep going."

"I went to the precinct today that Calvin works at."

"Why?"

I shrugged. "Not sure," I said, failing to mention the roses and note. "He wasn't happy to see me."

"He was probably busy," my dad supplied.

"He's closeted," I blurted out. "I don't know why I assumed he wasn't."

"What exactly do you feel for him, kiddo? You're sending conflicting reports."

I laughed out loud. "I'll say. So does he. I don't know, Dad. When it's just the two of us, he's so different. Calvin is quiet and charming and sweet. I've never been treated like that by a guy—like I'm a prince."

"Does he treat you like Neil did in public?" he asked, that sharp tone in his voice again.

"No. I mean, not really. I don't know. It's usually been a professional setting when I see him in public. He's stern."

Pop set his fork down and leaned back in his seat. "Are you fishing for an opinion?"

"Am I getting a bite?"

"He's a nice boy."

"He's forty-two, Dad."

"A nice man," he corrected. "But I don't think it's wise of you to get involved with someone right now. Neil hasn't even moved out yet."

"I know. I *know* you're right," I insisted. "And I don't think he's interested in a relationship anyway. At least, he's made no indication that it was more than sex."

Dad held his hand up. "Seb, you slept with him?"

"Uh. Did I say that?"

*Motherfucker.*

My dad sighed. "Were you safe?"

"Of course, Dad. Come on. I'm not a teenager." I finished the last of my drink. "I just wish I didn't have such shitty luck. I meet a guy I really click with and it's another closeted cop."

"Don't push him. If it's meant to be...."

I felt I had been quite calm and down-to-earth about all of the events the past week. Two dead bodies—one that I found, no less—the break-in, getting knocked out, losing Neil, the harassing notes—I'd taken it all in stride. I'd been able to deal with a murder investigation pretty damn well. God, I was even sleuthing around despite the threats of being in hot water with a certain redheaded cop.

But it was that same cop that made me feel like my heart was breaking.

It's a bizarre sensation, the feeling that you've met your other half, but that's really what Calvin made me feel. Like I've been wandering through life with a half a circle on my chest and everyone I've been with had a square on theirs. Except that when I finally found the guy that completes my circle, it turns out he can't stay mine.

For whatever reason it was. Married to the job, not a relationship sort of guy, too closeted—maybe he was even the self-loathing gay man who marries a woman to try to be "normal." Thinking of Calvin asleep in that chair at the hospital when he was unwilling to leave my side, coming back to drive me home, cuddling after sex—it had all meant so much to me.

"Sebastian?"

I picked up my napkin and reached under my sunglasses to wipe my eyes. "Yeah?"

"Kiddo, I'm sorry. I didn't... I don't want you crying," my dad said quietly as he reached out to pat my hand.

"I'm okay," I heard myself insist, my voice sounding very unlike my own. "It's not your fault."

"Did Calvin say something to you this morning?" Pop asked, on the defense again, seeing his adult son was actually a pathetic baby crying in public.

"No. Dad, don't worry." I finished drying my eyes.

"It's hard not to when you're this upset."

I steered the topic away from myself after that. We finished brunch with an uncomfortable weight over us, me avoiding discussion of Calvin and my dad trying not to press his concern onto me.

Maybe some people just weren't meant to have a partner in life. I suppose I could deal with that reality.

It was just lonely.

MAX CALLED when I was walking back to the subway. "Seb?" He sounded concerned.

"What's wrong?" I immediately asked. "I'm on my way back now."

"Okay. Cool."

"Max?"

"I was just finishing with all those boxes of books.... Sebastian, I think someone went through them. Nothing is missing! But my organization is all messed up, and I swear when your dad and I were here yesterday, it was perfect."

I stopped walking and moved to the edge of the sidewalk, out of the way. "Are you sure no one this morning—?"

"No. Only two customers have come in so far, and I had eyes on them the entire time," Max insisted. "Can you please come back soon? This place is starting to freak me out a little."

"Is Beth open?"

"I assume so," he answered.

I took a breath. "If you're nervous to be there alone, Max, lock up and go next door."

"Really?"

"Yes, really. Something weird is—" My breath caught.

Holy shit. *Holy shit.*

I'd completely forgot. I fucking *forgot*!

Holy—

"Seb? Hello?"

"I'll be there soon, okay? Go next door." I hung up and flagged a taxi.

I went back to my apartment instead of the Emporium. Sidetracked by my argument with Calvin and the brief period of self-loathing that followed, I'd overlooked the fact that the books from the estate sale in my shop were not the complete inventory.

I still had several boxes sitting in my living room that I hadn't even gone through.

If our mysterious, Poe-obsessed killer was anything to go by, there was a thirteenth copy of *Tamerlane* in existence that they were hell-bent on finding, and the way it played out to me was that it was part of my estate winnings. But the joke was on them, because it was starting to look like I did have it.

A book thought not to exist—just sitting in my apartment.

I raced up the stairs, my stomach making nervous flips. I was excited, like I were opening an ancient tomb only to find that grave robbers had never looted it and all of the mysterious and rich artifacts were still intact.

What sort of condition would the book be in? Poor? Fine? *Very fine*?

My fingers shook as I tried to unlock my door.

That book would have been around when Edgar Allan Poe was alive. For all I knew, he could have touched it—held it.

God, that rush of excitement I got from treasure hunting was back.

I shoved open my door and stopped dead.

My apartment was a mess.

The boxes were all open and tipped over, books strewn across the floor without worry or care to their condition. My personal books had been pulled from the bookcase against the wall, mystery novels tiling the wooden floor.

Someone broke into my home.

As if it was hard to guess who.

I looked down at the doorknob before crouching to examine the lock. The door had been securely fastened—how had they gotten inside? Pick the lock? How were they managing to get in and out of both my shop and apartment without breaking locks or tripping alarms?

They couldn't have had a key. The only people who had a key to both were Neil and me.

I cursed loudly and walked inside. I started scanning the covers and spines of the books thrown around, hunting for *Tamerlane*, but I didn't find it. I didn't find any Poe. I checked under the couch, the coffee table, everywhere in the house to make sure I didn't miss something amongst the disarray. If I had had it in a box without knowing it, I sure as fuck didn't have it now.

But if the creep found it and had it, in theory, people were safe now.

"No," I said out loud. He couldn't get away with this. He couldn't get away with robbery, assault, *murder*.

I sat on the couch and pulled out my phone. I had intended on calling Calvin, but paused. I couldn't keep defaulting to him. It was sort of pathetic. Of course, he was the detective leading this case, but fuck it. I could handle this without having to call the cops and get tied up in bullshit for the rest of the day.

I opened the Internet browser on my phone and pulled up the New York Public Library. After a short read about the rare books collection, I filled out the online form to get permission to see their copy of Poe's *Tamerlane* for myself. I had to choose a time for the next morning, due to them being closed on Sunday. I submitted the form, and tomorrow would just need to flash my ID and library card and I'd be able to get a glimpse of this rare book for myself. I hoped to discuss the value and history of the book with the curator while I was there.

I left the mess as it was and ran out the door to get back to the Emporium.

# CHAPTER ELEVEN

"SEBASTIAN!" BETH said as I walked into Good Books. She was standing near a table display in the middle of the shop, talking with Max and a very tall stranger, who had dark, long hair for a man.

"I came to fetch my wayward assistant," I stated.

Beth hurried over instead, wearing her usual bedazzled spectacles and yet another cat skirt I hadn't seen before. She threw her arms around me, nearly knocking the air from my lungs. "You brave, stupid man!"

"Beth, you're sweet, but I definitely prefer men," I managed to wheeze out.

She pulled back with a scoff and hit my chest. "Don't joke. I'm being serious."

I rubbed the spot, making a face. "Sorry?"

"You and your hard head scared that son of a bitch off before he had a chance to do serious damage to my business."

"Hearing Beth swear is like my grandma swearing," Max piped up.

Beth turned and pointed a finger at him. "Watch it, young man."

"Sorry, grandma."

"You shouldn't be open today," she chastised while turning back to me. "Health comes first. You need to be resting."

"I've rested plenty," I insisted politely. "I'm fine, really."

Beth pursed her lips and put her hands on her hips. "Things sure are getting strange around here. These break-ins, and what's all this with Edgar Allan Poe?"

"That's a long story," I said, glancing at Max, who had to have told Beth everything.

Max motioned at himself and shook his head before pointing at the tall stranger.

Beth noticed and waved at the dark-haired man. "Greg here was telling us about his run-in."

"Greg?" I echoed.

The tall man approached us while saying, "Greg Thompson. We met earlier this year. Maybe you don't remember me."

Oh. Mr. Oddities. "No, I remember you," I replied with a polite smile while shaking his hand. *That you were a dick*, I added thoughtfully to myself.

"Word has gotten out that you've also got a guy knocking at your door about Poe," Greg said to me.

"Whose word is that?" I asked cautiously.

"Cops and newspapers," Greg replied, as if he couldn't believe I didn't know that already.

"Newspaper?"

Max wandered over to the three of us, holding up a folded paper. "Look, it made the news, Seb. They didn't know it was you that got attacked, but they mention Beth's shop and your old boss! He was *killed*!"

"That sexy detective from the newspaper interview even came over," Beth added.

I had taken the newspaper from Max and paused to ask, "Sexy detective?"

Max smirked but didn't say anything.

Beth nodded. "Tall guy, built out of rock."

"Detective Winter," Greg added helpfully.

"I'd do him in a heartbeat," Beth stated.

Max started laughing.

I cleared my throat and hid my face behind the newspaper. It was hard to read without a magnifying glass, but I got the gist of it, recapping the murder of both Merriam and Mike, as well as mentioning my shop and the break-in at Beth's. The reporter was doing his best to link all of the stories, despite the interview with Calvin, where he was quoted as refusing to give up the names of certain individuals, for the sake of their safety.

Great. Either Calvin didn't want reporters harassing me, or he suspected what I did—this wasn't over and I was still a target.

"Maybe it's my eyes," I said, looking up at Greg, "but I don't see you mentioned in this article."

"A harassing phone call is hardly as interesting as a pig's heart or dead cat," he stated.

Something about Greg's story wasn't right. I know I don't have any real detective training to back up my statement, just an apparent hard-on for cops and a joy of reading silly mysteries in my free time, but even Calvin had admitted to it being strange. Why would the killer suddenly speak to a potential victim? Why would he put himself out there—make himself vulnerable to being caught? Police can trace phones, zero in on where the call was made, stake out the area, all of that.

But would Greg Thompson make up the harassment? Why? For the attention?

Calvin had said that to me. People do a lot of crazy things for attention.

It wasn't so ridiculous to rule out.

"But I think you must know more about what's going on than the papers say," Greg said with a grin.

I was taken aback by the comment. "Why do you think that?"

"Detective Winter came to speak to you, but your helper here closed up shop," Greg explained while jutting a thumb over at Max. "He was also the one to arrive when you were attacked the other day."

Whoa.

Hold up.

Danger, danger.

"Who told you that?" I slowly asked. How would he have known? Both shops were closed, there was no one around to see, and I highly doubted Calvin was offering that information willingly.

"Sebastian?" a new voice chimed in.

We all turned toward the door, and I was surprised to see Duncan, the young guy I sold a Dickinson book to. He smiled brightly at me, pulling off his beanie and waving.

"Oh, Duncan, hi," I said, taking the opportunity to inch away from Greg.

"I came to see you, but your shop is closed."

"Yeah, sorry about that."

"Are you okay?" he asked worriedly.

"Sure. You know, I should get back, so if you want to come along...."
I turned around, feeling the need to make up an excuse for Beth to join
me, to get her away from Greg because I was very quickly drawing some
uncomfortable conclusions about him, but Greg was shrugging his coat
on with the clear intention of leaving as well.

"Let me know if you need anything today," Beth said.

"Thanks, Beth."

Max grabbed his coat and joined Duncan and me. As we were
walking to the door, I hung back to make sure Greg followed us out.

"Be careful, Sebastian," he said as we stepped into the freezing cold.

I glanced up at Greg. "Of? Stepping on cracks, lest I break my
mother's back?"

Greg laughed. "You're a bit of an asshole."

"Ah, well, much obliged."

"Keep me apprised on what's happening, will you? You've
obviously got an in with the cops."

"Not as much as you'd think." I had a cop in me the other day,
though. Did that count?

Greg said his good-byes, and I was left to reopen the Emporium.
"You put up your decorations," Duncan said with a smile as he looked
around at the lights and garland.

"Oh, well, Max and my dad did most of the work. I was in the
hospital briefly."

"But you're okay, right?" Duncan asked, his eyes growing big.

I waved a hand dismissively. "Very okay," I insisted. I was
trying to be nice, but so many people wishing me well was sort of
exhausting.

The speakers started playing Christmas tunes as Max hurriedly
made the shop customer-friendly again.

Duncan tugged at his scarf absently, looking around a moment. "I
wanted to take you out to lunch."

"Really?"

He nodded.

That was unexpectedly sweet. I remembered him saying he'd come
back, but had I really thought he would?

"Do you still have a boyfriend?" he asked next. "Last time you said
you weren't sure."

Duncan's question was innocent, but it hit me like a punch to the gut. No, I didn't have a boyfriend, but in true human fashion, the only thing I wanted was what I couldn't have. I stared at him again—Duncan was younger than me, which I was a little iffy about, but still, he was cute and persistent and was asking me out like it was normal. Like it was no big deal.

"I... don't," I slowly answered.

Duncan immediately looked up with a big smile. "Lunch, then?"

"What about Calvin?" Max spoke up from behind me.

I turned and waved a hand at him. "I don't need your help," I said through gritted teeth.

"Calvin?" Duncan echoed, his tone dropping.

I looked back at him. "It's... nothing like that, don't worry. Duncan, I'm not sure I can swing lunch today—I've been out all morning as it is and the shop has been closed." I felt like a shithead. "But what about tomorrow? Maybe we can get brunch together."

"Yeah! Please!" Duncan was grinning again. "Can I call you tomorrow?"

"Sure." I reached into my pockets and felt around. "Let me find something to write my number on."

But Duncan already had his cell out. "Just tell me and I'll put it in."

I recited the number to him.

Duncan programmed it into his phone before slowly saying, "Sebastian Snow," as he spelled my name. He looked up with a smile while tucking his phone into his pocket. "I added a heart next to your name."

"Oh." *Did people do that? Was that a good thing?*

"So, then, I'll call you in the morning," Duncan said.

"Sounds good."

"Is there anything I can do before I go?"

"Do? Oh, no, really. Thank you."

Duncan moved close and pecked me on the lips, giving me a little kiss before I realized what he was doing. "Good-bye, Sebastian." He smiled and tugged his scarf up close before leaving the shop.

Max was clucking his tongue behind me from the counter. "Hussy."

I snorted while turning. "That coming from you."

"You're the one with the spicy ginger, though."

"It's not like that."

Max laughed.

"What?" I asked, confused. "Why the hell are you laughing?"

"Nothing, Seb. You're just hilariously blind in every sense of the term."

"I don't follow."

Max leaned over the counter, resting a hand under his chin and grinning. "I saw Detective Winter's face when he came in the other morning. He's so hot and bothered for you."

"That doesn't mean anything."

"Means something to him."

"How do you know? Are you a traveling fortune teller by night?"

"No, but I can see his subtle changes around you better than you ever will." Max waved his hand at me. "I'm an objective witness."

I slowly walked across the shop to the counter. "He hasn't said anything of the sort," I admitted quietly.

"Maybe he's shy."

I was about to deny that, but the other day, when it was just the two of us, his demeanor was so different. It was calm and quiet and sweet and—maybe he was a little shy? "He's closeted, that's all," I said, hearing the defensiveness in my tone.

Max shrugged. "Whatever. All I'm saying is, I can see the little hearts in his eyes."

BETWEEN MY morning attempts at crime-solving and working a busy day at the Emporium while still recovering from a concussion, I was exhausted. All I wanted to do was drop my bag, get undressed, and crawl into bed to sleep for about a week. I was fantasizing about just how nice that sleep sounded, how great my pillow was going to feel with my face buried into it, when I stopped climbing the stairs to my apartment.

Sitting on the landing of the third floor was Calvin. His arms were crossed over his chest, and his head was leaning against the banister of the staircase. He was sleeping.

"Cal?" I asked quietly, not wanting to startle him like I had done before at the hospital.

Luckily he didn't snap to attention, because it sort of freaked me out the way he did that. Instead, Calvin looked groggy as he opened his eyes and raised his head. "Seb?"

"What're you doing here?" I asked, looking up the stairs at him.

Calvin rubbed his neck as he straightened his posture. "I was waiting for you."

"I see that."

He climbed to his feet. "Can we talk inside?"

Of course, I wasn't going to turn him away. I hiked up the last steps and went to my door to unlock it. "Come in," I said after shoving the door open with my shoulder.

"What the hell happened here?" Calvin asked as he stepped inside, looking around at the mess I had left.

"Oh God, I forgot about this," I groaned.

"Did you do this?"

I shook my head. "No. Someone broke in. Well, I say someone, but you know who."

"Wait, what?" Calvin suddenly sounded pissed, or defensive, or something close to it. "Why didn't you call me?"

"I don't have to run to you like a damsel in distress," I retorted. "There was no threat to me. I was fine."

"No threat—!" Calvin reached up and pinched the bridge of his nose. "You come to me," he said sternly. "For *anything* regarding this case. Do I make myself clear?"

"I tried to do that this morning, and you nearly bit my head off. You can't do this. You can't order me to do something, but only where no one may see us together. I've done that, I did it for four years, and I'm not fucking doing it again!" I shouted. Everything about Neil that enraged me was suddenly channeled right at Calvin, and I couldn't stop myself.

Calvin grew quiet. In fact, he didn't say anything for an extremely long time and it got awkward. Eventually he walked away, first going into the kitchen, then my bedroom. He looked into the bathroom last before returning to me.

"Where'd Millett go?"

Ah, was it the one toothbrush that gave it away?

"He's at his brother's."

"*Why?*" Calvin pressed.

I turned away to push aside some of the books that were strewn across the couch before sitting. "Because we broke up," I said quietly. "Last night. I wasn't happy anymore." I glanced up, watching Calvin push his coat back to rest his hands on his hips. *God, he's so sexy when he does that.*

"Does he still have his keys?"

"Huh? Yeah. He hasn't finished moving out yet. I told him to take his time."

"And the Emporium?"

"I haven't gotten back either key. Why are you asking?" Almost the same time I spoke, it dawned on me where Calvin was going, and it pissed me off. "You think Neil did this?" I stood back up.

"I didn't say that."

"No, but you think it."

Calvin looked at me, his expression as hard as stone. "I'm thinking a lot of things right now."

I didn't speak. Neither did he. The building was quiet, only the distant sound of the pipes knocking as the heat turned on, breaking the stillness. The energy between us crackled. Any minute we were either going to fistfight or fuck.

Calvin moved forward, dropping his hands from his hips and reaching out to cup my face.

I wrapped my hands around his wrists. "You can't do this to me. You can't be sweet and caring in private and then treat me like a disease in public."

Being so close, I could see the painful way Calvin swallowed, the way his Adam's apple jumped. I could see how his gray eyes looked like a storm was raging behind them. His mouth was tight and drawn.

"I'm in the back with the prom tux," he whispered.

"What?"

"In your stupid closet," Calvin said. "I'm… so far lost in the back I can't… find the door." He leaned forward to press his forehead against mine. "I'm sorry, baby."

"Calvin…."

"I've never felt like this for a guy. Goddamn it, Sebastian," he said without any malice.

"I just got out of a relationship with someone who hid me from the world," I said.

"I know. I'm not asking you to go through that again."

"I ran into Quinn when I left this morning."

Calvin was quiet for a minute. "I know what she said."

"You'll get in trouble if someone finds out."

"This is an active case," he agreed automatically, but it didn't seem to faze him. That wasn't his concern. The fucking closet was.

"Why do you have to be so nice?" I groaned. "It makes it even harder."

He smiled but looked sad. "I can't change who I am, just like you can't."

"Change being nice or change being closeted?"

He paused for a beat. "Both."

"Not true."

"Baby…."

"Cal," I whispered. "You're forty-two."

"I was in the military for twelve years," Calvin answered. "When being caught with a guy meant a dishonorable discharge."

"It doesn't mean that anymore," I insisted. "And you're retired from the military."

"I'm a cop."

"Boy, have I heard that excuse before."

Calvin's hands tightened instinctively on my face before loosening immediately. "I'm not asking anything of you."

"I want you to, though," I managed to say as my throat tightened. "I want you to want me like I do you."

"I can't date you. I'm not going to ask you to deny who you are for my sake," Calvin replied.

"That's sweet. But don't you think you shouldn't deny yourself either? Times are changing, you know."

"Not quickly enough."

"What?"

"My first case when I was promoted to homicide was a gay man who had been stomped to death by a group of men. Literally *stomped to death*, Sebastian."

"If you stay afraid, they win and nothing gets better," I whispered.

"I don't want that to happen to someone—" He didn't finish. He leaned close again and kissed me gently. It was so soft and simple and so fucking sweet, it turned my heart over.

I hated him for doing this to me.

"I need to ask you to do something for me," he said, dropping his hands.

"I thought you just said…?"

He raised a hand to stop me from finishing. "I don't want you staying here tonight."

"What?"

"It's not safe."

"Calvin, you're overreacting."

"I'm not," he said sternly.

I sighed and looked around at the books thrown everywhere. Honestly, now that I was standing among the mess again, sleeping here alone, knowing someone easily got in and out, made me a little nervous.

"I guess I can stay with my dad. I really don't want him to be freaking out about this case, but if it can't be avoided…."

"Stay with me."

I snorted. "I don't think that's a good idea."

"I'm not asking you to come over so we can screw," Calvin said quietly. "I want you somewhere safe." He added as an afterthought, "I need to run something by you, about this case."

That piqued my interest. Plus, I could tell Calvin what I'd learned from my morning excursions. "All right," I agreed after another moment of thought. "Let me pack a few things."

I went and gathered a change of clothes and a few items from the bathroom. It definitely wasn't a sleepover for sex if I was bringing my lens solution and toothbrush, right? I couldn't sleep with Calvin again. I couldn't. I wanted to be with him so badly that if I teased myself again, knowing now that he would simply never ask me to date him—no. It hurt too much. No sex with Calvin. I'd sleep on his couch, he'd be satisfied I was safe, and my heart would beat on for another day.

I came back into the front room. "Reporting for duty, Captain."

Calvin offered a lopsided smile. "Major," he corrected.

"My apologies, sir," I said with a grin.

"Dork. Come on." Calvin opened the door and held his hand out.

Was I supposed to take it?

At my hesitation Calvin made the decision for me. He took my hand into his and led me out. He kept holding it as I locked the door, his fingers woven into my own. This man would be the death of me.

*I can't date you.*

*I'm not asking you to go through that again.*

He basically told me he wasn't worth the inevitable heartache.

And yet Calvin acted against his own words, as if he couldn't bear to face his self-imposed loneliness yet. In the stairwell he held my hand with such obvious affection that it tore me apart, knowing once we stepped into the world outside, Snow and Winter would never be. And sure enough, too soon, the cold night greeted us and his hand slid free from mine.

CALVIN'S APARTMENT was nice.

In that *never been lived in* sort of way.

So really, it felt quite lonely.

It was very clean and very minimal, a stark contrast to my little abode crammed full with books, too much furniture for its size, and antique odds and ends I couldn't get myself to sell at the Emporium. It was actually smaller than mine, a true New York studio the size of a large closet. There was a decent-sized bed near the windows toward the back, pushed up against a bare brick wall. A string of lights had been nailed into the bricks, their subdued, warm glow just what my tired eyes needed.

I took off my sunglasses as Calvin shut the door behind us, putting my regular glasses on. There was a television across from the bed with a PlayStation hooked up, which made me realize how much more I had to learn about Calvin, as I hadn't thought him to be the video game sort. There was a small nightstand by the bed with a lamp, and then an open space before the kitchen started across from the door. It was smaller than my own, with a tiny vintage fridge and a stovetop with only two burners and no oven. There were two cupboards overhead and a standing shelf off to the side that had dried goods neatly organized on it.

Other than that, it was a bachelor pad to the extreme. There were no photos or pieces of art hanging, no knickknacks around that might have spoken as to the personality of the owner. I also noted he didn't have a couch I could crash on.

Calvin took off his coat and hung it on the back of the door before motioning for my own.

I handed it over. "Nice place," I said quietly.

He shrugged. "Bathroom is right there if you need it," he said, pointing to the closed door just past the kitchen.

I couldn't imagine how tiny that must have been.

"Hungry?" Calvin asked.

"Actually, yeah," I said in mild surprise. "I haven't eaten since I saw my dad late this morning."

Calvin raised an eyebrow as he pulled his cell from his pocket. "After you went to the precinct?"

I nodded.

He looked back down at his phone, swiping sideways a few times before opening an app. After a moment of scrolling, he asked, "Pizza?"

"Good pizza?"

"The best," he agreed. "What do you like?"

"Just cheese."

Calvin smiled as he picked from the menu and placed the order. "What?"

"Nothing. We just like the same pizza."

"Want to get married?"

"Shithead," he murmured.

I laughed, moved farther into the room, and set my bag down near the bed.

"Want a beer?" Calvin asked, opening the fridge.

"Sure. Thanks."

He pulled out two bottles and popped off the tops. He walked over and handed me one before dragging a stool from beside the dry-foods shelf. "Here, sit down." Calvin pulled up a matching stool from a tiny door near the bed that I figured was probably a closet, sitting down near me.

"What did you want to discuss with me, about the case?" I asked.

He took a drink, paused, then took another. "You won't like it."

"Oh great."

Calvin sighed, rubbing his hand absently on his thigh, and I noted with interest it was the same one he'd been shot in. I wondered if it hurt him still. Like when it rained.... "The evidence is beginning to stack up."

"Against me? Jesus—"

"No, not you."

Well, I was surprised. "Who, then?"

"Neil."

I almost dropped my beer. "W-Wait. You mean—holy hell, you weren't kidding, were you?"

Calvin shook his head.

"Why? How can he even be a suspect? *I* make a better suspect!"

"Because we've ruled you out based on your alibis. And you sure as hell didn't give yourself a concussion. Look. Neil has keys to the Emporium and knows the security access code, doesn't he?"

"Y-Yes," I stammered, trying to get in a word, but Calvin continued.

"And he has keys to your apartment. Still. And your place was broken into the day after you apparently broke up? How did he take it?" Calvin was all cop now, his tone different. Sterner. A bit harsh. He must have played the bad cop more often than not.

"Well, of course he wasn't thrilled about it," I protested. "I admitted to sleeping with you and then told him I wanted to end a four-year relationship."

"And the next morning you received flowers, which were left in the shop prior to your arrival," Calvin continued.

"Yeah, but—"

"You'd already been having difficulties in your relationship when this all began," Calvin said. "And these events are now fixating on you, more than any other victim."

My throat was so dry, I needed another drink of beer just to swallow. "Neil isn't—God no. He's not a killer! He's a cop."

"That doesn't always mean they're a good person," Calvin said quietly.

"You realize that you're suggesting I've been dating and sleeping with a deranged killer, don't you? Fuck me! I know my choice in guys isn't always stellar, but I'm not *that* bad!"

"I'm only presenting the facts the way I see them," Calvin said, a bit more gentle now.

My mind was racing.

This wasn't possible. Not even close.

Pop had said *Tamerlane* would be worth a pretty penny. Neil was dating an antique dealer. It would have been possible for him to realize that. He knew all about the estate sale and the banker, Merriam Byers. He had been disinterested in the pig-heart fiasco and insistent to not go to Mike's shop the day I found him dead. What if his anger toward me when I told Calvin he was gay wasn't because of his sexuality, but because I unknowingly had the cops shine their flashlights on him? And the threats? As easy as dropping it into a mailbox. Neil was a forensic cop—he knew how to cover tracks, what would be looked for.

I swear to God my heart stopped beating for a minute.

I must have gone white, because Calvin was on his feet and offering me a glass of water, his warm, heavy hand on my shoulder like an anchor.

"Drink," he insisted, exchanging the glass for my beer.

I drank the entire cup. "Evidence can be twisted to look like a lot of things," I said after a moment.

Calvin's hand moved down my back, rubbing gentle circles. He had to have thought of everything I did, otherwise he wouldn't logically suspect my ex-boyfriend of homicide. "Has Neil ever been violent toward you?"

"No!" I winced when I remembered being shoved into the doorframe during our fight.

"Strange behavior?"

I gripped the glass so hard in my hands, I was afraid it'd shatter. "No. I mean, his hours are weird sometimes, but you know what that's like. You're both cops. Cal, please, he didn't fucking do this."

"I'm sorry, baby."

I stood, looking up at Calvin. "It's my turn to tell you what I think."

He looked surprised and was about to speak when his cell rang. Calvin answered it, saying, "Be right down," before hanging up. "Pizza guy. I'll be right back." His hand lingered a fraction too long before he was out the door.

I immediately walked into the bathroom and shut the door behind me. I felt lightheaded and a little sick. I sat on the lid of the toilet, holding my head and taking long, deep breaths. I could see why Calvin was humoring me as to where the evidence was leading him—after all, it was his job to collect it and arrest the person most suspected. It wasn't up to him whether they were guilty or innocent; that was for lawyers and courts.

Regardless, that did not make me feel better. Despite telling myself, *knowing* Neil was incapable of such gruesome acts, I could not explain how the person got into my shop and my home.

"Sebastian?" Calvin called as he stepped back into the apartment.

I stood and exited the bathroom.

He set the box on the counter and walked close. He had a worried expression on his face. "Are you okay?"

"Yeah," I said, offering a smile that I'm sure was hardly convincing.

Calvin put a hand around my neck, squeezed the back lightly, and massaged the muscles. "Do you still want to eat?"

"Murder can't keep me from pizza."

Calvin didn't smile. He gently pushed me back to the stool before grabbing plates from a cupboard and putting a huge New York slice on each. "So what is it that you think?" he asked, and I could hear reluctance in his tone. He gave me a plate, sat, and devoured his slice in I swear less than three bites.

"Still waiting," he said, standing to fetch another slice.

"Greg Thompson," I finally spoke up before taking a bite of pizza.

Calvin turned around, already working on his second piece as he sat. Had he not eaten all day? "What about him?" he asked with a full mouth.

Manners. Good grief.

"He's shady," I answered. "He makes me uncomfortable."

"I thought you hadn't seen him since the beginning of the year."

"He was around this afternoon, when I returned to the Emporium." I explained that Max had closed up and been hiding out with Beth once his nerves got the best of him. I told Calvin how Greg, surprisingly, was also at Good Books when I stopped by.

Calvin didn't speak, just silently ate his second and third slice of pizza.

"He mentioned that he knew you'd been the first to arrive when I got knocked out."

That made Calvin's eyebrows rise. "How'd he know that?"

I shrugged. "He didn't say. Greg gives me bad vibes, Cal."

"I can't arrest someone because they're a dickhead."

"You sure?" I tried, offering a smile.

Calvin smiled back. "I'm sure."

"Oh well. Anyway, he wasn't a dickhead. Well, sort of, but mostly he made me nervous. When we left Good Books, he told me to be careful. The way he said it wasn't—" I failed to find the word I wanted and waved a hand idly.

"With sincerity?" Calvin offered.

"Right. He seemed to be hinting that I knew more than I was letting on or that I knew more because of you."

That made Calvin frown, and I knew he was suspecting someone thought there was a relationship between us. "I see," he muttered.

"Look, I'm not saying that Greg is the guy, but something isn't right."

Calvin nodded and stood, bringing his plate to the sink to wash.

"Want to hear something else?"

"I'm not so sure."

I brought my plate over, standing beside him. "African greys can learn to mimic words or sounds within a day if it's easy or something they like. That lady's bird, he can very well be repeating some of the last words heard in her apartment."

"This guy screaming for the book."

"*Tamerlane.*"

"Right," Calvin said, putting the plates away. "But if Greg was the guy, why would he show his hand and mention *Tamerlane* to me?"

I wasn't sure. "Desperation?"

Calvin shook his head. "I agree that something is off about his story—"

"Whoever came into my apartment this morning came for my books," I interrupted. "If you noticed."

Calvin turned back to me, crossing his arms. "I did. Are you certain it wasn't in your possession?"

"No. But now how am I supposed to know? If it was, it's not there now. I checked. Someone thought I did have it, though."

"Look, baby, I hate to bring it up again, but of all people, Neil knew you had some of the estate sale at your home. And he had a key."

"But the things Greg said…. I don't think this is over. Call it gut instinct, but I'm pretty convinced the book wasn't in my possession. This guy is still looking for it."

"Does Greg know where you live?"

I made a face. "You know as well as I do that information like that is hardly a secret these days."

Calvin nodded and left the counter, tugging his tie loose and tossing it into a small hamper near the television. He started to unbutton the cuffs of his shirt next.

"What about the phone call that Greg claims he got?" I asked.

"I'm still working on it. These things don't move as fast as—"

"On television," I finished. "I know."

Calvin turned around as he pulled his shirt off, his pale and freckled chest there for me to see but not touch. He tossed it into the hamper. "You don't mind if we go to bed, do you? I'm… kind of tired."

I remembered finding him asleep on the stairs, waiting for me. I got the impression that Calvin didn't easily admit to any sort of weakness, even being *kind of tired*.

"Sure." I grabbed my bag. "I'll go use the bathroom." I left him half-naked, most regretfully, and shut the door behind me. I changed into some dark-colored checkered pajama pants and a presumably black T-shirt. I washed my face, brushed my teeth, and took out my red-tinted contacts before leaving.

Calvin stood in the middle of the room, scrolling on his phone. He still didn't have a shirt on, but had what *looked* like Christmas-themed pajama pants on. Maybe my vision was really failing me there.

"Is everything okay?" I asked.

"Hmm. Yeah, just checking a few e-mails." He turned it off and set it down on the nightstand before going into the bathroom. He came back out a moment later with his toothbrush hanging from his mouth. Calvin moved by me as he returned to his phone.

He smelled good.

He looked good.

He was definitely wearing pajama pants with little Santa men and reindeer on them.

"You look quite jolly," I teased.

He glanced up, brushing absently. "What?" he asked around the toothbrush before looking down at himself. "Oh."

"Waiting on something important?"

"I've been requesting research on the *Tamerlane* book," he mumbled. "Haven't gotten it yet."

"I'm going to the library tomorrow. I have an appointment to inspect the copy of *Tamerlane* that they have."

Calvin turned to me in surprise.

"I thought it'd be useful."

"Did you plan on telling me?" he asked after taking the toothbrush from his mouth.

I shrugged. "Probably."

He frowned and walked back to the bathroom. "You're not a cop."

"I don't need to be a cop to go to the damn library."

When Calvin returned, he stepped close enough that the smell of mint and man made my head spin. "We'll discuss this later."

"Fine, whatever." I wasn't going to fight about a trip to the library. I was really only half listening to him anyway, not that it could be helped when he stood so close that I could count his freckles. I reached out to touch the fine, light-colored hair on his chest and followed it down.

Calvin reached under my chin and lifted it. "Go to bed."

"Uh, are you coming?"

"I'll sleep on the floor."

"Cal, you're not sleeping on the floor in your own home. Come on." I tugged him to the bed, threw the covers back, and slid over to the side against the wall. "See? Plenty of space."

"Fine." He walked over to the front door to check the lock and shut the lights off.

I leaned over to put my glasses on the nightstand, then turned onto my side, back to Calvin as he silently climbed into bed. It took all of my self-control not to curl up beside him, but he'd been firm in his decision with me, and neither of us were doing so well when it came to no more touching and nicknames. Someone had to stop first.

The bed shifted, and Calvin drew up close behind me. He snaked an arm between mine and wrapped it over my chest, holding me tight.

"Calvin," I said with a sigh. I rolled over to face him. "You can't keep being so sweet and touchy with me if I'm not allowed to have you."

"I'm sorry," he whispered. "I can't help myself."

"It's not fair."

Calvin removed his hand. "I know. I'm sorry."

I couldn't help but imagine that Calvin, with the way he touched— so gentle and as if it were the greatest experience of his life—had been denied intimate contact for a long, long time.

"I'm not asking you to wave a rainbow flag around," I said. "You don't have to announce to everyone you work with that you're fucking a guy."

"There's more to it than that, Sebastian," Calvin replied. "I'm... not a good choice for a partner. There's a lot wrong with me that I don't want to burden another person with."

"Sounds like an excuse."

Calvin laughed. "Believe me, baby, it's not." He reached out to touch my cheek. "I'm sorry."

I pushed his hand away and moved closer, firmly holding him. "Every time you call me baby, I'm going to hug you."

"What'll that accomplish?" he asked while planting his fingers in my hair.

"You drop it constantly, so maybe if you get enough hugs, you'll warm up to dating. I don't know." *I just know I want you and can't bear the thought of losing you.* But I didn't say that out loud.

# CHAPTER TWELVE

I HAD fallen into a sleep that I don't think even the dead can obtain. It had been great until I got punched in the face and knocked into the brick wall. I startled awake, the entire left side of my face hurting and the wall scratching uncomfortably on my back. I think I cursed, but it was drowned out by Calvin's screams. It took me a second to realize he wasn't being killed, though if I had been going by sound alone, that's what I'd have suspected.

I sat up, reached over the bed, and grabbed him by the shoulders. "Calvin!"

He was thrashing in a nightmare—there was no other explanation for me having been slammed so hard. His skin was clammy and damp to the touch.

"Calvin! Wake up! Jesus—! *Calvin*!"

He woke up with a start, sitting up and struggling to breathe. He was shaking and quickly covered his face with his hands as he sobbed uncontrollably.

Oh God. What was happening?

I removed my hands from his shoulders, and they sank while he cried.

His side of the bed was damp with sweat as I moved to climb off.

These were night terrors. True, actual terrors that could wake a man—a man who I suspected was stronger and braver than anyone I had ever known—from a deep sleep and reduce him to an emotional mess in seconds.

It was then that those little things I'd seen Calvin do started to connect. The moments he'd been startled—Max dropping the box, when I said his name while he was half-asleep, the squawking African grey.... And the twelve years of military service that Calvin refused to talk about.

It made sense now.

PTSD.

"Cal? Honey, you're okay," I said loudly, trying to be heard over his crying. "You're in bed, in your apartment in New York. You're here with me. Everything is okay," I insisted.

The moment was surreal, to see such a powerful man reduced to nothing but raw and bleeding heartache.

What had he been dreaming about? What haunted him? The war in the Middle East had gone on so long that many Americans just sort of forgot about it, myself included. Now that soldiers were home, just exactly how many of them were coming back with invisible wounds that the public still discriminated against out of sheer ignorance?

What can a man bear to see before he's seen too much?

"Cal?" I said again. I hastily grabbed my glasses so I could see what the hell I was doing before taking his wrists and gently tugging them down to reveal his face.

The dark was my friend, and I could see him in better detail. Calvin's eyes were bright with tears, his cheeks wet, and his hair a mess. He looked old. He looked vulnerable and broken. It made me realize that receiving the Medal of Honor and countless other awards issued by the police department and military did not make him invincible.

"I couldn't save them," he whispered. "There was so much fucking blood. I couldn't—I couldn't reach them."

I was sitting on my knees in front of the bed, staring up at him. It hurt to see this, hurt like nothing I'd ever experienced. I pulled him down, and Calvin slid off the bed. He sat on his knees in front of me, clinging fiercely and hugging me so hard that I could barely breathe.

I rubbed his back. "You're safe," I insisted.

"I let them die," Calvin cried.

I moved my hand up to his head and gripped his hair. "No. Don't think that. Please don't."

"I let that little boy die."

I maneuvered Calvin back enough so I could hold his face in my hands. "Calvin," I whispered. "Everything's going to be okay." I didn't know what else to do or say, and it was scary.

It was terrifying.

He was starting to calm down, though. Calvin wasn't shaking anymore and was wiping his eyes dry. *This* must have been the issues he didn't want to burden me with. How many nights a week did he wake up alone in utter fear and panic? Was he getting help?

"Calvin?" I asked quietly.

"I'm sorry," he whispered, avoiding eye contact. "I didn't think this would happen tonight. I'm just… stressed."

I wasn't sure what to do or say. I didn't want to set him off again. "Can you stand?" I asked. He nodded after a beat, and I helped him to his feet. "How about you go take a quick shower to cool down? Do you have clean sheets?"

"What?" He looked back at the bed, realizing he must have sweat so much I needed to bring it up. "I'm so sorry."

"No, it's okay. Don't worry." I gently pushed him toward the bathroom. "Go take a shower."

I waited until Calvin shut the bathroom door behind him and the water turned on, then went to the closet and felt around for a bit before finding folded bedsheets and pulling them out. I quickly remade the bed, tossing the old sheets in the hamper as Calvin came out of the bathroom, wet and naked. He changed into a clean pair of pajamas before sitting on the edge of the bed.

I crouched down in front of him. "Can I get you something?"

He shook his head. "I'm sorry you had to see that," he muttered.

"Please don't apologize."

"Did I hurt you?"

"No."

"I thrash around. I don't mean to."

"Cal, I'm okay," I insisted, not bothering to bring up the fact he had actually hit me pretty hard in his sleep.

He rubbed at his jaw in an agitated manner.

"Do you… need to talk about anything?" I asked quietly. "You can trust me, if you need to get something off your chest."

"No," he immediately answered.

"Calvin—"

"No, Sebastian," he said again, harder. "I'm not—I don't want to talk about it." Calvin's voice got thick again, and he covered his eyes with a hand.

I got up and sat beside him on the bed. "All right, all right. You don't have to." I reached over, took his free hand, and linked our fingers together.

He gripped my hand hard for several minutes. His hold eventually began to loosen as he seemed to mentally talk himself down from whatever ledge of memories he was looking off.

"Have you seen a doctor?" I asked quietly. My answer was silence, so I took it as a *no*. That worried me. "What about a VA hospital? They're trained to help with this sort of thing."

"I don't want to talk about it!" Calvin retorted angrily. "Seb. Please, just—stop. *Please*." He still held my hand and turned to look at me.

I'll be honest, it scared the shit out of me knowing that Calvin was suffering from some pretty intense PTSD that was apparently untreated, but it was the middle of the night and not the appropriate time to argue about seeing a doctor.

"Do you want to try to get some more sleep?" I asked. When he didn't respond, I leaned around him to set my glasses down again and lay back on the bed. "Cal, come here."

He obediently turned and lay down beside me, putting his head on my chest and wrapping himself around my body. I tugged the comforter back over us, and we were both quiet. I petted his head for a long time, and eventually his breathing evened out and I allowed myself to chase after sleep with him.


THE NEXT time I woke, I wasn't on the receiving end of a punch to the face, which was nice. It was still dark out, but I could tell from the subtle change in light through the closed blinds that it was about time to get up.

"Morning," Calvin grumbled.

"You're awake already?" I asked before yawning.

He grunted.

"Did you sleep much?"

"A little," he agreed after a moment. He rolled away and onto his back.

I moved on my side, leaned over, and kissed his chest.

Fuck it. Fuck all of it and everyone who said this was a bad idea, myself included.

What I felt for Calvin was very real, and no amount of being told I couldn't have him would sway me. Yes, I knew jumping out of one relationship and right into another was incredibly stupid. I knew what was even worse was leaving one man because he couldn't be open about loving me for another man with the same issue, but I was too taken with Calvin to put on the brakes.

And I knew what he felt for me was real and as intense as what I was struggling with. His shit about not being worth it wouldn't push me away, especially seeing now that he deemed himself a poor partner due to scars of war. We all have demons. If I had to rock him to sleep every night, telling him it was okay and I loved him, I would.

My breath caught.

God.

*I loved him.*

There really was no turning back.

His hand found my hair, and he hummed when I put my mouth over a nipple, sucking and gently biting. "You don't need to do this," he murmured.

"Do what?" I asked while moving over to the other nipple.

Calvin groaned quietly. "Feel bad for me."

I stopped and raised my head. "I don't pity you." I straddled Calvin's hips and leaned down close so I could see his face. "I want to be with you."

His hands found my hips and slowly moved to hold my ass. "I can't. I can't stomach being the cause of your broken heart."

"You haven't broken it, though."

"It's inevitable."

I leaned down and pressed my cheek to his, our rough jaws rubbing against each other. "Do you *want* to be with me?" I asked quietly.

His hands moved up my back and wrapped around me tight. "More than you know."

"Then let's see what happens," I replied, raising my face to find his mouth and kiss it.

Calvin slid his hands under my shirt and pulled it up over my head before tossing it to the floor. He grabbed my ass again, pushing me down while thrusting up to grind against me. He bit my neck and started sucking the skin.

"Oh God," I groaned. "Cal, I need you."

"What do you want, baby?"

I could feel a bashful heat spread over my face, and I dropped my forehead to his chest, nipping him in response.

Calvin growled playfully. "You want my cock, don't you? You want me to fuck your tight ass until you're screaming, right?"

I rubbed myself hard against him. "Yes, I do."

"I want you to suck me first." Calvin roughly raised my head. "Get me nice and wet for you."

There was nothing sexier, nothing more erotic, than waking up on a Monday morning and being ordered to suck the cock of this delicious man. God, yes, I wanted to taste him so bad I could barely manage to tug his pants off in my excitement. Calvin's erection jumped up, the head huge and already dripping. I got down and held the base while licking the salty liquid.

Calvin groaned appreciatively.

I wrapped my mouth around him, bobbing up and down on as much length as I could manage.

Calvin murmured words of approval. He gripped my hair and thrust up a few times, trying to get more. "Yeah, baby," he said. "That's good. Suck harder."

I hummed in response and tightened my mouth around him, moving up and down quickly. I came back to the head, sucking hard, then soft, hard, soft, over and over.

"Fuck! Sebastian!" Calvin pushed me off, sat up, and grabbed me into a rough kiss. His tongue pushed into my mouth, tasting himself. "Finish getting undressed," he ordered after pulling back. He turned to the nightstand and opened the drawer, searching inside as I hastily kicked my pants off and threw them to the floor with the rest of our pajamas. Calvin turned back to me, grabbing me in another fierce kiss and tugging on my cock a few times. "Hands and knees," he ordered.

I moved into the requested position, waiting to hear the snap of a bottle of lube, but I didn't.

Instead, Calvin grabbed my asscheeks firmly, groping and pulling them apart. "Look how pretty," he murmured.

Then I felt his tongue pressing against my entrance. I jumped forward, but Calvin held my hips firmly as he continued thrusting his tongue in and out. I moaned quietly and dropped my head. I'd never been rimmed before, and it was exciting and bizarre and felt really good.

Calvin stopped and bit one cheek. "Like that?"

"Yes," I whispered.

"Want more?"

I nodded.

"I can't hear you," Calvin purred.

"Yes," I groaned. "I want more, please. *Please*."

A hand came down firmly on my ass, and I jumped again. Then Calvin's tongue was pushing in and out, and good God, was it fucking incredible. I leaned down on my forearms and just *felt*. Calvin continued to lick and bite until I was a quivering mess.

He sat up, breathing hard as he placed kisses along my spine. Then I heard the snap of the bottle, and a blunt finger pressed into me. "I love your ass," Calvin murmured. "The way it's sucking on my finger, desperate for more."

I moaned in response, pushing back to meet Calvin's hand.

He hushed me. "Be patient."

"*Cal—*"

Calvin pulled his finger free and slapped my ass hard. He soothed the skin and murmured something under his breath before shoving two fingers in. He took his time to stretch and prepare me again, pausing time and again to smack my ass. It hurt in an erotic way. I'd never experienced it before but definitely wanted it again in the future.

"Cal," I whispered as he pushed three fingers in and out.

Calvin stopped and leaned over me. "You okay, baby?"

"Yeah."

"Is it too rough?"

I shook my head. "No, I like it."

I felt his smile as he kissed the side of my head. "Ready for my cock, then?"

"I—uh—"

Calvin petted my head. "No? Tell me what you want."

"I want you to fuck me," I insisted.

Calvin rubbed my ass again. "You like when I slap your ass? Is that it?"

"Yes," I said quietly, burying my face into my arms.

Calvin chuckled. "Don't be embarrassed. I'll give you whatever you want, sweetie." He moved back behind me, and I listened to the foil of a condom wrapper and more lube. The head of Calvin's cock gently pressed against me, then eased in, breaching and filling me.

Then he smacked me hard, and my muscles tightened instinctively around him.

"Oh fuck," he groaned while rubbing my ass. "That's right. You like that, don't you?"

I shivered and shook on my hands and knees, my cock hard as a rock between my legs. "Yes, do it again!"

Calvin shoved in a bit more, moving slowly when I hissed and cursed under my breath. "Okay?" he murmured.

I moaned some kind of response, glad Calvin was pushing in slow. He smacked me again when he was about halfway in, and the groan he made when I tightened around him was so incredible. I felt good knowing I was giving him the same sort of pleasure he was able to give me. I got one more hard smack before he was inside me completely.

Calvin's hands ran up and down my back, soothing my ass and up my sides. "Ready?"

"Just fuck me!"

He grabbed onto my shoulders and started pounding into me. I felt as if I were completely at his will. From behind, on my knees with my ass in the air, Calvin was able to fuck me fast and hard. Every time I shoved back to meet him, he'd smack my cheeks. They were hot and stung a little, but the pain was so fucking pleasurable, all I could do was helplessly beg for *more*.

More of Calvin's cock in me, more of his hands on me, more of him dictating the speed, the angle, the roughness. More of every dirty little thing he said as he lost himself in pleasure. He told me how good I was, how my ass was the best he'd ever had, how he wanted to come inside me and lick me clean.

I cried out loudly, moving my weight onto one hand to stroke myself. I was so hard, it hurt—I'd never needed a release as much as I needed one in that moment.

"You ready to come?" Calvin asked, one hand gripping my hair as he fucked me.

"Yes! I need to come," I begged.

"That's good, baby. Keep stroking yourself."

"Don't stop, don't stop," I said while awkwardly trying to keep moving back to meet him. My breath caught in my chest, and every muscle in my body tightened. "Oh God! Calvin!" And then I was coming hard, spurting onto the clean sheets and whimpering when he smacked my ass again, harder than he had yet.

I could feel Calvin coming, and his hands moved down to my hips, keeping me pressed against him as he rode out the sensations.

"You're so gorgeous," he said. "*Fuck.*" Calvin pulled out and flipped me onto my back, leaned down over me, and kissed me with a sort of aggressive possession.

I wrapped my arms around his neck, pulling him down on top of me, our kisses eventually calming as our blood cooled. "Wow," I finally said, laughing.

Calvin grinned and kissed my nose, my cheeks, my forehead. "You liked that?"

"Yeah. I've never had that before."

"Seems to me you've been denied a lot of sexual pleasures."

I pursed my lips and shrugged one shoulder. "Sort of, I guess."

Calvin hummed quietly, brushing damp hair from my forehead. "We should get going. You have to work today, don't you?"

I stretched lazily. "No. Emporium is closed on Mondays."

"Oh. What are your plans, then?"

"Shit."

"What?"

"I have a brunch date."

I could feel Calvin tense beside me. "I see."

I grabbed my glasses off the nightstand so I could see him. "It's not what you think."

"Then what is it?"

It was a strange revelation to see he was jealous. "It's just a customer. He's asked me out a few times, and yesterday, after you got angry at me, I didn't think I'd end up here with you. I plan on nicely letting him down."

Calvin frowned and put an arm around me firmly. "Is that all?"

"The library," I mentioned again. "Clean my house, I guess."

"No, don't go home."

"I can't live in your closet with you," I said, before amending the comment, "I mean, the size of your apartment."

"I need to have forensics check out your place."

"Calvin, what's the point? I've already been home twice. I've touched everything, moved books around."

"Doesn't matter, Sebastian. If we can find one fingerprint—a partial print, even. Besides, you need the locks changed too. It's not safe." He sat up, running his fingers through his hair until it stuck up comically. "Want to shower with me?"

"Together?" I asked with a chuckle. "Will we both fit in that tiny-ass little bathroom?"

"Unless you want to lay there covered in drying cum?" Calvin offered as he stood and tugged his condom off.

"Jesus, when you put it that way." I stood and followed him.

Calvin tossed the condom as he turned the light on in the bathroom, then turned it back off. "There's enough light coming through the window, right?" he asked, motioning to the small opening.

The fact that he noted I didn't have contacts in and the light of the bathroom was too harsh was extremely thoughtful.

Calvin turned the shower on and then moved under the stream of warm water, tugging me in with him. He kissed me a few times, hands moving over me. "I hope you're wearing a turtleneck to your date," he murmured, maneuvering me under the water while he grabbed shampoo.

I opened my eyes, watching his blurry figure in the dim light. "Why do you say that?"

Calvin reached out and ran his fingers through my wet hair, soaping it up. He leaned down to kiss the side of my neck. "Because I left a mark."

My hand reached up instinctively, touching the spot he kissed. "You did?"

Calvin hummed absently in response. "Sorry."

"Actually, I don't mind."

He must have been smiling because I could hear a note of amusement in his tone. "Really?"

"It's kind of hot."

"You're kind of hot. Rinse your hair."

"Yes, sir." I laughed to myself as I leaned back into the spray, letting it wash the soap out. I switched places with Calvin so he could wash his own hair next. "You know," I said quietly while feeling around for soap and snagging a washcloth. "I think I'm going to have a thing about you and showers."

"Why's that?" Calvin asked.

"Because just a few days ago, I was jacking off in mine to thoughts of you."

His hands came over mine, and he took the soap while kissing my mouth. "Good."

"Good?" I repeated.

His hands were on me again, washing me with the cloth. "Yeah, because I was doing the same thing."

"I can't imagine that."

"You doubt how sexy you are."

I snorted. "Have you been paying much attention?"

"Plenty." Calvin bent down to scrub my legs. "I'm not the one with a vision impairment."

"Oh, low blow."

He chuckled. "I think you're fucking gorgeous, baby. Whether you want to believe that or not is your call." He stood, turned me around, and ran the washcloth over my back and ass. "Just know that no amount of frumpy sweaters will ever make me think different."

"Shopping is difficult for me," I admitted.

"Why?"

"Colors. The world depends so much on its ability to see color. Colors provoke emotions, and maybe it sounds stupid to you, but I get so stressed out trying to understand if a yellow shirt is going to clash with the rest of my attire that I want... to cry." Now I knew how dumb that sounded. I was essentially crying over spilled milk while an Army veteran cried over massacred children.

Calvin turned me around and kissed me.

I wrapped my arms underneath his and held on to him for a moment. "I used to try more," I added. "I had a fashion color wheel and everything, but it was just too much work. It's easier to trust my dad to buy a bag of secondhand crap for me in white, gray, and black, which he says can't clash no matter what."

"I can solve this for you," Calvin said.

"Really? Complete human eye transplants?" I asked hopefully.

"No, just go around naked."

"That doesn't solve shit."

"It'll make me happy, though."

I laughed and shoved Calvin playfully. "Ass. Give me that," I said, grabbing the cloth and soap. I started scrubbing his chest and arms.

When we finished washing each other down, which I've never ever done with a guy before but was pretty fun and intimate, we got out and toweled off. I popped my lenses in so Calvin wouldn't have to shave in the dark.

He paused from lathering his face to hold mine and stare curiously at my eyes. "So they do make your eyes dark."

"Yeah. Extra protection, like a second pair of sunglasses."

"And if you don't wear them?"

"Everything's just too bright."

He rubbed the side of my face with the pad of his thumb before letting go.

I fetched my bag and glasses from the other room and joined him again, not daring to manually shave like Calvin. "I cannot see well enough to trust a razor against my jugular," I explained, making a half-assed effort on my face with an electric razor.

Calvin smiled and continued shaving in silence.

I sort of liked this. Neil and I had never shared the bathroom to get ready, but it was sort of sweet and domestic to be shaving together, even if it was too cramped and crowded. "Have you been with a lot of guys?" I asked while brushing my teeth.

Calvin had finished shaving and was washing the soap off. "Define 'a lot,'" he answered.

"More than one by several."

"Then yes," he answered dryly.

"A lot of boyfriends?"

He shook his head. "No."

"How many?"

He started brushing and didn't answer until he finished. "One or two."

"That's it?"

Calvin nodded and grabbed deodorant and cologne. "Yeah." He looked over at me. "Why, you know someone who's interested?"

I snorted and washed my mouth out. "I know a guy," I agreed.

"I think I've told him no a few times."

"He's a persistent shit."

"I'll say."

I laughed and leaned over to read the label on Calvin's cologne.

"What?" he asked.

"Nothing. I just like that smell."

Calvin started coffee after finishing in the bathroom. "Can you stay, or do you have to drink coffee with your date?" he asked, and don't think I didn't notice the tone in which he said *date*.

"I can stay," I replied, voice muffled as I tugged a T-shirt over my head.

Calvin stood in front of his closet in nothing but a pair of boxer briefs that hugged his upper thighs, his cock and balls heavy and snug in the soft cotton.

I moved up behind him and wrapped my arms around him, pressing up close.

"Hello," he said, still sorting through hung up shirts.

"Hey."

"I don't have time to go a second round, baby, so don't get me excited."

"I'll try not to." I leaned my forehead against his warm back for a beat before kissing his freckled shoulder. "How long would it take for me to kiss each freckle you have?"

"You'd be dead before you finished."

I laughed and let him go so he could dress. "Do you not like them?"

"I don't mind. I hated them as a kid."

"Why?"

"I got picked on a lot."

It was extremely difficult to imagine anyone being dumb enough to pick on someone as hot and dangerous as Calvin Winter.

"Before I figured out I was into guys, I couldn't get a girlfriend because none of them wanted to date a ginger." He turned while pulling a shirt over his shoulders. "It's easier for girls with red hair—everyone thinks they're cute. Not so easy for guys."

"I'll keep you," I offered.

He smiled slightly. "Yeah, I know you will."

"What do you want in your coffee?" I asked, walking back the whole two feet to the kitchen.

"Cream," he said, pulling on trousers and tucking his shirt in.

Good grief, the way Calvin's muscles rippled and pulled the fabric.... *Look away, look away.*

I offered him a fresh cup once he came over to the counter. "Hold on," I said, reaching for his tie. "It's crooked."

He held still as I adjusted the knot before taking a sip. "Thanks."

"Do you have time to eat?"

"I'll grab a bagel before I get to work," he answered.

"When are you sending forensics to my apartment?"

Calvin sat on a stool. "First thing."

I nodded. "All right." I reached into my pocket and pulled a key off a ring. "In case you need it."

Calvin accepted the key without question. He took another sip of coffee before standing and reaching around me to pick up his keys from the counter. I thought he was going to put mine on the ring so he wouldn't lose it, but instead he shifted one of his own off and passed it over.

"What's this?"

"I don't know how long it's going to take," Calvin answered. "So if you need to go somewhere, just come home. *Here*—I mean."

"Oh... thank you."

He nodded and finished his cup before going to put his shoes on. Well-worn Oxfords with the wide, flat toe. Classy and handsome on Calvin.

I followed after, and soon both of us were bundled up against the cold and ready to go.

"Call me after your visit to the library," he said as he locked the door.

"Sure."

"Or if... anything happens."

"Should something happen?" I asked warily.

He turned and looked down. "Just be careful, okay?"

"Will do, Officer."

"And don't go digging around where you shouldn't."

"Who, *me*?"

"Seb, I'm serious. No sleuthing around."

I waved a hand at him before tucking it into my jacket pocket. "I won't."

"All right."

"You be careful too," I said.

He leaned down and kissed me in the privacy of his doorway. "Have a good day."

I smiled as I followed him down the stairs to leave the building. It was all very sweet and domestic.

Except for the ongoing murder investigation.

But it's always something.

# CHAPTER THIRTEEN

THE NEW York Public Library took their rare books collection seriously. I signed in with my library card and ID, and checked my coat. No bag, pens, or anything of the sort allowed into the room. For those there to study the books, notes could only be taken with pencils, and photographs were at the discretion of the curator.

"Sebastian Snow," a woman spoke as I was allowed inside. "You're here to examine *Tamerlane* by Edgar Allan Poe, correct?"

"Yes, ma'am," I replied.

She was a tall, broad-shouldered, pretty woman with her hair tied back elegantly and a suit that made her look extremely dashing. "My name's Kate Bell. I'll be showing you the book."

"Wonderful." I followed behind her as she motioned me along.

"Professor?" she asked.

"What? Oh, no. I'm an antique dealer, actually. I've sort of become interested in Poe lately." *Sort of.*

"I see."

She didn't offer further conversation, but I needed to keep asking questions. About anything. I'd strike at something important sooner or later. As much as I believed Calvin was working his ass off to get to the bottom of this case, I was afraid he wouldn't get there in time. Pesky things like paperwork and legal proceedings held him up, and with already two dead and this creep zeroing in on me, I wasn't willing to stand by idly anymore.

I technically hadn't *promised* Calvin I wouldn't snoop about. I'd help, whether he wanted the assistance or not.

"Do many people ask to see *Tamerlane*?"

"Now and then," Kate answered, slowing her walk to look at me. "It's not the work he's known for."

"Written by a Bostonian."

She smiled. "That's correct. Poe published the work anonymously. The printer was a young man named Calvin F. S. Thomas, whom Poe hired and paid to produce the copies of *Tamerlane*. The production amount is rather disputed, but in general it is believed that no more than fifty copies were made."

"My father is a retired professor of American literature," I said. "He told me there's only twelve copies known to exist today. Is that so?"

"Very true." Kate stopped walking. "It is known today as the Holy Grail of American literature. To find one, especially any copy not already accounted for, would be priceless."

"How much is it worth? Of course, its condition taken into consideration."

"The last copy that sold at Christie's auction went for over half a million dollars," Kate answered. "A few years ago."

"To a private buyer?"

"Yes. One or two I believe are owned by individuals. The rest are in universities, libraries, and the Poe museum," she said, ticking off the points on her fingers.

We started walking again. I was sort of amused by the fact that Poe's printer had been a man named Calvin. Here I was, on a search for *Tamerlane* like Poe would have been looking for someone to bring his book to realization, and in swoops a man named Calvin. Not that I wanted to be Poe. I was more than happy with my own appearance, had no desire to marry my cousin—or a woman at all, for that matter—and I'd prefer not to die under tragic, mysterious circumstances in a few years.

*Calvin F. S. Thomas. If it wasn't for you, we may not be in this mess today.*

Or perhaps Poe never would have published his work at all.

Imagine a world without Edgar Allan Poe.

A more surprising, selfish thought occurred to me: I'd have never met *my* Calvin.

Kate brought me to a desk that had been prepared, and *Tamerlane* was brought out. After I put my regular glasses on and explained my vision issues, I was allowed to look at the book with my magnifying glass.

The book was surprisingly simple. It wasn't even a book. It was a pamphlet. Forty pages entitled *Tamerlane and Other Poems*. The paper was fragile and discolored from all the years it could have been stored in an attic before finding the light of the literary world. It was small too. A lot smaller than I thought it would have been.

"It didn't receive any real critical acclaim," Kate explained. "Much of it was inspired by Lord Byron. Are you familiar with him?"

"I studied his work in college for a time."

I was allowed to sit and read the poem of "Tamerlane," which was an incredible experience. And my curator, Kate Bell, was something else. She had endless facts to share about both Poe and the book, which I was sucking up like a sponge.


"DETECTIVE WINTER," Calvin said when answering his cell.

"It's me."

"I know."

*Was that some kind of code? I'm in public so I have to pretend this is a work-related call?*

I frowned but didn't say anything about it. "I'm just calling to say I finished at the library."

"Where are you going now?" Calvin asked quietly. I could hear other voices in the background.

"Patty's Diner. Some place a few blocks from the library, actually."

"For the… brunch."

"The brunch date," I corrected. "Yes. Hey, for the record, the last copy of *Tamerlane* that went to auction sold for over half a million dollars. That's some serious motive right there."

"When was this?"

"Few years ago. Twelve copies are known to exist. The curator was saying the sky's the limit if there was a thirteenth copy found."

"And you saw the book?"

"It's actually a pamphlet, but yeah. Pretty amazing."

"I need the curator's name," Calvin said.

"Why don't you just ask me for what information you need?"

"You're not a cop, Sebastian."

"I'm aware of that," I said sternly. "But I'm also not an idiot."

"I never said—"

"It hasn't been requested in a while. No one recently, for sure, so no leads there. In fact, she asked if *I* was there because of the news."

"Fucking reporters," Calvin muttered. "Sebastian, I appreciate the... help, but that's not enough. I can request far more information than you. I need her name."

"Why didn't you just fucking come with me, then?" I don't know why I was getting so defensive. I knew I wasn't a cop and I was only trying to help, but it had reached beyond that now. The attacks against me were personal. The people in my immediate circle were being affected because of this psycho.

"Why are you getting so pissed?" Calvin asked in a harsh whisper.

"I'm not helpless," I said firmly. I had been standing at the south exit of the library beside one of the two great lion sculptures. Ironic that I was giving Calvin so much unnecessary shit while standing beside the lion known as Patience.

"I don't know why you keep insisting I think these things," Calvin said.

I raised my head to look up at Patience. The lions were over a century old and had a few names throughout the years, but in the thirties, the mayor of New York City had renamed them Patience and Fortitude, qualities he said that all citizens needed to survive the Great Depression. Patience had weathered far more in life than I had or ever would. Over a hundred years of joy and celebration, sorrow and loss, destruction and construction, the lions had endured with unwavering dignity. Perhaps I was giving a slab of marble too much credit, but I put my hand against the cold pedestal Patience sat upon and took a breath.

"I'm sorry," I said to Calvin.

"What?"

"I'm sorry," I repeated.

He was quiet for a beat. "It's okay. I know this is stressing you out."

And the fight was over.

Had this been with Neil, we'd still be going at it.

"I've got to go."

"Kate Bell was the woman I spoke to," I said.

"Thank you." Calvin said good-bye and hung up.

ADMITTEDLY, BY the time I got to the diner Duncan had texted me to meet him at, I was feeling a little guilty about having a date with him. It's not like I had expected to end up at Calvin's the night before. I certainly hadn't thought I'd be getting more phenomenal sex or skirting around a potential relationship.

Were we dating? No.

Would we? Hard to tell. I was not oblivious to how he evaded a direct answer that morning when I brought it up.

And I certainly hadn't expected to learn about Calvin's PTSD. That worried me. I had never seen a man break down so suddenly the way he had last night, and this morning it was like it hadn't happened. It was like watching a knight put his armor on. Nothing could reach Calvin when he was at work; he was focused solely on his job as a detective. But how long can a knight endure the weight before it becomes too heavy and he has to remove pieces of his chainmail? Before he must make himself vulnerable in order to breathe?

I had learned through my initial research on Calvin that he had left the military just a few years ago, but how many times in those years had he awakened like he had last night? It had to be exhausting. Physically, mentally, emotionally. I literally could not imagine what he was going through, but it hurt to see him suffer alone. I decided while sitting at a booth in the back that once this shitstorm of a case was over, I'd approach Calvin about seeking help.

A soldier shouldn't fight a war alone. There were people who could help him.

I felt my phone buzz in my pocket and tugged it free. Text from Calvin Winter. I smiled and unlocked the phone with a swipe, not sure what to expect after our last conversation.

*Forensics at apartment now.*

What a romantic.

Another text popped up on my phone while I had been trying to peck my way through a response. Beth Harrison. Wow, wasn't I the popular sort today?

*Celebrate the Master of Horror and Macabre with a surprise unveiling! Sure to capture the hearts of the literary world! Tonight at Good Books, 7:00!*

What?

I didn't bother with texts and immediately called Beth. "What the hell is that text about?" I asked when she picked up.

"Good morning to you too, Sebby."

"Good morning. What surprise unveiling?"

"Did your father never teach you what *surprise* meant?"

"Beth, come on. What is this about?"

"Oh good grief, Sebastian. It's. A. Surprise. Come by tonight, understand? I mean it. Don't miss this. It's going to be huge."

"In what way?" I was almost hesitant to ask.

"Great for business. Really great."

That's when I began to wonder… If I didn't have the copy of *Tamerlane* in with my antique books, could it have accidently ended up with Beth's secondhand paperbacks? All of this time, the killer had been targeting antique shops because it made sense that that would be where the book would have ended up.

But it was so easy to mistake *Tamerlane* as nothing but junk.

Kate had told me about the antique dealer in the eighties who sold it for a whopping *fifteen bucks*. They clearly didn't know who either a Bostonian was, or thought it to be a facsimile.

Just a little six-inch pamphlet.

*Shit.*

"Beth, I have to go. I'll call you back."

"You're going to come tonight, right?"

"Yes, of course," I quickly answered before saying good-bye and hanging up. I called Calvin next.

"I don't have time," he stated upon answering my call. His tone was very official. Man, he could turn off that sweet side real fucking fast.

"It'll be quick. Have you confirmed that Mike was one of the antique shops that put in a bid for the estate's book collection?"

A moment's pause. "Sebastian," he said quietly. "What did I tell you this morning?"

"Just answer me. You've told me everything else."

"No, I haven't."

"*Calvin.*"

"Where are you?"

"I'm at the diner, behaving like a good boy and waiting for Duncan."

"Duncan?"

"Andrews. The date. The guy. Come on. Tell me."

He sighed with such a level of exasperation that if I hadn't known better, I'd tell him he needed to get laid. "Yes, Sebastian. He did."

"And Greg?"

"Seb."

"He didn't, right?"

"All three of you did."

That surprised me. "Are you sure about Greg? Was there anything strange about his bid?"

"Other than he offered more than what he appears to be financially capable of," Calvin said. "Why are you calling?"

My train of thought was halted when I glanced up and saw Duncan stepping inside. He immediately spotted me and waved before hurrying over. "I have to go," I told Calvin.

"Stop. Sleuthing." He hung up.

I set my phone down. "Good morning," I said with a forced smile while looking up at Duncan. My mind was racing a million miles an hour. I didn't have time for this.

"Good morning! I'm sorry you've been waiting." He removed his hand from behind his back and produced a bouquet of roses. "For you."

"W-What? Oh—Duncan, this wasn't necessary." Now the guilt was coming on hard. I hesitantly accepted the flowers.

"Don't be silly," he replied, removing his coat and taking a seat across from me. "It's the least I can do."

*Least you can do?* "Thank you," I said slowly.

"So is that... other guy watching your shop today?"

"Other.... *Max*?"

Duncan shrugged. "I guess."

"No. We usually aren't open on Mondays."

"That's good."

"Why?"

He grabbed his menu, staring hard at the breakfast options. "He just gets to be around you all day."

"How unfortunate for him."

A waiter came over and poured us each a mug of coffee before taking orders. Morning sex left me famished, and I was even hungrier after my meeting at the library. I ordered waffles with a side of bacon and briefly wondered what Calvin would have ordered. After seeing how he could put pizza away when denied a meal, I'd imagine he could have easily eaten two of the waffle specials. Duncan asked for eggs and toast, and the waiter left.

"So," I said. "What do you do? Are you—you're not still in school, are you?"

He grinned. "No. I'm not *that* young."

"Oh?"

"I'm twenty-four."

I laughed quietly and sipped my coffee. "I don't remember being twenty-four."

"How old are you? Twenty-eight?"

"Flattering."

"Thirty?"

I jutted my thumb up in the air to indicate higher.

Duncan made a face. "You are not."

"I'm thirty-three," I said with a smile. "A nice boring age. I'm in bed by ten."

"You're not boring!" Duncan insisted. "I think you're very interesting."

I bit my tongue as I tried to delicately navigate these dark waters without insulting the guy. "Well, you don't really know me."

"I know enough."

"You do?"

"I know that you're really smart. You wouldn't be able to run an antique shop if you weren't. You like literature too."

"I also like silly mystery novels," I pointed out.

"Why do you wear sunglasses so often?" Duncan asked, ignoring my comment.

Had I worn them a lot around him? "I have a sensitivity to light."

"Your eyes are very pretty. 'Whose luminous eyes, brightly expressive as the twins of Lœda,'" he quoted with a grin.

"Ah, thanks," I replied, ignoring the heat rising to my cheeks.

Duncan was still smiling widely, looking terribly excited. "Is your head okay?"

"My head?"

"You got hurt," he said with a worried tone.

"I'm fine—how did you know it was my head?"

"I heard the bookstore woman mention it."

"Beth? Ah, yes, I'm fine. Thank you for asking."

Our meals came fairly quickly after. Thank God, because my stomach was about to let out some of those cavernous growls, like a monster from the depths coming up to feed. The waffles were delicious. Warm, with melted butter and syrup. The bacon had just the perfect crunch to it too. I had devoured half of my meal within minutes.

I listened to Duncan talk about books, a subject he was quite passionate about, and gave my polite comments in between bites of food. To be honest, between the bacon and my curiosity over Greg's large bid that he was financially unable to see through, I was only half paying Duncan any attention.

"Sebastian?"

"Hmm?" I quickly wiped my mouth on a napkin. "Sorry. What?"

"I asked what you were doing this evening."

Uh-oh. Time to let the guy down. "I was thinking about going to Beth's shop. She's having some big book unveiling."

Duncan tilted his head curiously. "Really…?" He set his fork and knife down. "Can we go together?"

*Crap.*

"Actually," I said slowly. "Duncan, you're a really sweet guy, but I think I'm a little old for you."

"No, you're not," he said simply.

"Well, I mean to say that there may be someone else—"

"But you told me you didn't have a boyfriend."

"I don't. Not really. But there was someone I met before you."

"How?" Duncan asked, with such a desperate tone you'd think I had absolutely broken his heart. "It's that fucking redhead, isn't it?"

I blinked in surprise at his tone. "Hey. Come on. Don't be rude. How do you even know who it is?"

Duncan shook his head and grabbed his scarf and jacket. "I can't believe you would do this."

"Do what?" I asked defensively.

"Betray me!"

"Jesus, Duncan. You need to calm down."

"Shut up!" Duncan looked like he was going to cry. "I'm leaving." He stood from the booth and left, pulling his coat on as he walked out the door.

That's how I ended up paying for two meals.

I WAS waiting for the train at Bryant Park, although where I was going, I wasn't entirely sure. I could just go to the Emporium, do some work until Beth's exhibit.

Fuck.

*Fuck.*

*Beth.*

Duncan had thrown me off my game!

Beth and her stupid surprise unveiling! Assuming there was in fact, a long lost thirteenth copy of *Tamerlane* being tossed as part of that estate sale, it ended up in one of two places. Either my shop, with the haul of antique books it should have been a part of, or in Beth's haul of secondhand paperbacks, where it could have easily been mistaken as junk and tossed in. I had to assume, despite never having looked in my boxes at home before someone had taken the opportunity to investigate themselves, that I didn't have *Tamerlane*. I had to assume I *never* had it.

Why?

Because Beth did. How long had she known, I don't know, but somewhere along the way, she found it. Being a serious person in the business, she knew who the author was and the goldmine she had stumbled upon. An unveiling of that book for the general public to see, exclusive to Good Books, before putting it up for auction—her brick-and-mortar shop would be safe for years and years to come.

The problem with Beth having the book was that I was pretty sure our killer knew she did too. Otherwise they wouldn't have broken into her store and I wouldn't have nearly been killed. And it didn't matter if there wasn't evidence as to who it was that snuck into Good Books. It made no sense for it to be anyone but this EAP freak. They'd managed to discover I was the antique dealer with the winning bid for the expensive collection. It should have only been a matter of time for them to determine who won the cheap paperbacks and come to the same conclusion I did.

The fact that our shops were neighbors was just too convenient.

Beth was undoubtedly pulling out all the stops to promote this surprise event. It was like ringing the dinner bell for a hungry bear. The killer would come. He *had* to. He had already killed two people in his fanatical search for the book. He'd have no qualms about offing a third.

But I was stuck between a rock and a hard place. If I told Beth and she called off the event, the man would just lie in wait and strike when we wouldn't expect him. If I told Calvin, he'd have cops there and maybe this guy wouldn't appear. He'd still be out there, still ready and willing to hurt more people—maybe still me, and most certainly Beth. And I might gripe about Beth not paying her account on time, but I've known her for years. She's a good person. A *friend*. I wouldn't let someone hurt her.

Having the book unveiling go on without commotion might be the only way to corner the killer and catch him. The only way to keep everyone safe, the book in the right hands, and get him behind bars. My number one problem still was: who.

I knew what it was: A thirteenth copy of *Tamerlane and Other Poems*.

I knew why: Money. Lots of it.

I knew where: Beth's shop.

I knew when: Seven o'clock tonight.

But I didn't know who.

I had more clues than I knew what to do with, and none of them could draw a line to who the fuck this guy was. My best bet was still Greg. Maybe Calvin had my ex-boyfriend pinned as the most interesting guy, but that was just simply ludicrous.

I had decided where to go.

# CHAPTER FOURTEEN

MARSHALL'S ODDITIES. I'd never actually been inside. It was an extremely small store—two or three of them would fit inside the Emporium easily. There was only enough space for a few customers to skirt around the displays at a time, but it was empty that Monday afternoon.

Empty, save for myself and Greg Thompson.

He was sitting behind the counter, reading the newspaper, and looked up when the door opened. "Sebastian?"

"Hi." I looked around the shop as he shut the page he was reading and put his hands on the countertop.

The shop was brightly lit and was starting to annoy the growing headache I had. The shelves weren't stocked as heavily as my own, but the items were similar. What my returning customers told me of Greg's business was that he had interesting wares, but was priced higher than what the market asked and wasn't as knowledgeable on particular subjects. I was full of random facts, for sure, and took it as a compliment that my customers trusted me and my research, despite being one of the younger antique dealers in the city.

"Can I help you?" Greg asked. "Or have you come to spy on my shop?"

"Ha-ha." I pressed a smile to my face and stopped a foot or two from the counter. I steeled myself to continue on. I believed this was the man who killed Mike Rodriguez and Merriam Byers, and I'll be honest, my heart was pounding pretty hard. "No, I came to see if you heard about Beth's book event."

"The mysterious unveiling? Oh, yes. I'll be there."

"Any idea what it's about?"

Greg shrugged. "Can't say. The Master of Horror and Macabre, though. Sounds like you know who."

"I heard you were one of the bidders for the estate sale that I won."

Greg was quiet for a beat, and I wish I had been closer so I could better read his expression. "I bet you heard that from your detective buddy, huh?"

"I'm not sure why you think I have a friend among the police on this case."

"I know you do. Max was telling us," Greg said.

*Note to self: kill Max.*

"I'm sure he's mistaken."

"What do you really want? I know you don't like me, Sebastian, so I highly doubt it was to invite me to Beth's event if I hadn't already heard about it."

"How did you know that it was Detective Winter who found me when I was attacked?" I asked. The fact that he had that knowledge had been bothering me.

"The newspapers say a detective on the case arrived before uniformed officers. I'm assuming it was him since he's appeared to be the lead on the investigation," Greg replied.

"I know why you did it," I stated abruptly.

Greg slowly stood from the stool behind the counter. "Did what?"

"Reported the bogus phone call. No one had figured out this was regarding *Tamerlane*, so you showed your hand to see who would scare first. Whoever did would be the one with the book, right?"

Greg took a step around the counter.

"Except that didn't work either. It just made you suspicious."

"You think I reported a fake threat?" Greg asked slowly.

"I know you did. You're hard up for cash and a good reputation."

"Excuse me?"

"How often does your store have no customers in it?" I asked. "Having that book would give you prestige, not to mention half a million dollars."

"What are you fucking talking about?" Greg asked defensively. "I don't even know what the hell *Tamerlane* is, just that some psycho called me screaming about it!"

"*Tamerlane and Other Poems*, by Edgar Allan Poe. His first publication—one of the most priceless books in American literature today!"

My customers had said Greg wasn't as knowledgeable.

*I don't even know what the hell* Tamerlane *is*.

"Shit," I whispered.

How many revelations were considered too many in the course of two days? I felt sick to my stomach.

Greg must have noticed. "Are you okay?" he asked hesitantly.

"What? Yes. No. Yes."

"Which one?"

"Don't go to Beth's tonight," I said firmly, taking a step back.

"Fuck you," Greg retorted.

"I'm goddamn serious, Greg!" I snapped. "If you want to live to see the new year, don't go." I turned and walked out of the shop, flagging down the nearest taxi.


I HAD gone back to Calvin's apartment and let myself in with the key he'd given me. The place was quiet. Still. A silence that I didn't think could exist in a place like New York. I sat on the edge of his bed, listening to that high-pitched hum that fills an empty space.

I don't know for how long. Twenty minutes. An hour. Two?

Eventually I stood and started searching for a notepad. I ended up rummaging under Calvin's bed and finding a box that had some discarded office supplies. I took one of the legal pads and a pen, then paused when I unveiled a small black box. Calvin had trusted me not to go digging about his private things when he gave me his key, but I was about to do something *very stupid*, and if something happened to me... I wanted to know just a bit more about him.

Inside the box were his medals from his military service. There was a photo of Calvin in his police cadet uniform, smile so big and, daresay, a little dorky. He looked innocent. I turned it over to see the date on the back. So he'd been in the police academy before he went off to war.

Innocent indeed.

There were a few more photos buried at the bottom. In one, Calvin posed beside several other men in uniform, the backdrop of some far-off desert in the Middle East. The back had a few names scribbled on it. Some more photos showed the same men, a face or two missing this time, and smiles more drawn and worn. At the bottom of the pile was a photo of Calvin that someone must have taken without his knowledge and given to him later. He was crouched on one knee, face dirty and helmet missing. A young girl was in his arms and appeared to be crying while holding on to Calvin tightly.

My throat tightened as I looked through the box. Small snapshots of Calvin's past, moments he was unable to let go of but that tore at his mind day in and day out. Among the military photos was one of a family in front of a home, including Calvin in dress uniform with a somber expression. An older man and woman posed with him, along with another young man and woman. Brother and sister? Calvin's family? I wondered what their reason was for being locked away in this box.

Maybe Calvin would tell me about them one day.

Assuming I lived through the night.

I put the memories away and pushed the box back in its place under the bed. I sat once again and started writing. I wrote down everything I knew about the victims and the events that had led up to this moment. I put down all of my suspicions and evidence that Duncan Andrews was the man who had killed two people, assaulted me, and broken into numerous establishments in his search for *Tamerlane*. I did it so that if I wasn't here to explain it myself, Calvin would still have my notes. Maybe he'd be able to catch that bastard in my name.

I couldn't get the cops involved now. Duncan knew who Calvin was, and he'd be looking for him. If I was at Beth's without backup, Duncan would feel safe. It'd be my only chance to stop him in a place I knew to expect him.

I turned the page and wrote another quick note to my dad. I kept it simple, because to think much more into it would be like admitting I was going to be killed.

*I love you, Pop.*
*Thank you for being there for me, always.*

I quickly turned the page again, biting back the urge to cry.

*Calvin—*
*Please visit a VA hospital. Don't do this alone.*
*I love you.*

I pulled the pages back to the beginning and let out a breath. I left the notebook on the pillow before standing and going to the clock on the wall to check the time.

Six o'clock.

Showtime.


GOOD BOOKS was packed by the time I arrived at quarter to seven. People drank champagne from plastic flutes and chatted happily in groups throughout the store. The shop was bright with twinkling Christmas lights and electric candles among the front window displays and bookshelves. Fake snow and garland decorated end tables, and holiday cookies were being served alongside the bubbly alcohol. Festive music played overhead.

The aesthetic didn't really fit Poe, but then again, what would Beth have done to decorate for the Master of Macabre? Play recordings of a beating heart and splatter fake blood across the floors and tables?

Christmas was a safer theme. And cleaner.

Ella Fitzgerald came up next on the mix. Next year all of my troubles would be out of sight, if I was inclined to believe her.

I smiled and shook my head. *I hope so, Ella. I really do.*

I had to keep my sunglasses on because of all of the extra lighting, despite it being dark outside. Scanning the faces for a few moments, I did see Greg, who briefly met my eyes and probably scowled, though it was hard to tell at this distance, before turning back to his conversation. Yeah, well, he could screw himself. I was looking for Beth, anyway.

"Sebastian!"

I turned quickly to see Max coming over with two glasses and offering me one. "Max? What are you doing here?"

"Beth invited me. Here. You look like you need a drink."

"Max, you need to leave."

"What? Why? I just got here."

"It's not safe to be here," I replied.

"Safe? Sebastian, are you drunk already?"

"No, God, I wish I was. Max, please just—" I paused when I saw Beth over Max's shoulder. She was hanging up the phone behind the counter before waving at me.

Beth rushed into the storage room before coming back pushing a display on wheels, the top covered in a heavy cloth. "Ladies and gentlemen!" she called, clapping her hands after stopping in the middle of the room. "Thank you everyone for bearing these frigid temperatures and coming out tonight. I've invited you all here to take part in the unveiling of a magnificent piece of history thought not to exist to the literary world."

I left Max and started looking around for Duncan. He was here; he had to be. This was what he was waiting for. *Tamerlane* was here. *His Tamerlane* was within grasp.

"Edgar Allan Poe's first publication was in 1827 and was a small collection of poetry entitled *Tamerlane and Other Poems*. The simple, forty-page pamphlet was released in July, when Poe was just eighteen years old. It was published under the pseudonym, a Bostonian, and received little acclaim from the literary world," Beth explained to her enraptured audience. "In fact, it is such a rare piece of work that after Poe's death, it was thought to never exist at all! Only twelve copies were thought to survive of the original fifty. Until today."

A hushed whisper moved throughout the crowd.

I wove in between people, searching for Duncan.

"Today, my dear friends," Beth said, "I give to you the long lost thirteenth copy of Edgar Allan Poe's priceless first publication." She removed the cloth on the glass display.

Inside was a copy of *Tamerlane* that looked much like the one I'd seen at the library earlier. It was in remarkable condition, with an intact cover and little discoloration. I was sidetracked for a moment, moving closer to get a look at the history Beth was sharing. I had a hundred questions about the condition on the inside, and more importantly, how Beth had found it, but those thoughts were all brought to a screeching halt when all of the lights in the shop went out.

Candles and Christmas strings too. Someone had flipped the switches.

A second of silence, then murmuring voices. I could hear Beth cursing and moving away from the display, most likely to the back room.

"B-Beth!" I shouted. *Not back there. Don't go back there.*

Then there was a gunshot, and people screamed.

I ducked and covered my ears, the ringing making my head spin. I raised my head and looked around. *Thank you for the darkness, Duncan, you little fuck.* I moved toward Beth now that I could see better. I put a hand on her shoulder.

"Are you okay?" I asked loudly, speaking over the buzz in my ears.

Beth was lying on the floor but lifted her head and looked at me. Terrified, but alive. She nodded.

There was another shot and then shouting. "Don't fucking move!" Duncan.

I was crouched in front of the display, and he was still deeper in the shop, having come out of the back after turning off the lights. I knew he'd come after I had mentioned Beth's book event. I had realized that by mentioning it, he'd know immediately which book it would be in regards to. I also knew he had fixated on me and felt I'd betrayed some relationship he thought we were in. He wouldn't hurt anyone else once he knew I was here.

He'd follow me. He'd follow the book.

My plan seemed really, really stupid now.

Get the book out of the store. He'd follow after me. I hadn't thought about what would happen after that.

Maybe the shots fired would alert someone to call the police. Maybe I'd be able to outrun Duncan long enough until cops arrived.

*Don't second-guess yourself.*

I stood up among the people crouching and trying to hide. "Duncan! Stop it!" I could see him waving a gun around frantically before pausing at the sound of my voice.

"Sebastian?"

"I said I was coming, didn't I?"

"You didn't come with me!" he shouted. "You—you're a whore! You're a slut! You betrayed me!"

"Duncan, I don't know what you thought was going on between the two of us, but—"

"Shut up!" he screamed, waving the gun again. "I knew you wouldn't steal my book! I knew you were better than all those other greedy pigs! I apologized! I brought you fucking roses!"

I hoped to God someone was recording this on a phone.

"But you're worse than all the others! You and that cop! Did you laugh about me while you fucked him?"

"Duncan—"

"*Did you!*" he screamed again.

"Let's talk about this outside," I said calmly, despite my heart racing so hard that I felt sick. "Let's get away from these people."

"No! You'll call the police and blame it all on me! They'll believe you because of your pig boyfriend!"

"How about I leave my phone here?" I slowly reached into my pocket to take my cell out and set it on the nearest table. "See? Come outside with me."

Then I heard the shop door open behind me, and Duncan screamed before firing another round. It missed me, but I swear to God I felt the breeze of the bullet as it whizzed by and hit the door, shattering the glass window. Among the sudden chaos and renewed screams of terrified patrons, I grabbed the hefty metal tray the Christmas cookies were sitting on and slammed it down onto the glass display *Tamerlane* sat inside.

I reached inside through the shards, cutting myself as I grabbed the book and tucked it into my coat.

"No!" Duncan cried, and I could hear him running toward me.

I dodged the closest people as I made for the door.

*Don't stop*, I told myself. *Just run. Get him away from Max. Away from Beth. Away from everyone.*

I had just opened the shop door, barely stepped into the freezing night, when a hand grabbed mine. I startled but didn't break free.

I knew that hand.

"*Run*," Calvin said sternly. He took off into the dark, hand tight around mine, never letting go.

I slipped and skidded on the frozen sidewalk, but Calvin's footing never wavered. He held on, keeping me on my feet as we ran down the block and crossed the street. The air froze my lungs as we ran, the wind burning my face with its freezing temperature.

But we kept running.

Calvin's coat billowed open around him, like dark wings that would lift us off the ground and bring us to safety. The wind tore down the street, and Calvin's scarf was tugged free from his neck.

Everything happened so quickly, it seemed to actually slow down. The minute details I remember seem almost silly now. The strange glow of freshly falling snow in the streetlamps. The echoing pound of our steps, as if the city were completely empty, save for the two of us. The strides Calvin took, too powerful for me to keep up, and he had to yank me forward.

A gun fired behind us, and Calvin skidded to a stop. He spun around, pulling me to stand behind him as if he were a shield, while reaching into his coat to pull his pistol free. Calvin raised his gun, not even managing to take aim at the figure standing in the middle of the street between the blocks before another crack echoed into the frozen night.

And then Calvin fell.

He crashed backward onto the pavement, gun sliding free from his hand. He was staring up at the clouded sky as if in surprise. And then pain.

He took a breath that sounded so scary.

Duncan was laughing. Screeching and bellowing as if he'd finally lost his fucking mind.

I dropped to my knees beside Calvin and reached over his chest. His right side was wet and warm, and he made another pained sound at my touch.

"Oh God," I whispered when my hands came up covered in blood. I was shaking so badly, I could barely control my limbs. "Cal? Oh God, oh God." I yanked my jacket off and pressed it down against the bullet wound.

Stop the bleeding. Put as much pressure on it as you could.

"That's what you deserve, you son of a bitch, disgusting *pig*!" Duncan was screaming. "*Sebastian*! Don't touch Sebastian! Don't touch *Tamerlane*! It's mine, mine, mine!" He waved his gun at us.

I looked down at Calvin. "Please," I whispered. I needed to call for help. He wasn't going to make it. I reached down and gripped his hand tight.

"Sebastian!" Duncan shouted.

I looked up.

"Get away from him!"

"Duncan, put the fucking gun down!" I cried. "You shot him—aren't you happy now? Put it down!"

"Get away from him!" he shouted again. "Bring *Tamerlane*!"

I glanced at my coat, which was soaking up Calvin's blood, before digging inside to remove the pamphlet. It was covered in blood.

Priceless to worthless. "Is this what you fucking want?" I raised it up and tore it in two.

"*No!*" Duncan screamed. "No, no, no! Sebastian! *What have you done!*"

He was going to kill us both.

When Duncan raised his gun again, I dropped the book and grabbed Calvin's fallen pistol. I'd never touched a gun before, and the weight was cold and deadly. All I knew was aim and pull the trigger.

So I did.

The kickback was strong, and I dropped the pistol out of fright. The crack was so loud, like thunder had struck my brain. While my ears hummed and buzzed, I watched Duncan drop to the ground.

I had no idea where I'd struck him. Didn't even realize I would be able to hit him. But what if he were okay? He still had his gun.

I stumbled to my feet, tripping over myself as my legs refused to function. I moved closer to Duncan and looked at him warily. He had blood running from his mouth, but his lips were still moving, saying something I didn't care to hear.

I picked up his gun and ran back to Calvin.

"Cal! Cal! Don't you fucking die, do you hear me?" I begged when I got back on my knees beside him. "Cal?" I shook him hard. "*Calvin!*"

I reached into his coat, took out his cell, and called 911. I told the dispatcher a policeman had been shot and gave the cross streets.

The wait for the ambulance was the longest five minutes of my life.

This wasn't how it was supposed to end.

# CHAPTER FIFTEEN

MY KNOWLEDGE that Duncan Andrews was the killer was based on nothing but circumstantial evidence at best. It was my gut that told me, like when he mentioned loving Poe when we first met. His adoration of literature, and the roses he'd brought me at the diner, which were identical to the ones left in my shop. Especially the comment about my eyes, which I learned was from Poe's poem, "A Valentine." Nothing but circumstantial evidence.

Thank God I was right.

Not that it fucking mattered.

I needed to see Calvin, but no one would let me. When the ambulance came to pick him up, I wasn't allowed to go with him. When I went to the hospital myself, I was turned away. I wasn't a cop. I wasn't family.

*So scram.*

My heart was fucking breaking. I was the reason for it all. If I'd just called Calvin instead of going to Beth's with a half-formed, dumbass plan, none of this would have happened. Was he even alive? No one would tell me anything. I just needed to be assured he was okay. Even if he never wanted to see me again, I'd be okay with that. As long as he was *alive*.

"Sebastian?"

I had been prowling the hospital waiting room like an insane person but stopped at the sound of my name. I looked over, pushing up my glasses. "Quinn." My heart dropped to my gut.

She motioned with a curt wave of her hand for me to follow away from the strangers in the room and down a quiet hallway.

I rushed after her. I had been awake for nearly two days straight and was fueled on nothing but coffee, adrenaline, and absolute fear. By the time Calvin had been rushed to the hospital and into surgery, visiting hours were long over and I had been told to leave. No one could make me rest, not Pop, Max—Jesus, even Beth came to my apartment to see I was tended to. I returned to the hospital that morning and stubbornly sat in the lobby, hoping, *praying* a nurse or passing cop would feel bad for me and let me in to see Calvin.

"Quinn," I said, and my own voice sounded very strange and far away.

She stopped and looked up at me, holding out her hand and taking a breath. "Why are you here?"

"You *know* why. I only want to know if he's… no one will tell me anything."

Quinn pulled her coat off. She looked dapper in a suit and tie. Goddamn, I was so tired. She looked back up while holding the jacket against her chest with both arms crossed. "Calvin's okay."

I let out a shuddering breath and had to grab the banister on the wall.

"You know, the boys all call him Mr. Invincible," she pointed out with a small smile.

I closed my eyes, took off my sunglasses, and quickly rubbed them dry on my sleeve. "He's really okay?"

"Yes. They took him out of the ICU already."

I put my glasses back on and looked at her. "Thank you," I whispered.

Quinn seemed to hesitate for a minute, looking back over her shoulder once or twice. "Look. I know that Calvin's family is here now. They were notified last night."

I thought of the photograph in Calvin's box under the bed.

"But I can go speak to Calvin and get you permission to see him."

I wanted that. More than anything. To see him alive and breathing and to apologize until I was hoarse, but it didn't seem right. I couldn't make him feel obligated to see me.

And that photo. Calvin's expression in that picture nagged at me. An unhappy man. A man with secrets. I knew in that moment that his own family didn't know he was gay.

What a nightmare.

"No," I said, having to clear my voice. "It's okay."

"You sure?" Quinn asked in surprise.

I nodded and took a step back. "He needs to rest." I paused. "Can I ask you a question? About the case?"

Quinn shrugged a shoulder and nodded. "Sure."

"Duncan—"

"He's alive. You didn't kill him," she interjected.

"Oh."

Okay. Good. I guess.

"How did Calvin know where to find me?"

"They found one print at your apartment. It got rushed through the system and came back matching Duncan Andrews. He was convicted of assault against his great uncle a year or so back. The late Edward Andrews, I should say."

"The estate," I replied.

She nodded. "He had no will, left Duncan nothing. Calvin mentioned he talked to you on the phone and that you were having lunch with that guy. When the prints came back and we realized it was the same Duncan, he tried calling to warn you to stay away, but you never answered."

"I went to the library and left my phone on vibrate. Sometimes I don't... notice it."

"Yeah, well, he called the Emporium, your dad, and then he tried Good Books. Ms. Harrison said you were there for an event. Calvin went off fucking half-cocked without me."

I remembered, when I had caught sight of Beth the night before, she had been hanging up the phone. Talking to Calvin moments before unveiling *Tamerlane*, and the entire event went to hell, courtesy of me.

"How'd he get into my shop and apartment?"

"Stole your keys and made copies, it looks like," Quinn replied.

"Will I be arrested?" I asked next, sort of surprised by my question. "I had to shoot him—Duncan." I had already gone through this with the responding officers, but if I couldn't get confirmation from Calvin himself, his partner's word was just as comforting.

"No. *Hell no.* Duncan Andrews brutally killed two people and assaulted you and his own uncle. He shot a detective. He's definitely unstable and will probably plead insanity, but no, Sebastian. You aren't going to jail," Quinn answered.

There was that, at least.

I DIDN'T hear from Calvin the rest of the week.

So I guess whatever could have happened between us was over.

I know I had said I'd be okay with that so long as he was alive and well, but in all honesty, I wasn't okay. I had never felt like this. Never felt so fucking helpless and broken and devastated. I'd only known Calvin for two weeks, but it felt as if everything in life had led up to us meeting. We were supposed to meet. I was supposed to love him.

I tried to placate the bitterness inside me with the knowledge that our relationship would have surely soured like mine had with Neil. If you've dated one closeted cop, you've dated them all. But that only made me have to lock myself in the bathroom of the Emporium for a bit so I could sob my fucking eyes out. I couldn't win.

And so the days went until Christmas. It was snowing as I was getting ready to go to my dad's place. He had offered to come to me, but I needed to get out. Needed to walk and breathe in that cold, festive air, and once and for all come to terms with what the universe had laid out for me. I wouldn't start the new year with such blackness in my life.

There was a quick knock at my door, and I cursed at the thought that Pop felt he needed to come over and make sure I got to his apartment okay. "Coming," I called, leaving the bathroom and drying my hands on my pants. "Pop," I grumbled as I tugged open the door.

Calvin looked up.

My breath caught, and my stomach felt full of butterflies. "Cal," I whispered.

"Am I interrupting?" he asked.

"N-No, no. I just—" I looked him over. Standing, breathing, arm in a sling with his jacket resting over his shoulder. "You're really here."

He held up a few folded pieces of paper. "I needed to return your letters."

"Letters?"

He handed them over. "Smart. About Duncan. You figured all of that out without any of the information I had available."

I felt my face heat up when I opened the notes I had all but forgotten about. My evidence against Duncan, should I have been hurt. My good-bye letters to Pop and to Calvin. "I didn't—I'm sorry I left these. I wasn't thinking."

"Seb," he said. "Can I tell you something?"

I swallowed painfully and nodded. His expression was raw and naked, so exposed from the usual guarded appearance Calvin wore.

"I know you couldn't be with Neil because he denied his relationship with you. Look... baby... I'm no better."

I gritted my teeth hard but nodded. How much of a hypocrite would I be to deny Neil but go through the same issue with Calvin? This was for the best.

"So I told my family."

I immediately looked up. "What?"

Calvin looked a little sad. "They came to see me while I was in the hospital. I've never told any of them that I'm... gay."

"Is everything okay?" I asked, but I knew it wasn't.

Calvin forced a smile onto his face. "I know it's not much, but if it's a step in the right direction for you—"

I dropped the papers to the floor and grabbed him in a hug.

"Ouch! *Fuck*, baby!"

"I'm so sorry!" I exclaimed, pulling back.

Calvin winced and put a hand on my shoulder, managing another smile. "I love you, Sebastian."

You know that whole *cry because you're so happy* thing? I was *so close* to that. I smiled and wiped under my glasses. "Yeah, well, you're not so bad yourself," I said, grinning.

"Merry Christmas."

"Merry Christmas, Cal."

"Can I come in? Or are we going to stay in the hallway for this?"

I scoffed and laughed. "Want to come have breakfast with my dad and me?"

Calvin smiled, and it was beautiful. "I would."

C.S. Poe is an author of gay mystery and romance. She believes that happily ever after is an attainable goal for any character, given enough elbow grease and legwork is provided.

C.S. lives in New York City, but has called a host of different locations home in the past, most recently Ibaraki, Japan. She regrets no longer having easy access to limited-edition candy, capsule toy machines, and clean trains, but over ten years in New York has proved to her there is no place quite like it.

She has an affinity for all things cute and colorful. C.S. is an avid fan of coffee, reading, and cats, in no particular order. She's rescued three cats, including one found in a drain pipe in Japan who flew back to the States with her. Zak, Milo, and Kasper do their best on a daily basis to sidetrack her from work.

C.S. Poe can be followed on her website, which also has links to her Goodreads and social media pages. She can also be followed via her e-mail newsletter on the website.

Website: www.cspoe.com

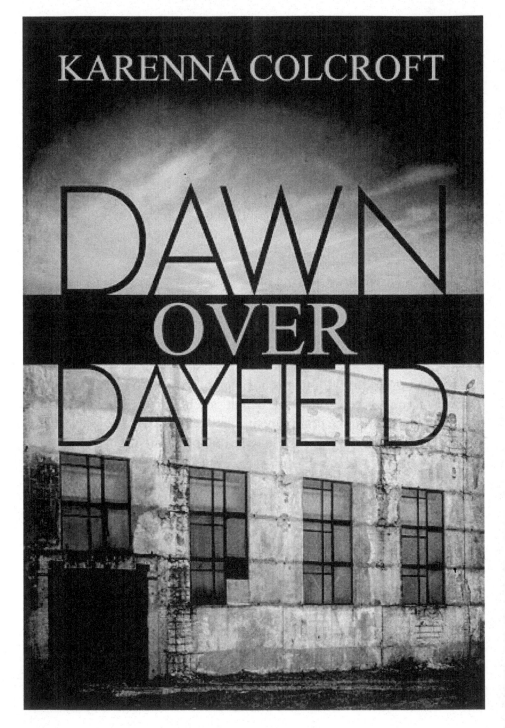

KARENNA COLCROFT

DAWN OVER DAYFIELD

After the death of his adoptive mother, Andy Forrest decides to track down his biological family. The search leads him to the struggling central Massachusetts town of Dayfield—and local historian Weston Thibeault, the town's only other openly gay man. With the help of Weston, Andy uncovers secrets about his birth father, the youngest son of the Chaffees, the family that once owned Dayfield's largest employer, a furniture factory that closed thirty years earlier.

As Andy and Weston work together, they find a connection to a scandal that rocked the Chaffee family over 125 years ago. But small towns like to bury their secrets, and many of the older residents of Dayfield will do anything to stop Andy and Weston from discovering the truth about the town and its inhabitants.

# www.dsppublications.com

BENJAMIN DAHLBECK

# MOUNTAIN
## MURDER MYSTERY

The Severn family—Jeff and his wife Phyllis, Lynette and her new fiancé, and single Andy—has gathered at the mountain home of their grandmother, Mary Agnes Severn, to celebrate Thanksgiving and hear an announcement regarding their late grandfather's will. With news of an escaped convict in the hills, everyone is barely settled in before a huge snowstorm strands them in the large old house with only gas lamps and lanterns to keep the darkness away.

Local sheriff Roger Dickerson arrives to check on the family and seek shelter from the storm. Sparks fly between him and Andy as long-held passions bubble just under the surface, but before they can address them, Mary Agnes's three servants are murdered one by one. Who is the murderer? Is it the escaped convict? Is it someone in the house? Everyone has a motive, and everyone has the means. What's going on between Andy and Marcus the handyman? What's going on between Phyllis and Marcus? Is there something going on between Roger and Marcus? It's (snow)bound to be a wild week of murder, mystery, and mayhem!

# www.dsppublications.com

I am the conductor,
leading the sweet symphony
of pain and agony.

# SPLINTERED
## SJD PETERSON

A string of murders targeting effeminate gay men has the GLBTQ community of Chicago on alert, but budget cuts have left many precincts understaffed and overworked, and homophobia is alive and well within the law enforcement community so little has been done to solve the mystery. When the FBI calls in Special Agent Todd Hutchinson and his team, the locals are glad to hand the case off. But Hutch finds a bigger mystery than anyone originally realized—seventeen linked murders committed in several different jurisdictions. Hutch's clues lead him to Noah Walker.

Working on his PhD in forensic psychology, Noah has been obsessed with serial murders since he was a child. Noah finds himself hunted, striking him off Hutch's suspect list, but not off his radar. To catch the killer before anyone else falls victim, they'll have to work together, and quickly, to bring him to justice.

# www.dsppublications.com

For more
great fiction
from

DSP PUBLICATIONS

visit us online.

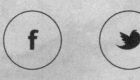

CPSIA information can be obtained
at www.ICGtesting.com
Printed in the USA
LVOW13s2310110318

569504LV00006B/149/P